DEAD SILENCE

They Steal Your Thoughts, Your Body
and Leave You In the Afterlife

Craig A. Brockman

Curve of the Earth Publishing

Dead Silence: They Steal Your Thoughts, Your Body and Leave You in the Afterlife

Copyright © 2024 by Craig A. Brockman

Curve of the Earth Publishing

All rights reserved.

ISBN: 979-8-218-35963-8

No portion of this book may be reproduced in any form without written permission from the publisher or author, except as permitted by U.S. copyright law.

This book is a work of fiction. All people, places, and events are works of the author's imagination and are used fictitiously. All resemblances to people living or dead is purely coincidental.

Editor: Michaela Bush

Cover and interior layout: Craig A. Brockman

Contact: craig@craigabrockman.com

Visit: craigabrockman.com

Printed in the United States of America

Aaida's Song

CROSSING IS PERILOUS FOR every child. Some do not survive.

The girl sits in the bow and the canoe tilts as the man launches from shore and steps in: He is a man in the moonlight and a coyote when in shadow.

Like the stark and steady drum of the winter dance, their paddles ply southward following the milky stream of light on the water. The child's white hair, caressed by the sad moon, entwines with the wavering silver trail.

The boat slides over yawning chasms and glides above the deep like an owl in flight, its wings spanning silent in the night sky, its back skimming the stars. Beneath in dead silence lay infinite depths black and cold.

Water burbles at the sides of the canoe like the gentle suckling of a cub.

"Daughter, I long to meet you." Her mother prays from the southern shore. "I wait here for you."

"Sing for your mother and sing to me the song of the Acudo: the one who creeps from the water," Coyote says.

The girl points with her lips at the stream of moonlight and broods with her inscrutable face.

She sings.

"*The loon keens while lost in gray, wandering on still water.*" Her voice carries across the water like the bird of which she sings.

"*Silent Manitou; wraiths cloaked in ragged plumes of fog,*
Transparent against the rock, sweep across the damp sand.

Enfolded by the green-black limbs of spruce and hemlock...they vanish.
From shore, the gentle waves whisper incantations to these spirits.
The warbling call echoes off cliffs and forests, over beaches and grass,
Onto stones and fallen birches, and back over infinite water.
In boundless depths, leviathan phantoms glide in darkness over bones and ballast."

She pauses and runs a hand through her hair.

"We come back," she sings the last refrain.

"We always come back," Coyote replies.

Chapter 1

Confession

"And you never told anyone about your affair?" the priest said.

"Well, hardly an affair," Ron Jarvin said. "More of an indiscretion, a dalliance."

"Seriously?" the priest huffed. "Can you make it any more trivial? One night stand? Slam, bam, thank you--"

"Please, Brian. You're better than that," Ron said. He pretended to throw the contents of his empty cup and the priest flinched. "I thought we were friends."

"Well, you came to me, and I'm glad you did. I can't believe you kept this bottled up all these years," Brian said. His big hands moved restlessly, and he swiped at the short hairs above his ear where a band of surviving wisps circled his head.

"As a confessor, you've heard all this before," Ron said. "You know how it is, the excuses. I was embarrassed." He pinched the bridge of his nose. "I'd just washed out of my priestly calling. I suppose I wanted to establish myself as a free man."

There was a pause.

"You're smiling. What?" Ron asked.

"Sounds like a brilliant rationalization. But she was a younger woman. And a patient of yours. Seriously, what could be worse?" Brian said.

"*Former* patient," Ron said.

The priest lowered his chin, turned his head sideways a notch, and shot Ron a doubting glance.

Ron scratched his short beard and waved his hand. "I know. It's awful. Awful."

Brian examined his friend's features. His clear eyes and easy smile had made him an engaging psychologist. But in only a few years his face had begun to sag, wrinkles had deepened around his eyes, and streaks of gray were chasing through his red hair.

"But she was not *that* much younger," Ron said.

"C'mon. You're only digging the hole deeper," Brian said.

"Well, yes. She was a few years younger." Ron twitched a shrug.

"You never said a word to me about this. So, what makes you want to confess to me now?" The priest quickly lifted his palm. "Sorry. Since you no longer consider yourself part of the Church, this is not a sacramental confession."

"Church or not, you're the only one for me to confess to." Ron grinned.

"Why? What prompted you to tell me? I'm curious about these things, what prompts people to come forward after so long?"

Ron leaned back in the chair holding his hands behind his head, elbows flared. He inhaled deeply. "A girl—a young woman contacted me, and she thinks I am her father."

"That's it? Does she have proof?"

"Well, yeah. DNA. She sent me a link to one of those ancestry sites and..."

"And what?" the priest asked.

"Like I said, she contacted me about this."

"Out of the blue, a girl tells you she's your daughter?"

"Not exactly out of the blue. Actually, I've known her a long time and I think you and I may have even talked about her once or twice," Ron said.

"Who is she?" Brian asked.

"Gracie Bird. Gracie Knowles, now. The woman, Dee Bird, was her mother."

Chapter 2

Roads, Dreams, and Regrets.

IN ANOTHER DAY THE car ferry, *SS Badger* out of Ludington would take him across Lake Michigan where he would meet Gracie and Adam. Ron had known both of them for years, but this would be the first time to see her face to face knowing that she was his daughter.

He had been tossing and turning through the night, lying awake, his body feeling raunchy. Old wounds were flaring up. There was a night when he was being the hero and tried to stop an insane man. He kneaded the fingers on his right hand that had been severed in the assault and reattached. Though they were numb, at times like this they would burn and tingle. In the same assault he had received an injury to the back of his head. Now that he was getting sick he felt a piercing headache coming on, and his throat bristled with pain. Either he was developing some kind of flu, or he had more apprehension about the whole trip and seeing Gracie than he had been willing to admit.

He had more to worry about: Gracie was pregnant, and he did not want to expose her to anything and make her sick.

And then there was Adam, who had been his friend and had worked for Ron for a long time. Since the story had come out about Ron being Gracie's father, they had texted only a few times. But how had Adam really taken the news? How would Adam take it that Ron had withheld a serious indiscretion from his best friend all these years. And now Adam had been made aware of it only because it concerned Adam's wife, Gracie.

Throughout the long night, whenever he drifted back to sleep, there were only nightmares. Each dream was more vivid and haunting than the one before.

He dreamt of the ferry crossing Lake Michigan. The ship was under weigh, and he was peering out of his cabin into the darkened passageway. There was an ominous sound that was at first far away along the iron corridors, then nearer. *Scrape. Pause. Scrape. Pause.* He looked left and right trying to see into the rolling hallway. It began as a lone, fleshy rasping, then it spread throughout the great vessel. Joining in unison: *Scrape. Pause. Scrape. Pause.* The deathly rhythm grew nearer and nearer until the sound entered the side passage toward his cabin. A gelatinous stench, a draft of carrion brushed his cheek. He gagged and slapped a hand over his mouth, straining to see into the gloom. Emerging from shadows, the first forms swayed into view. Tightly packed, flesh-on-flesh, drool-on-drool decrepit corpses neared. Their faces were downcast and gray, rotting arms swung in pace to the tempo of their shuffling gait. To the beat of a stygian drummer, like slaves rowing a Roman galley, they swayed nearer as if to a shambling sea chanty.

Their last living thoughts wriggled from their heads like escaping tapeworms, writhing from holes in their skulls and drifting over them as they passed in their macabre meander.

A corpulent woman dragged near, and Ron could read the thoughts she extruded: *We will want to thaw the ham Thursday eve if it shall be ready by Sunday morn.*

"What is this?" Ron mouthed.

Trailing above a dangling ear, the thoughts of a nattily dressed gentleman with a massive abscess on his jaw: *Brace yourselves, there will still be time if I can just beat this damn septicity.*

A girl with wide milky eyes and a rope at her throat: *She should not have spoken to me that way, but now she will receive her comeuppance.*

I shan't be here to see them leave when their train goes home to Cleveland, was the last thought an old man with a sad, friendly smile.

And a young Native woman in a white buckskin dress—

"Dee," he whispered.

He awoke gasping, his sheets clinging with sweat. Rolling onto his back, he laid his arm across his forehead and stared at the ceiling.

He had played that night with Dee over and over in his mind nearly every day for—how long? Thirty years? At the time she was no longer his patient, not anymore. They were friends. And being admitted to rehab again was embarrassing for her, so she did not want to have her father or anyone else take her to that facility in Appleton. She had asked Ron to drive. Of course, he would do it. It was an eight-hour trip, stay overnight, and return on Sunday. An easy favor for a friend.

When they arrived, her paperwork was messed up, it was a Saturday, so she would need to be admitted through the Emergency Room. And there were other loose ends. It got late, so she would just get a room at the hotel where Ron was staying and go in on Sunday. The rest of the scene was as sordid and stupid as any affair. After that night together, she was admitted on Sunday, and he drove home with a hangover and a truckload of regrets.

So long ago.

Restless and awake in his apartment, he threw off the covers and decided to get an early start for Ludington. There was little point in sleeping. And his headache was worse.

In a few hours, he was driving over the Mackinac Bridge, rubbing his forehead and massaging his temples. High over the water he glided, tires humming as the bridge arched toward heaven. His headache grew to daggers looking into the crackling glint of the rising sun like quicksilver ladled over the sea-green expanse of Lake Huron.

More reels played in his mind.

He never imagined Dee would become pregnant. She probably had been with a half dozen men that summer and she certainly would have had birth control. He had been too naïve—selfish? to take responsibility for protection that night. Of course, he had been too mortified to keep in touch. Then two years later, she died. When he heard about her death it felt like tearing off a scab. He didn't mention it to anyone. He hadn't even known Dee had a little girl until he read the obituary: *Survived by two children, Duane and Grace Bird.*

That was before the Rising. They called it the Crisis, the Turning, or the Rising. A few years ago, ghosts walked the Upper Peninsula of Michigan and monsters swam in the depths of Lake Superior. *Ha!* He laughed to himself. It seemed crazy to even think about it. And most people didn't. All major news outlets and even the locals who had lived through it had already explained it away as just another climate phenomenon, pseudoscience, or mass hysteria. The good, level-headed citizens of the U.P. were once again ridiculed as hicks who could not understand the complexities of meteorological phenomenon or simple physics, and it was concluded that thousands of people had merely been hoodwinked into believing that it was some sort of supernatural phenomenon.

So, people were afraid to mention it. Forgotten.

Soon after, his friend, Adam Knowles, a fellow psychologist, moved to Wisconsin and, after a short courtship, married Gracie Bird. It seemed everything returned to normal. But in the aftermath and in the vacuum that it created, his regret over his affair simmered.

Now it had boiled to the surface.

Through a DNA ancestry site Gracie had uncovered a connection to Ron's niece, Samantha. It was not hard to trace the relationships from there. Awkward emails and texts between Gracie and Ron ensued. It was more of a curiosity at first. There was never condemnation or recrimination. Finally, Gracie made the invitation for him to meet them at their home in Keshena. But there was so much to wrestle with, and he was still not sure if going to Wisconsin to meet Gracie and Adam was a good idea. With all his experience as a psychologist, he still could not counsel himself. Everyone looked up to him. He was the steady hand, the sober presence, and he was not used to feeling anxious and exposed. Leader, psychologist, former priest, and marginal Christian: with all his dirty laundry on display. Because in this sordid tale, he deserved to lose everyone's respect. He had gotten drunk, and no one would be wrong to accuse him of taking advantage of a troubled young woman—a former client. A fiasco that resulted in a daughter.

It was torture to realize that he was capable of such callous disregard: That he could have a one-night stand with a former patient that would leave him with a daughter he'd never known. It was a mess. He had been fraught and sleepless for days, and the closer he came to facing Gracie again—as his daughter, the more he was overcome by anxiety. Like anyone else, he'd had his share of mistakes and screwups in life and there were things that he regretted. But most of those blunders had affected no one but himself. How would his shame and overwhelming anxiety play out in front of his old friend Adam and Gracie, his daughter—*daughter for God's sake!* He had no context to deal with this. He was nervous and beside himself.

Ron had heard only rumors about Dee and her notoriety after she returned from rehab. She had rapidly and mysteriously inherited a significant role in the spirituality and Native lore of the Lake Superior region. He did not know more. He did not want to know more.

But he understood that Gracie had inherited that mantel. And because of her mother's mysterious death and because of the position Gracie had inherited, she was surrounded and protected. She was also a leader within a group that Ron had known about and had contact with for a long time.

This group had contacted Ron occasionally through the years because he was considered an expert without peer when it came to understanding the lore and science of the Great Lakes and specifically Lake Superior. He had long been sought as a speaker and writer on the topic. It was much more than a hobby. Like Dee, he too had inherited a role from his ancestors. The walls of his small apartment were stacked with collections of books and volumes—some ancient, that were part of an assortment like none in the world.

The group that Gracie was a part of was vast and secretive. It was referred to simply as the Lake Council or the Lake Council of Keepers and only they understood their mission entirely and who comprised their membership. Even their official title, *The Kitchi-Gami Council of Keepers*, was an oversimplification and possibly a deflection. Ron understood them to be a clandestine alliance of Native men and women who protected and monitored Lake Superior generation upon generation. They had the duty to monitor the big lake for threats and they tapped into the spiritual climate of the region while ceremonially beseeching the gods that be to protect this vast inland sea. Their umbrella of protection had been more powerful and effective than anyone could know. They deemed Kitchi-Gami a spiritual entity and the health of its waters and shores would only be as good as its spiritual integrity. Beyond these parameters, the purpose of the Lake Council was vague to Ron. Their origin might go back centuries or even millennia.

Ron had maintained this loose relationship with them ever since he had discovered his own special relationship to Lake Superior and had been bequeathed the trove of materials and ancient books from his grandfather. Ron had majored in limnology for a semester or two before entering seminary. He always had a relentless curiosity about the lake. But through these materials he learned that among his family he was not alone. He had inherited not only a dusty pile of books, documents, and artifacts, but he had also inherited a vocation—a calling as he came to understand it. His lineage went back to some of the first Jesuits that had followed the ancient waterways and whose sandals had first tread the ancient trails to the shores of these fresh sparkling seas. And the hearts of these men had not been intent only on the souls of the Native people who inhabited the shores, but also intent on learning about and chronicling the nature of this cold, dark body of water and its shores. He had inherited an ancient trust. He relished the time he spent recording and studying the soul of this vast living entity.

Personally, he did not entirely understand or subscribe to Native spiritual beliefs, but he understood enough to know that the supernatural integrity of the lake was somehow intrinsic to its survival. Maybe it was as simple as the relationship of humans to the land. People are charged with taking care of the land, with stewardship, or they will die when the land no longer supports them. But both his faith and that of the Native people went much deeper, to something akin to a divine contract.

But there was also ominous opposition. Deadly. There were those who wanted to tap into this reserve of spiritual energy and harness it for their gain. Ron did not know their intentions, and he doubted that even the council understood. And this cabal, this pack of dogs had been tenacious. If the spiritual canopy protecting the lake could be fractured, they would take control of the waters and take control of the spirit of *Kitchi-Gami:* Lake Superior. The Dark Council could harness it for evil.

But so far, their attempts had been fruitless. First they killed a rising spiritual leader like Gracie's mother, Dee, then they used a hopeless shaman to try to martial the deep forces of the lake. The Keepers thought the Dark Council had been defeated when Dee's daughter, Gracie, destroyed the shaman. The story had been embellished until it was whispered that the shaman, James Graves, had fallen into the very jaws of the mythical Great Lynx, Mishipezhu. Ron's sensibilities were not prepared to go that far. But he knew that the Dark Council was on the move again and it appeared they would not stop until they eliminated the Lake Council, Gracie, and anyone associated with them.

As he drove toward his meeting with his daughter, he had much to wrestle with. From the Mackinac Bridge he would continue south, then west to take the ferry across Lake Michigan from Ludington to Manitowoc, Wisconsin. His plan was to stay overnight in Ludington, and board early. On the four-hour journey across Lake Michigan he could rest, think—and pray. Sailing on the massive *SS Badger* ferry was one of those things he had always wanted to do but had never had the time or the luxury to afford. If there was ever a time to slow down and unwind, it was now.

But as he accelerated off the bridge, he felt completely drained. His skin crawled with fever; his muscles twitched with chills. But he refused to believe he was getting sick. He brushed it off to weariness from days of sleeplessness and fretting.

The farther he drove, the drowsier he became until he felt himself drifting off. He swiped his phone to play something loud, but even that did not keep him alert. His uneasy stomach resisted food, but when he got off the interstate and headed west, he would find someplace to get some coffee and stretch his legs.

He would try to get his bearings as he edged off the map into his uncharted life of fatherhood.

Chapter 3

A Lunch with Providence

AN ANOMALY, AS IF a colossal sea serpent had been flung to the earth by the gods, a freeway cuts north-south through the woods and arcs above the highway that enters the town of Cadillac. Just before the overpass sits a gas station with a convenience store and a Tim Horton's donut place. Ron shambled in. The change of scenery was reviving, but his headache and chills were not improving.

And his anxiety was riveting. He couldn't shake it.

Prompted by the odor of sugar and grease, he ordered an egg and sausage thing along with a bucket of caffeine. While he waited for his order, he noticed out of the corner of his eye a man who was watching him intently from the booth near the door. The man's table was empty without food or a tray, so Ron thought he must have been waiting for someone. Maybe the guy was trying to decide if Ron was the one he was supposed to meet. Or maybe the man recognized him from somewhere else. Having seen thousands of clients, Ron never knew where he would run into one. At the moment, he was in no mood to engage in a counselling session, so he looked away and pivoted back to the counter.

He grabbed his order and looked around briefly to find a place to sit. But the place was crowded, so he headed for the door. It was an easy choice to go back to the car and listen to the radio. Or just sit alone in silence.

He was almost out the door and he had purposely not made eye contact with the guy who had been staring at him.

Then the man raised his arm and made a circling motion. "Plenty of room right here," he said.

Ron glanced at the man and had to smile. If they'd held a look-alike contest for the late actor Wilford Brimley, this guy would at least have been the runner up.

"You can park right ch'ere, I was just about to head on out," the man said.

Ron didn't have the heart or the energy to refuse.

"You look like you was rode hard and put up wet," the man said as Ron slid into the booth. The guy already had the handlebar mustache and all he would need was a cowboy hat and a pair of suspenders to complete the dead actor's persona. Instead, he wore one of those old red woodsman's caps known most commonly as a Stormy Kromer.

"I'm Malachy." He offered a meaty hand with stout fingers. His grip was firm.

"Ron Jarvin. Malachy. That's Irish."

"Yep. For Malachi, I am told." He looked thoughtfully at Ron. "But you look weary, my man. Anything I can do to lend a hand?"

Ron thought it was a bold offer from a total stranger, but when their eyes met, something made him hold his gaze a moment longer. The man was being utterly sincere, as if he had a willingness, and more remarkably, the actual ability to help. As a psychologist, Ron had always wished he could have honed such a face for his clients.

"Well, since you asked…" Ron hesitated, unwrapping his meal and prying the lid off his large coffee. "Let's just say I'm embarking on a difficult journey." He smoothed the wrapper on the table while thoughtfully regarding the egg and sausage sandwich. His weak stomach flipped at the sight of the food.

"Are you an escaped convict? Family troubles? I've had my share. I had myself a brother or two that, let's just say, had a fall from, er…grace." A side of the man's big mustache ticked upward into a smile.

Ron stopped mid-bite.

"So, a fall. From grace. Was that it?" Malachy said. A gentle breaker of laughter washed acceptance and warmth across the booth.

It took Ron a moment to catch his composure and smile. He set down his food. "Well, yeah. But I suppose you can't just say *fall from grace* lightly to a man who left the priesthood long ago and now just discovered that he has a daughter named *Grace* who is having his grandchild." *Why in hell am I telling him all this?*

The man raised his eyebrows. "Well, I'm always prime for a good story. And I got all the time in the world." He leaned back with one hand splayed on the table while he loosely cupped the other over his mustache and stroked down to his chin and studied Ron.

"Ha! Where would I start?" Ron said.

"Let me ask. Are you married? You ever had kids before?" Malachy said slowly, as if sliding the first card onto the table. But he asked in a tone that implied he already surmised the answer.

Ron gave a half-shake of his head.

"So, you ain't had kids. Never married."

Ron weighed how much to say. "The priesthood kept me out of circulation, and after I got away from being a priest, I was wrestling with my place in the world." He scratched his beard. "I guess I wrestled too long."

"So, you've always been single?"

"Mostly. Here and there, but nothing that I could sustain."

Malachy patted his big hand on the table. "Nothing that you could sustain or nothing that a woman wanted to sustain?" He huffed and grinned.

Ron smiled. "I would say that you are nosey, but I just met you so I…"

"No. No, I apologize." Malachy held up his palm. "I s'pose I am just fascinated by the way folks make their way in the world. No offense."

"None taken." Ron spun his coffee between his thumb and finger, thinking. "It was my fault that my relationships didn't work. I've dealt with that. I can be honest."

The noise and bustle of the restaurant closed around them again for a while.

Malachy studied him. "Anyways. All that aside. I bet you worry about what it's like being a dad and more important, how to be a good dad." The man's gaze was level, challenging, yet unwaveringly compassionate.

Ron was reaching his fingers under the sandwich again as the man spoke but stopped. Out of nowhere, as sudden and random as a meteor flashing across the night sky, emotion burbled up inside him and threatened to spill over. Without looking up, he carefully laid aside the food, folded the paper over it, creased his napkin and folded his hands for an instant. His open hand moved upward to cover his mouth, he inhaled, and he slid the hand down, across his chest and folded it into his other hand on the table.

Malachy was patient. Ron clenched his jaw, swallowed the lump in his throat, and lifted his brows once.

"I am so sorry, partner. I should've kept my yap shut," Malachy said.

Ron sniffed, waggled a hand, and shook his head. How had this total stranger laid bare the essence of what Ron had been fearing? All of Ron's years of counselling and even his session with his priest friend Brian had not been able to tease this from his soul.

Ron nodded slowly, looking down at his coffee, turning it with his fingers. "I am afraid you hit it." He smiled. "You're pretty good. I'm a psychologist and could not have cut to the chase like you just did."

"You've been a failed priest, a psychologist, and you've made some whopper mistakes. Heck. Looks to me like you have just about all it takes to be a good dad."

"Oh, I don't know. I really don't—"

Malachy reached his big paw across the table and patted Ron's hand. "No worries, friend. No worries."

Ron covered his mouth again as a small sob caught in his throat. He flashed a look around the restaurant, quickly regained his composure, and wiped the corner of an eye with his napkin. "Whew. I am so-o sorry."

"Nothing to apologize for. Never. I am sure you are forgiven."

"But how? How would you know?"

"Well, as a former priest you should know darn well how that works. And if you don't accept the forgiveness you've been offered, it will only cloud your relationship with your new daughter. And you don't want that."

Ron tried to say more, then waved a hand and just said, "No. I do not."

Malachy sighed. "Well, it's about time for me to ride into the sunset. Your Grace is a lucky gal."

"Thank you. I hope I didn't ruin your day," Ron said.

"Oh no, quite the opposite." Malachy leaned back, pressed his big hands on the table, wrenched sideways in the booth, and stood. He lifted his chin. "See ya on the other side...of the lake."

As the man left, Ron felt that a weight of doubt had lifted. Assurance, and maybe even an edge of excitement crept in. He still felt tired, and his headache was pestering again, but he felt more relieved and whole than he had in days.

Wait. How did he know...?

He twisted to see where the man had gone, but he was gone. Disappeared.

Chapter 4

Boarding the Badger

THE FERRY WOULD LEAVE the next morning, and he was still weary, sick, and aching by the time he reached Ludington. Arriving at the hotel, he dragged his pack into the room, dropped it on the floor, and went to the bathroom. In a couple of minutes, he had flopped onto the bed, exhausted.

It seemed only moments had passed when he awoke in a sweat to the radio blaring and his head pounding. Morning. Fortunately, the last occupant of the room must have been a ferry traveler who had set the alarm on the clock next to the bed.

He rolled off the bed, staggered into the bathroom, and felt like death while hovering over the toilet waiting for his stomach to either settle or let loose. He splashed through a quick shower and hedged around his beard with a few scrapes of a razor. In a daze, he picked up his pack from where he had dropped it and was out the door and stumbling through the lobby to grab a cup of coffee.

Throwing his stuff in the car, he drove to the ferry feeling weak and feverish. Because he was sick, he regretted that he would not have the full experience of crossing Lake Michigan on the big ferry. But he was gratified that he'd paid the extra fee to have a cabin on board. He would have a bed.

Arriving at the ferry dock, he pulled his car up to the agents who asked a few questions about weapons and contraband while one agent circled his car with a dog. They waved him ahead and he was eventually directed into a slot for the car. Everyone seemed pleasant, out of proportion to his mood and to the damp morning hung in gray.

Standing in line with his leather pack, a stiff breeze caused chills to rise to his core. Men and women in fluorescent oranges and limes bustled everywhere. Further ahead, a sad lady carried a three-legged dog next to an equally sad man with another brutish dog. Dealing with dogs on a ship seemed like an unnecessary recipe for trouble. And true-to-form, trouble arrived. As he shuffled ahead in line, moving closer to the ship, one of the fluorescent-clad men was pointing at the ramp. "Watch your step there, sir. Watch your step."

Ron thought the man was indicating the step up to the ramp and just as Ron was about to step on the ramp the man said, "Stop, pardon the mess. We're cleaning it up." One of the dogs had left a neat, steaming line of turds. Ron's stomach pitched, and even his normally tolerant self was in no mood. He was unusually irritable and grimaced at having to endure such mindless carelessness and conceit.

Get a grip, he said to himself.

Ahead, the line was backing up at the bottom of a long flight of steps. Two obese women were unable to navigate the steps and the staff was bringing down a large lift that would carry them upward one at a time. Fortunately, the dogs had been ushered to kennels. *Be nice. One step at a time. One foot after the other,* he told himself, feeling sicker by the minute.

This would have all been a minor nuisance that would never have troubled him if he weren't feeling so awful.

While he waited, he could glimpse deep into the belly of the great ferry where cars were being lined up and stacked one by one. The full, ancient aroma of coal fumes and grease wafted from the engine room that hummed below his feet. He closed his eyes and inhaled while imagining old cities, train engines, and seafaring vessels.

On board, he paused at the Cruise Director's office and got the key for his cabin. Shuffling along the passageway, reading the numbers on the doors, he was flooded with all those strange sensations of a mind and body that was under siege with illness. Sounds made him jump. Each of his joints and muscles ached and twitched, his mind was in a fog, and his gut made him hope there was a functioning head in the cabin and that it was stocked with at least two rolls of paper.

Every surface of the ship was coated in layers of paint thick as porcelain. Encased in the iron hull of the great ferry, everything clanged or banged, and there was a constant thrumming that felt as though it arose from a flow of crackling magnetism within each atom and molecule of the eight million pounds of iron surrounding him. He ran a hand over his damp forehead, trying to settle his fever thoughts.

He looked at the *13* on the key and back again to the placard on the door. "Thirteen? That's my room? Why not?" He smiled to himself.

The narrow cabin smelled like paint and disinfectant. It had two beds with bright blue bedspreads, a small window, a sink, and *yes!* a narrow door that opened into a miniscule triangle room with a toilet. But in his fatigue, he just tossed his pack on the spare bed and collapsed onto the other. The hull of the ship rang with a sharp bang about every fifteen seconds as the heat poured through the vents and into the passageways. The sound was slow and ominous as if between the decks some gremlin with a silver hammer had slipped unknown. The leering creature crouched with one hand clawed over a knee while with the other: *Bang. Ting. Bang. Ting.*

And soon he slept.

HE DREAMED A GREEN and purple carpet in a restaurant that featured a pork chop special. Across from him in the dream sat Dee, in that same sad restaurant attached to the cheap hotel where they had stayed in Appleton. In a corner, there were folding banquet tables and chairs stacked behind a booth that was piled with cases of paper products.

Dee seemed a little stoned as she picked apart her wilted salad. He hadn't known what a patty melt was, and now as it lay splayed before him, he wished it had remained a mystery.

Having honed his celibacy over ten years of seminary and priesthood, he was never comfortable alone with a woman unless it was in a professional setting. Now that he was a rebellious, long-haired former priest, he figured he could lay aside the jitters and loosen up. But it was hard not to think of Dee as his client. In fact, it was only recently, since they had become friends, that he felt comfortable no longer addressing her by her full name, Rose Delight Bird.

"Do you need anything else?" he asked.

She made a sad half-smile, shook her head, and scanned the depressing dining room. "Do you just want to go back to the room?" she asked.

Your room or my room? He was afraid to ask. Dee was a friend and he intended to keep it that way.

"I have a teeny bottle." She held up thumb and finger. "They say you should go into treatment drunk or stoned so you don't go into withdrawal or something."

With a motion of his head, Ron disagreed. "I don't know if that's true. Maybe it's just an excuse." He smiled. He could be frank with her.

Of course, he followed her back to her room. He took a sip from the not-so-tiny bottle, then another. They sat too close while they talked. Finally, she was absently tracing through the hair on his arm. While still talking, her fingers trailed across his shoulder and finally to his chest. He pretended not to notice.

She looked up at him with heavy lids over her deep brown eyes. She parted her lips to kiss. But a sound loud as rasping cicadas pulsed from her open mouth. It reverberated in the room until a fat beetle crawled over her tongue. It launched from her lips, and he flinched as it flew at him. She vomited a swirl of flies and bugs that filled the room with angry buzzing. He twisted away with his arms flailing at the swarms, stumbled, and fell back onto the bed. Spinning his head, he found himself face to face with Dee's desiccated corpse that lay sprawled on the bed. To escape the stench, he wrapped his arm across his face.

The flesh on her face was riffling with vermin and she spoke. "Gracie and Duane are in danger. Help them. Your daughter needs you."

"No...!" He stood and twisted away, launching toward the window. Tearing aside the curtains, he fumbled to find a latch, lift a sash, or smash the window. From outside, a creamy glow brightened the glass. Far away, through a torrent of glittering crystals, a woman approached as if drifting through driven snows.

He did not recognize her for a moment because he'd never known this woman with the level gaze of confidence and conviction, only the damaged, downcast, and drug-addled Dee.

As she drew near, her lips were moving, but she was too far away to be heard or understood.

She touched the window with her fingertips, then pressed her palm against the glass and he could hear the edge of desperation in her voice.

"Gracie and Duane are in danger. Help them. Your daughter needs you," she repeated. Their eyes met and the glass no longer separated them. She reached toward him, but just as quickly her form was drawn away again, her arms still outstretched. Further, smaller, she receded into the distance. Until she vanished.

Chapter 5

A Ferry Frozen

Weeping, he thought he had awakened. As if he had swallowed glass shards, his throat ached, his head pulsed so badly he was afraid to move, his flesh crawled, and chills wracked his body.

But he had not awakened. The symptoms of fever and infection that he had tried to ignore for the past two days had grown much worse and now he was rapidly sinking from deep sleep into the realm of semi-coma.

In his delirium and chills, he imagined that his tiny cabin had grown freezing cold. He could see his breath. Pulling the blankets off of the spare bed, he rolled into a cocoon of coarse covers.

Like a scream drowned in a snowstorm, he could barely understand the muffled shout coming from far away outside the small window of his cabin. "She. Needs. Your. Help."

Puzzled, he threw back the covers and stood. The room was washed in the dull snow-glow that fills windows on early winter mornings. He dipped his head to see out the window and pushed the curtain aside. He expected to see waves and water to the horizon, but the window was glazed with frost. He rubbed the glass with his elbow and stared through the milky smear.

He gaped at a sea of white where whirlwinds of snow and slithering snow devils chased across the frozen scape. The ferry was frozen in place miles from shore. He swept a bedspread around his shoulders and stepped into the frosted hall. The clanging and thrumming had stopped, leaving the ship empty and shrouded in silence.

The corridor was covered in a layer of snow. A solitary figure approached; a slender man dressed like a porter. His steps were plodding, and his arms swung slowly. Ron was about to speak until he realized the man wore a blue ceramic mask. For a moment, Ron smiled to himself. Was there to be a costume party on board the ferry? But the man only stared at him and never interrupted his pace as he strode past. The mask had long, pointed ears, slanting eyes, and a narrow snout lined with sharp, bloody teeth. The man with the coyote mask watched over his shoulder briefly, then turned his head forward, and walked on, his bare feet silent on the frozen floor.

Ron watched as the figure of the strange man vanished down the hallway, then he cinched his blanket close around his neck and shuffled through the passageways until he emerged onto a deck glazed and slippery. He inhaled the crisp, open air and felt the alkaline sub-zero cold on his tongue. Like rows of daggers, long icicles hung from the decks above and from the gunwales. He leaned over the edge. Rope ladders hung over the sides, swaying in the wind. Meandering footprints led away from the ferry and were quickly devoured in the flurry.

Squinting into the shifting sheets of snow, he watched for any stragglers or frozen bodies lying in the drifts. The winds grew to a howling crescendo until finally, like a great roller breaking on shore, the gales subsided, simmering and hissing to a whisper. In moments, the last of the snow swirls pirouetted, bowed, and laid in repose on the frozen surface. It was silent except for the tiny, restless fractures in the icicles or the scattered musical chatter like glass chimes as ice shards separated and fell.

A great tremor shook the ice, and the sides of the ferry pitched and shrieked against the shifting tectonics of the frozen sea. Another tremor was attended by the metallic zing of fault lines screaming across the petrified surface. After a brief silence, another cascade of thunder and movement shook the vessel. Several hundred yards from the trapped ferry, the ice suddenly tented like a pyramid and thrust upward, large as a glacier, until it burst open with a booming crash.

Within the explosion of ice slabs and water, a great head thrust upward with curving horns big as spruce trunks and pointed ears like a lynx.

Ron knew. Few people could know more than he about the lore and legends of those mythical beasts, the creatures of Native lore, or the denizens of the Great Lakes. Especially since the Rising several years ago, these myths and creatures seemed often to play in his dreams and nightmares.

Big as a whale, the creature shook off the remaining blue shards of ice, clawed its way onto the ice, shook itself of the cold lake water, and preened and licked its shaggy coat: Mishipezhu, the Great Lynx. The beast was a chimera of cat, scaly dragon, and horned monstrosity.

Fascinated by the raw splendor of the creature, Ron found himself edging across the ice, closer. But typical for a dream, as he neared it, the animal only grew smaller and smaller until it had diminished to a cat no larger than a leopard. Soon it was nipping the ice off it paws, smoothing its flanks, and pawing behind its ear. It purred contentedly as Ron approached. Bemused by the ancient wonder, he reached forward cautiously and petted its broad head, scratching around the horns and behind its ears.

Like a lazy pet, this horror of Lake Superior circled Ron's ankles and curled at his feet. "Nothing to fear," Ron said to himself nervously.

But the mythic creature had arisen from the wrong lake. The ferry was not on the beast's home water, but it was on Lake Michigan.

The beast suddenly stood and whipped its snout toward the ship. It crouched on its haunches, eyes wide with ears laid back, and hissed as deep and loud as a blacksmith's bellows. Ron spun to see what had riled the big cat. At first there was only the black monolith of the massive ferry inexplicably wedged in a sheet of ice that stretched from horizon to horizon.

Then, from around the bow, almost indistinguishable from the snow, the slight figure of a spindly-legged albino fawn wobbled hesitantly onto the ice, followed immediately by a wary doe just as white as her fawn. Ron smiled and looked back at the lynx. But the big cat had not seen the deer. With fur bristling and teeth bared, Mishipezhu's yellow eyes were fixed on the upper decks of the ferry.

Mishipezhu bolted, growing larger with each leap as it galloped across the ice and disappeared in a trail of swirling snow.

Ron pivoted back toward the ship and saw movement along the lower deck. At first it was only the dark outline of a large animal until it skirted one of the lifeboats and could be seen in silhouette. It was a canine form slinking along the rail, tilting its head, raising its ears, and stopping to scrutinize the white deer that faltered on the ice and snow. Step by step it edged toward the bow, stalking the deer below. Ron's first thought was that one of the dogs had escaped from the kennels below decks. But this was no one's domesticated pet. It stalked with the skill of a wild animal. He shouted at the deer and waved his arms, trying to frighten the doe, but it was like his words froze in the air and fell to the snow. In a fluid movement, the animal bounded to the front of the ship and rested paws on the top rail of the gunwale, looking down at its prey. It was huge, much larger than a wolf, but its reddish-gray disheveled fur and long pointed ears were not those of a wolf. It poked its pointed nose in the air, sniffing, and swiveled its head until it saw Ron. The lips on the narrow snout curled in a deadly sneer: Coyote. An enormous coyote.

In a moment, the dream-scene altered, and he was back on the ferry, no longer was the ferry frozen in ice, but it had sunk into the depths of Lake Michigan. As if drifting in a current, he glided through the darkened passageways with the bedspread still flowing from his shoulders. Ropes of mossy algae brushed his face and tangled in his hair. Cabin doors stood ajar. He braced as a square leather and tweed suitcase bobbed in the doorway of a dark room. A white hand wrapped around the handle and a corpse sprawled, floating in the vacant cabin. With dead fisheyes, a woman regarded him in silent confusion.

He drifted further, insensate, unfeeling while scanning the gray passageways for his cabin. Other corpses dipped, heads bobbing in the stale current and he pressed against the bulkhead to slip past them.

Some had decayed longer than others. They floated naked, their filmy flesh hanging and fluttering in the flux. And though he drifted in deep water, the scent of bilge and death invaded his senses and encased him.

When he found Cabin 13, the metal door creaked on its hinges, but inside was only darkness.

He was no longer underwater; the dream was changing again and this was not his cabin. The dream had morphed into something else. Something familiar to him from long ago in his childhood. Maybe it was an odor, an ambience, but he knew this was now the tiny bedroom he had as a teenager.

He had thrilled at the challenge of darkness, of plunging into darkness. As a youth, he could have flipped the switch on the wall of his bedroom or turned on the light in the hall and opened the bedroom door wide enough to allow the hall light to illuminate his room. But each night was like a test for him. The ritual was simple, almost silly, but it quenched a budding thirst for adventure that he'd inherited in his blood. What else could lure him to walk alone down the long passage to his bedroom? Like a ghost, he would slip from low light into darkness, then under the curtain of night he steadied himself with a hand on the door jamb before stepping into his bedroom. Blindly skirting the rickety chair, the chaos of clothes, shoes, and books, he would fumble for the wooden lamp next to his bed. All in the dark. As a lad he relished the shudder it gave him to test the unknown. He imagined what might be lurking in the corners of his room, what apparitions he nearly brushed past to reach his bedside.

Maybe at that age his quest, this pressing into the realm of shadows, challenging the darkness, came from the same source as his budding quest for faith and truth. Or was it simply to contest the bounds of his pre-adolescent courage?

When he turned on his light, all fear would vanish.

He had recurring dreams that were similar to his experience of venturing into his dark bedroom. What others may call nightmares, he imagined it as holding out against the darkness. He might hold on for a few seconds longer as a decrepit wraith embraced him. Or he recalled dreams of venturing into a darkened church—each time the same darkened church with the same faceless statues carved in black, the bleeding figures in stained glass, and the insipid, judgmental icons glaring down at him. From there, he would be exhilarated as he pressed forward venturing toward the altar and into a sacristy cast in shadows.

When he had been an altar boy, he had been enthralled to pull the gown over his shirt and jeans and prepare to participate in the magical rituals and ceremony. He would have dreams of being in the church preparing for mass near the closet where vestments hung. And though these were dreams, he relished that feather-tickle up the back of his neck, that electric thrill to push through and go beyond the musty robes into a secret passage. He remembered how the way would grow smaller and smaller. Each time in his dreams he would try to squeeze through—because he knew there must be a fantastical world beyond. Each time the dream would shatter, or he would awaken before entering the enchanted land. The disappointment would stay with him into his waking hours.

If he could reach into a realm beyond, then he would have proof: Proof of eternity and of the supernatural. His dreams imagined that if he pushed through fear, he could discover Truth.

Truth. It had always been nebulous and seemingly unattainable to him. But he knew it was the vital force of the universe. He thirsted for it.

In his delirious fever dream, he stood at that yawning cabin door on the *SS Badger*: the cabin that had become the bedroom of his youth. He took one step forward into the gloom and knew that if he could make it to his lamp, then all fear would dissipate with the light. He delighted in the terror.

But this darkness was deeper, more viscous, and damp. He shuffled ahead, stretching a hand in front of him. Only ten or twelve steps to his lamp by the bed. On and on he went, cautious step by cautious step, deeper and deeper into the room. His hand was extended and shook like a palsy. The floor felt metallic, and his scraping steps resonated cavernous and deep as if in the belly of a great ship. Twenty steps in and reaching for his lamp, electric fear fizzled up his spine. But there was still nothing in front of him. He took tiny steps a few to the left and then to the right trying to find his way in the darkness. He imagined that he heard breathing nearby, and he could sense a presence, the presence that he had always imagined as a child but was now very real.

Something fleshy and covered in bristle brushed past his wrist, then his elbow pressed into doughy tissue mottled with tumorous growths. Several moist huffs and a cough burst into an angry porcine squeal that rose higher, and louder, until piercing like a raging siren. Ron covered his ears, but it made no difference. The din wavered and altered until it was the laughing cackle of the coyote.

Chapter 6

Hospital

Dee's face floated above, bright and serene, filling the night sky like a full moon. Ron furrowed his brow, trying to fathom. He blinked.

"He's coming around," she said while looking up at someone standing at the other side of the bed.

Ron slowly hunted her gaze, following until he saw another face. "Adam?" he whispered. "Is that...you? Where...? Am I...dead?"

He squinted again, trying to see the woman. "Dee?" he managed. But it was not Dee. Each thought had to be carefully extracted and etched on his brain. He concentrated hard like the toddler who would sit with his tongue at the corner of his mouth, trying to sketch each letter of his name with a crayon.

It was not Dee; it was her daughter. Another phrase came slowly to mind, pressed in crayon: *Their* daughter.

"Gracie..." He began to speak, but his voice only trailed into simpering before he closed his eyes and lost consciousness again.

Adam Knowles walked around the bed and stood beside his wife. With fingers splayed, she caressed her swollen abdomen.

"He thought I was my mom." She smiled at Adam.

"I know," Adam said. "Will he be alright?"

"Before you got here, the nurse said that it's a good sign that he's coming out of the coma so quickly. The bloodwork looks like he had bacterial sepsis. He nearly died of infection. But now that the fever is down and he's responding to antibiotics, he should be alright."

"Are you worried? Do you want me to stay? I can take as much time from work as I need, now." Adam said. "You've been here for almost three days."

"No. He'll probably be out for a long time again. Now that he has seen us, I think we can leave for a while. I might want to go back to the hotel and take a nap."

"When do you want to go home?" Adam said.

"I don't want to stay any longer than we're needed. I don't want to draw anyone's attention to us or to Ron. If we stay too long and they know we're here, they might..."

Adam laid a hand on her arm. "Do we need to contact your brother?"

Gracie bit her lower lip and shook her head slowly. "No. I don't want to call Duane yet. Ron should be fine. Leo or Donnie will be here shortly. They are going to drive over and get his car from the ferry dock and then they'll stay around here to keep a look out. I'll talk to the doctors and see how soon we can get him out of here. We can decide what to do after that." She sighed. "I'm all the family—" She looked up at Adam. "*We're* all the family this guy has here."

"His brother Jan is up in Canada. I know him a little. And Sam, his niece," Adam said. "Should I try to get hold of them?"

"I don't know. I thought about reaching out to Samantha after she came up as a possible cousin on the DNA site, but I'm worried about drawing any attention to her, too."

Adam shrugged. "More and more, it seems pretty obvious that trying to draw out the Dark Council by creating that fake account on the DNA site was not such a good idea."

"No. It certainly was not our best move. The Lake Council of Keepers has discussed it. I suppose I can understand what Duane was thinking, but it has created some complications. It could have helped Duane to pin the Dark Council down and figure out what they were looking for.

"Yeah. Doing the ancestry program had some consequences." She touched Ron's shoulder. "But not all bad."

"No. Not all bad." Adam agreed.

"But we can't be sure of all the other consequences, the other possibilities," she said. "And surely we don't know everything—or even *who* those characters are looking for. But I know Ron is not the one they want. They should have learned a lesson after that ridiculous shaman, James Graves."

Watching her father, she was silent for a while, remembering that terrible night when James Graves was pitched into Lake Superior after nearly killing Ron.

"I remember Graves too well. He was creepy," Adam said.

"He was," she said thoughtfully. "That Dark Council assumed they had found an important shaman, but they were stupid to use him. Every big bird is not an eagle."

"Um…what does that mean? You know that I'm still not up to speed on all your Native sayings and jargon. I've only known I was Native for a couple of years, you know." Adam said.

Gracie's laugh jingled like a music box. "I know. You're not up to speed on lots of stuff." She bumped his shoulder. "But I still love you."

"What did you mean about Big Bird and the eagle?" Adam asked.

Now she held her stomach with both hands as laughter shook her small body. "Not Big Bird!" She covered her mouth, caught her breath, and looked around. "They are going to kick us outta here." She stepped away from the bed. "My Pops used that saying about the big bird and the eagle. It's about exaggeration. It means that just because you see a big bird flying across the sky it doesn't mean that it was an eagle. People who like to tell big stories may see things that aren't there. They will try to impress you by saying they saw an eagle, when they probably only saw a vulture or heron. That bunch thought that James Graves was an eagle when he was only a filthy vulture."

"Okay. I get it. But you're sure they don't want Ron? Won't they follow him to get at you?"

"I don't know if they will follow the DNA trail that far. And even if they find out he is related, the people we are dealing with do not want to risk blowing their cover, just because Ron Jarvin happens to take a ferry across the lake and ends up in the hospital." She looked at Ron again. "In hindsight, it was probably a mistake to do that DNA site, but we did that test because we knew they would be watching. We hoped it would draw them out. And Duane thinks it did."

"I started it," Adam said. "Maybe I shouldn't have tried to figure out my DNA."

She looked at Adam again, grinning. "Yes. You sort of started this. I think Duane got the idea after you did the DNA. But it wasn't your fault. You just wanted to find out what kind of mutt you were before I had your baby."

Adam rolled his eyes, and she winked in return.

She walked back to the bed and patted Ron's shoulder. "I hope we didn't create a mess. We just never expected all this to turn up. I feel responsible. Like I let it happen. Maybe subconsciously, I just had selfish motives for finding my father. It's all confusing."

Silently they watched Ron for a time, made small talk, then gathered themselves to leave.

Suddenly the heart monitor next to Ron's bed started to scream, thin and piercing like a new widow. Before Gracie and Adam could think, two nurses were crashing into the room.

"Excuse us. Step back, please." A man in scrubs touched Gracie's shoulder as he plowed ahead with a medical cart in tow. More staff rolled in.

Gracie and Adam watched in a daze as nurses flung back linen, repositioned, attached electrodes, and positioned needles over the ports to his IV. "No pulse? Confirm. I need a read-out." A man said with unsettling calm while his hands locked over Ron's chest, ready to deliver CPR.

Amid all the confusion, a nurse hurried into the room, holding a tablet. She tapped and swept at her screen a couple of times and rested her hand on Gracie's shoulder. "Are you his daughter? A relative?"

Gracie couldn't answer for a moment. "Well, I, uh… What's happening!"

Chapter 7
Yet a Girl with Imagination…

Yet a girl with imagination lives a life not quite her own.

Often Gracie read the letter: A note central to her life. And because she did not want it entombed in a dark envelope or embalmed in plastic laminate, she had stored the letter in a simple clear sleeve. It became a ritual to slide the paper from its protection and run a finger across the yellowed creases that she had tried to heal over the years with dressings of clear tape.

By the time this young woman had turned thirteen, she could have claimed responsibility for giving her grandparents their gray hairs and worn wrinkles. This was a tough time in their home. Aunt Nessa had moved out. As soon as her mother's sister was old enough, she left home for work and college. And she would rarely return, even for holidays or special occasions. Nessa had experienced a jealous rebellion of her own that had started when her dead sister's kids came to live with her parents a decade before.

Nessa had been only a girl when her sister, Dee, died. Then all of her parent's attention was turned toward grief and toward providing for her sister's kids, Duane and Gracie. Dee had been older than Nessa and she had doted on her younger sister. To Nessa, the loss cut deeply.

And even Gracie's quiet, thoughtful older brother Duane had left home for college. Despite the age gap, he had been her faithful ally and tried to be her counselor and confidant.

But by thirteen, Gracie seemed beyond help—from anyone. Not even Duane could reach her. The young girl had thought Duane was only trying to comfort her when he told her that story over and over; a fantasy that held no more credence to her than Santa Claus. He tried to explain that their mother had died trying to rescue him from the underworld. In Duane's story, their mother had trusted a bunch of charlatans to ceremonially induce a dream state so that she could reach out to Duane while he was in a coma. But Duane suspected that those bad men had intended to murder their mother all along. Gracie had no interest in her family's culture or tradition. Back then it had all been stories, myths, and nonsense to the girl. Just Duane's clumsy solace.

It didn't matter to Gracie how her mother had died. Dee had been heartlessly torn from Gracie and no one could take her place. She blamed everyone; even her brother, her grandparents, and certainly her mother. Secretly she suspected Dee had probably just fallen back into drugging, and she had OD'd. And Duane was just making up a fanciful story to gloss over it.

So, the insurrection against her young life had raged on.

Then on her thirteenth birthday, her grandparents had handed her the faded envelope. Her black hair was worn in a boy cut with one purple wave cascading down the side of her face. While she slumped at the table, arms folded across her black hoodie, a reflex jerk of her head flipped the hair covering one eye. Birthdays were fraught with strife for as long as her grandparents could recall. Especially for this couple who loved their granddaughter like their own lost daughter yet who knew too well that no one on this side of eternity could give the girl what she really wanted: her mother. But on that day, the girl's discontent had boiled into rage: the headphones were not the ones she wanted, the gift card was only $25, and she was too damn old for that backpack. *Pink? Are you serious?* The clothes were tossed aside, ignored. Totally stupid.

She'd pushed aside her favorite meal of fries and chicken nuggets and ignored her grandmother's gasps while she snuffed each of her thirteen candles with her fingers one by one. She picked at the birthday cake.

Finally, Pops returned from the other room holding an envelope close to his heart. His arm extended gracefully like a heron, and he laid the envelope in front of Gracie. Grandma drew near, trying to see. Grandma knew this was an important moment. Her vision had been diminished by raging diabetes and fiercely refusing to control the disease was her own act of rebellion.

Inscribed in delicate cursive the envelope said *To my beloved girl on her 13th birthday.* Reading the inscription, the girl had enough and stomped to her room and slammed the door. When she was alone she carelessly tore away the envelope that had been untouched for all these years. She had no idea who it was from, but it had better be at least a $50 bill. But no. She huffed. It was just a note. But it was a note that was about to alter the tortured path of a slight and very troubled girl.

It was a simple letter that began *Dear Gracie* and after only a few paragraphs ended *I pray that you live both intentionally and with imagination. Yet a girl with imagination lives a life not quite her own. I will love you forever and ever. Your Mother, Rose Delight Bird.*

The old couple were shuffling plates to the sink and talking in worried, hushed tones when the bedroom door burst open. They were prepared for another onslaught of screams and curses but the little girl that had stormed into her room was not the same one who emerged. Holding up the note, her face washed with tears, she wailed. She could not speak, but threw her arms around her grandpa and squeezed his waist. After a while, they moved to the couch where the girl sat between them for a long while, not speaking or even looking at them. They stroked her hair. Over and again, quiet tears would grow to breakers of gasping sobs shameless as a toddler.

She finally trailed off and went to bed without a word. A different person awoke the next morning. She had left the girl behind and was on the path to becoming a woman, the uncommon daughter of an uncommon woman: Rose Delight Bird. Known as the White Doe.

Her mother had written the note to Gracie because she knew that what she was doing to rescue Duane was risky and that she may not return. When Gracie was a child, she had disregarded Duane's stories, yet the legend of her mother had secretly grown in her mind. She imagined Dee as a shapeshifter because her mother had changed from something damaged and hurtful into something loving and powerful. Despite her skepticism, Duane's stories of Dee's voyage into the underworld had left a mark on Gracie. It was a myth that she wanted to believe, doubted, then believed sincerely later in life when she came to know her brother as a man.

The truth had been made known.

To *live a life not quite her own* this girl with imagination would become not only more than she had been, but she would learn to live beyond herself. Applying her fancy not to music, or art, or words, but applying her thoughts and vision to transforming her small body into a force like her mother.

And by the time her 14th birthday arrived, her gifts became nunchucks and Jiu-Jitsu lessons.

Chapter 8

Juan and Rosaria

HIS EYES WERE OPEN, so Rosaria instilled the drops, then gently massaged his lids and held them for a moment until they stayed shut. While she waited she fussed with his hair lovingly and tried to reset his ponytail, but he was as restless and twitchy as a yellow perch on ice, gasping and freezing all at the same time.

It was spooky. They were in a damp cavern with a few bare pieces of lawn furniture and a low light. She did not like it and was afraid of what she would have to do if something really bad happened to Juan, but he had assured her he would be safe.

She was worried and he was too restless. It was clearly more difficult for him this time. Her hair was in a loose bun, and she tucked a wisp of dark hair behind her ear. With pursed lips, her fine features were focused and intense. Her husband was fidgety this time, but during the other sessions he laid as quietly as their sleeping tabby cat, Chatsworth. The cat had been sleeping on a corner of the cot until the restlessness woke him and he arose in sleepy disgust, circled twice, looked at Rosaria, and seemed to roll his eyes before dropping off the end, the sandy floor chuffing under his paws. The cat padded silently away.

He was emerging early this time. Previous sessions had been infrequent, but for the past month he insisted on going under every week. And each time seemed longer. It was getting hard to hide it from Annabelle and Aiden. The twins were nearly three and it was difficult to convince them to stay with the sitter down the road for a few hours until he was ready to come around.

Sometimes he would be out of it for a while after the sessions. She could run the shop and even do many of the fixes and uploads for the devices that locals entrusted to them. And she also managed all the business that was connected with the online sales side of the shop.

Juan and Rosaria Baptiste were the aliases, but they had grown into their role after purchasing the ramshackle house and restoring it into a home and computer shop just after the twins were born. It sat on fifteen acres just off Highway 28 in Michigan's Upper Peninsula. No one paid much attention to the Baptistes. And *Yoopers,* as Upper Peninsula natives are known, didn't pry into other people's business. This had been a major factor in helping them decide to relocate back to the U.P. Unless you needed help, people minded their own business.

Privacy was one reason they lived here. But so was the proximity to the work that *Juan and Rosaria* were really there to do.

A computer shop was a good front, and they could keep track of a variety of criminal activities and chatter from the threads of data they could glean from the computers they serviced in the shop. It was done legally with orders if needed, and at this level none of it would be used to convict anyone. It was more for their security and to protect those they loved.

But the location and history of this house were crucial. It had been a rock shop before the old spur of highway had been abandoned and the new Highways 28 and 41 had been constructed. Not even a handful of locals were alive to remember the history of the establishment, and they had long forgotten the ancient mine just a stone's throw from the back door. The mine penetrated deep and forgotten, far into one of the oldest igneous layers on earth.

It was little more than a rough cave that meandered a couple hundred yards and the outer digs probably predated European settlers. With input from a couple of the wise council members of the Kitchi-Gami Council of Keepers it was no accident the Baptistes had found and restored the rock shop.

Everything is by design. Her husband had convinced her of this long ago, and his certainty and conviction were some of the qualities that had drawn her to him even before they were lovers and even further back to when they were coworkers consulting on difficult federal cases. Back then she was the computer and data expert, and he was the investigator. Now they were a team and their skills converged seamlessly.

Their relationship had deepened, they married, and the Federal Marshals had helped them hide while they did their work undisturbed—for now. Their identities had been changed but their commitment to one another did not falter.

His eyes snapped open, terrified, and he gasped and pumped his knees under the blanket.

She leaned near and whispered, "Shh...Duane, it's okay. You're back."

He clasped her hand, his grip squeezing harder until she had to pry her fingers away. Still looking up at the ceiling, his eyes wide, Duane said, "Maura." He found her face. "I think we found them. The walls there are like that red sandstone cut from the Soo locks in Sault Ste Marie."

They knew there were countless buildings and basements in that region that had been built out of the stone that had been quarried from the site of the Soo locks.

"There are a lot of places to consider, but we only have to find one," Duane said. "And, based on what we know, if any part of Maggie's former bed and breakfast is built of red sandstone, I think we know what we might find there."

"You mean that group that may have bought that inn? You said there was a rumor the cabal—or cartel or whatever you called it—had bought that place," she said.

"Yes. The Dark Council. And I think that their purchase of the inn may be more than a rumor now," Duane said.

Chapter 9

Beyond Naomikong Bay

Ron had awakened briefly to see Gracie's face, then fell deeper into unconsciousness than before.

Then as soft and rhythmic as a brush through flowing hair, he heard waves stroke the sand, murmuring as delicately as willow leaves.

He grinned as carefree as a child; his eyes lit for adventure. He could not recall how he had arrived at this familiar expanse of hidden beach along Lake Superior. Several times, he'd canoed alone to the Naomikong beaches. He'd camped somewhere here, but after a restless and haunted night, he had left the next morning.

Naomikong Bay had always seemed bewitching and serene. Now it was hypnotizing. The night choir of crickets, katydids, and other unknown species from the Insecta class of arthropods, along with the Amphibians: *Salientia to be specific,* Ron recited to himself, *frogs, toads, and their relatives.*

Along with the meteorology, limnology, hydrology and any other *-ology* relative to this deep, cold lake and its surrounding beaches and forests, the flora and fauna were also one of his loves.

But he sensed something different. Something had been altered along this stretch of beach. The colors were deeper, the sand softer, and the water more sensual—if that were possible. Golden rays threaded through leaves and branches like woven strands of glass from where the sun seemed permanently perched just below the tree line.

He hadn't noticed the old rowboat pulled up on the beach. *Is that how I got here?* Rowing a boat, paddling a canoe, or hiking would be the only way he could have arrived, and he remembered none of it.

Across the bow of the boat was written *Shirley's Cabins*. He wouldn't have rented a boat—not from Shirley's Cabins. *I think that place changed hands a couple of years ago, or it may have closed.*

A frantic rustling in the brush startled him. Service berry and tag alder hedged a forest that stepped upward from birch trunks gleaming white and thick as mammoth bones, then to spruce, and finally to great white pine, their tops washed in the molten bronze of sunset.

As though a conductor had swept the chorus to an abrupt pause, the night sounds ceased. Even the waves no longer whispered, and everything was heartbeat silent. Trying to discern the reason for the silence, Ron stepped nearer the forest, gazed up and down the beach, then turned to look across the water. Only silence.

Then came a sound far away at first, yet clear and placid as the last vibrating tones of a bell. A woman's voice, at first low and breathy, it swelled, wavered, then gathered and folded layer upon layer to a deep and brittle sadness. He pondered. *A Celtic dirge. No, a nun's chant—a Buddhist nun? It may have been Tibetan, no, definitely Irish. No. Not that.* The voice was high, sweet, and innocent more like a young girl than a woman.

The evening seemed to have dimmed another turn, so he had not noticed what lay ahead through the trees along the beach. Peering into darkness amid soaring white pine trunks, a row of flames flickered along a wall of log and stone. Through the brush that hemmed the beach, he looked for a path. But there was no pathway. He swiped his way through the dense brush until he found himself standing in front of a long porch lit by a row of oil lamps that stretched far away in each direction until disappearing into haze and branches. The woman's voice had ceased, and it left him with a sad longing for something vitally needed but forever out of reach. The smooth rumble of the doors in motion drew his head around just as the hem of a gown whisked through the door and disappeared as the doors shut.

He stepped onto the deck of the porch.

The posts were big as barrels and the walls of the lodge were set with arching stained-glass windows. The woman had retreated through great wooden double doors that were intricately carved in scenes of harvest. The longer he looked at the carvings, the more intricate the scenes became. He imagined the muscles straining on the arms of the threshers as they swung their scythes, sweat rolled off their brow as sunlight glinted from the blades of their tools. The long skirts of the women rustled in a cool breeze, their baskets overflowing.

A man suddenly rushed up behind him, pushed past, and shouldered into one of the heavy doors and rushed inside.

Startled, the door had nearly swung shut again before Ron could collect his thoughts. He pushed against the door and stepped in. The man was sprinting across a cavernous lobby that seemed to stretch both ways into infinity. Wearing a T-shirt and cutoffs, the man's bare feet thumped on the worn carpet.

"Hey, wait," Ron shouted.

The Native man slid to a halt, a ponytail swishing around his shoulders as he spun.

The man looked stunned. "Ron Jarvin. What are you doing here? Why are you here? How did you—?"

"Duane Bird?" Ron said.

Chapter 10

There Is a Lodge

"Ron, do you know where you are?" Duane said.

In confusion, Ron scanned across the endless lobby furnished with log and leather chairs and fires crackling in great fireplaces framed by wooden statues that angled from their perch like ship's mastheads. His head swiveled back toward the stained-glass windows, now darkened. He still could not remember how he had arrived here, and now even the beach outside was fading into memory. He glanced down at the shoddy carpet, as if searching for an answer, then with a sad, worried face like a lost child, he met Duane's gaze. "I have no idea. I-I can't remember how I got here." He stepped closer. "You are Duane Bird, right?"

"Yeah." Duane looked around quickly and held up a finger. "But, man, I can't stop here. I'm sure that you arrived here for a reason, but we don't have much time. What is the last thing that you remember?"

"Your sister." Ron's face brightened. "And Adam. I was sick. I felt awful. They were there beside my bed."

"Mmm...that doesn't help much. But Gracie told me how you had showed up through that ancestry site. That's all water under the bridge. But it sounds like you were in a hospital." Duane paused. "That might not be good."

"What do you mean? Where are we? Is this—?"

"I don't know." Duane scratched his head. "I can't tell you why you're here. I was first here long ago with my friend Scotty when I was just a child." His hands drifted downward, presenting his tee shirt and shorts. "Thus, my third-grade outfit." He grinned. "You're not wearing a hospital gown. That has to be a good thing." He flapped his hand. "But it's too much to explain and there are too many possibilities as to why you are here at this particular moment. But we just don't have time to sort it out. The window into this place can close at any moment, and I think I am close to discovering why I keep returning here. But we have to move. We have to get going." He swiped a hand, *c'mon,* and took off down the main hallway leading away from the lobby.

"But…" Ron had little choice. He loped after Duane, twisting left and right through a maze, down one hallway and across another, each corridor looked just like the last: the walls were covered in dull wallpaper that was a gray shade of yellow patterned with thin blue and green vertical stripes disrupted only by mold, water stains, or a peeling edge. The blue carpet ran along all the hallways, moldy-smelling in the warm, moist air, and patterned with tiny flowers that could just as well have been fungus.

The men were moving quickly, but Ron kept up with the younger man easily. He should have been bending over, hands on knees, gasping for air. He had probably not done any meaningful exercise in years.

They passed hundreds of doors that lined passageways. On each heavy wooden door, a different scene was carved into a panel. The scenes were similar to those on the front doors; the images seemed alive as they swept past. But these were not only scenes of harvest. There were scenes of urbanscapes, too, and woodlands, villages—old villages, modern towns, ranches, and placid lake fronts. Any life that could be imagined.

"Down here." Duane disappeared into a side door and down into darkness along narrow steps.

Ron paused at the top staring downward into the shadows with mushroom-damp basement odor seeping upward toward the arched doorway. "Duane." He called. No answer. But he could hear the slap of Duane's bare feet fading below him.

He plunged forward down bare wooden steps slippery with moisture, bracing his hand against the moldering wall. In a moment, his eyes adjusted to an ambient glow dim as starlight. He saw Duane thump onto a landing and wheel around the corner onto another descending flight.

As Ron flashed around the corner, he recognized that they had come to a floor much like the one above, except it appeared to have been empty for decades or more. The wallpaper sagged from the walls, the doors to rooms were open or canted off their hinges. Each room lay dark and still. He felt a chill. Then like the sound of a cold, eerie draft seeping through a broken window Ron heard moaning. Was it merely a draft or was it a lost soul held captive in one of these rooms? His heart surged and he paused.

"Ron, keep up!" Duane's voice came upward from the next flight of stairs.

He followed downward another flight, deeper into the gloom until his feet grated when wooden steps transitioned to stone.

At the bottom, Duane stood in a hidden cove that covered a landing barely larger than a closet. There were no more flights of stairs going further down. A low, narrow cavern led away from the landing in both directions. A greenish phosphorescence marbled the walls and reflected in the wet path. The scent was no longer the moldy rot from the floors above, but earthy, like moss and pond water.

Duane tucked the hair behind his ear, looking left and right, trying to recall. Along these halls, time and place could roil and become irrelevant. But he had been at this landing twice, and both times he had been yanked away as some portal or crevasse in his consciousness had closed.

Decades ago, he and his boyhood friend, Scotty, had been here in this *other* world. They had veered right and were eventually led out of the maze of deep, sunken floors and found their way out of the lodge. He recalled what lay in that direction. Now he was compelled to go the other way. Duane went left and Ron followed, calling from behind.

"Duane, wait up. Where are we? Just tell me what we're doing down here?" Ron asked.

Duane plunged into the darkness. Ron sighed; not wanting to be left behind, he followed. But the blackness was palpable, substantial like a thin wall of congealed grease that seemed to cling to hands and face as he clawed through. Breaching the film, he found himself in a dimly-lit hallway, similar to the maze of hallways above. But within these hallways amber sconces flickered along the walls, illuminating ornate wooden trim, moldering tapestries, and threadbare rugs that could have been from millennia gone by. There were again many rooms. Arched wooden doors tilted, decaying in their frames.

Duane had vanished.

In silence, he cautiously stepped forward while listening for Duane's footsteps. He was fearful to call out. He stopped when he heard what could have been the creaking of a floorboard from somewhere above or the rasp of one of the rotting hinges. He edged forward, looking away from doorways that yawned like cavernous throats. He scurried past. A thin whimpering hung in the dank air for a moment; a voice between whining and a phlegmy rumble in the throat. When he paused the eerie sound paused. He still could not hear Duane.

Searching for Duane, he forced himself to peer longer into each gloomy room. Whether it was a trick of his vision or something more sinister, milky forms shifted about in the abandoned chambers.

He hurried ahead.

He stopped suddenly and twirled around. A filmy apparition trailed behind him. Shapeless and void at first, but as it neared, it coalesced into a figure. As it took form he could see the tilted head, sockets for eyes, the corners of the mouth, and a brow deeply saddened, like a caricature of grief. The form was a shirtless man, his chest and belly a bloated curve from neck to pelvis. The grating moan returned as the dead man reached toward Ron with a muttering that swelled to a soulless bleating. "Blah...blah...blah."

As Ron pivoted to flee there were more of the sorrowful dead oozing from darkened rooms on either side. The groaning grew to a dirge of the hopeless and lost. Ron covered his face. On the verge of tears, he pitched forward and fled, stumbling and gabbling. Uncovering his face, he flailed ahead, pitching side to side seeking a way out. A hand clawed at his arm until it gained purchase and gripped him tightly. He cried out and shook his sleeve, desperately trying to break free. He smacked the hand that grasped him.

"Keep moving," Duane said, continuing to grip Ron's arm. "Ignore these souls. Ignore all this." Duane did not slow or look sideways as he spoke. Fearfully, Ron was dragged along until they took another corner and Duane slowed, studying each door.

"This has to be a nightmare. A bad dream," Ron said. "Why can't I wake up?"

"Not a dream, definitely not a dream," Duane said. They faced one another.

"Then where are we? You have to tell me."

Duane gripped Ron's shoulders. "You will be alright." He stepped back.

Ron's head spun to look back over his shoulder and around at the moldy hallway. "I can't believe this is anything but a terrible dream."

"No. This is beyond dreams. A delirium wilderness. That beach where you landed may have looked familiar. But that beach, this lodge, and everything beyond is a land that dreams only presume. It's the place that dreams have been trying to tell us about. Our dreams are just a thin gauze between our lives and this wilderness."

"I can't believe it. How do you know?"

"I told you. I was here before. I survived. I was rescued by my mother, Dee." Duane hesitated. "But she never returned, and neither did my friend Scotty."

"What the hell do you mean? Am I dead? Is this purgatory—hell?" Ron's voice was raising.

Duane patted the air with his palm. "Be calm. You're okay." He gazed at Ron a moment longer. "But I can't say why you're here. If you were in the hospital, you may be in some kind of coma or...dead."

Ron was silent. Duane waited, allowing the man to gather his thoughts.

"Then how did you get here? Are you dead?" Ron asked.

"Because I was here and found my way out, I can return. My wife watches over me as I make a transition." Duane waved his hand. "None of this matters right now. I absolutely must move on before I run out of time. I must find them this time, or it will be too late."

"Find who?" Ron said.

"It should be right here. It will be easier to show you." Pointing a finger, Duane began counting off the doors, "One, two, three...the serpent." The fourth was a closed door with a stained-glass panel. He leaned with his shoulder and the rotten door frame crumbled. He looked back to Ron with a broad smile. "We found them."

Ron approached the broken door but recoiled at the vivid figure of a poised serpent. It took a moment to realize that the form was a representation of the Rod of Asclepius, the medical symbol, that had been precisely rendered in a stained-glass panel. The snake seemed to slither in the murky glass. Ron reached out and cautiously traced a finger around the flawless image.

Ron stepped beside Duane into a room encircled by more amber sconces. The scene left them speechless.

The large room was set with twenty stone slabs or more. A few of the slabs were empty, but on most of the others lay a girl or young woman. A blanket had been neatly draped over each, leaving only their bare shoulders exposed.

The room was built with irregular blocks of red stone and the humid ether made the walls greasy damp. Pieces of old metal hospital furniture lay bent and twisted like angled bones disappearing in murky haze into the corners of the large room.

Duane walked among the women, studying each one as if he were trying to recognize them or memorize their features. Each had long hair spread carefully across their shoulders. Their perfection and precise arrangement brought to mind a sordid collection of dolls. Most had long black hair over their brown shoulders and could have been Asian—or Native. Two or three of the young women were black, and a few had hair that was red or blond.

"Who are they?" Ron whispered as he stepped beside one of the slabs.

Duane only held up a hand and spoke as if to himself, "They are not actually here. This is storage, the place of dead silence where they are being held."

Ron looked down at one of the women on the slab. Her glossy hair surrounded her and flowed nearly to her waist like a cape. She was peaceful, the corners of her mouth turned slightly upward as if merely catching a restful nap. Her features reminded him more of an Indigenous woman from South America or Mexico rather than Woodland or Plains Natives.

Her eyes flashed open. Ron started. "Duane," he whispered.

It was as if she were trying to mouth something. Fearful, her eyes pierced into Ron, but she seemed frozen. Trapped. Only her eyes and lips could move.

She tried to form a hoarse whisper and kept repeating with her lips.

Duane rushed over and looked down on her. "I recognize her from the files. Salvia Lopez. Salvi, they called her."

Duane leaned near, trying to hear.

She swallowed hard and said hoarsely, "Find the key. Truth is the key. The Truth will make us free." Then her eyes closed abruptly, and she was still again.

"What's wrong with her? What's happening here?" Ron asked.

"Salvi Lopez is from New Mexico. But she was hanging out with friends in Rapid City, South Dakota when the three of them suddenly went missing. We've been searching for these girls. They've disappeared from all over and we had suspected many were abducted and possibly trafficked. But this is not like any trafficking we've seen. They were not lured with drugs or snatched from troubled homes." Duane put his hand to his chin. "They were selected and pursued. Chosen somehow. We don't know how or why." Duane looked around the room. "And I think that's Missie Beals from Fort Berthold. And Angie Perth from Rosebud." He pointed.

"What she said is so cryptic. Find…wait! Find the key…Truth is the key?" Ron scratched a finger above his brow. "And something about 'set them free.'" Ron looked at Duane. "This is crazy. It's like some kind of bizarre script, right? I still can't believe this is not a dream."

"It might be like a dream for them. I just don't know where they are or how we reach them."

"You said that they are not actually here. You mean…"

The scrape of boots on wet stone snapped their attention to a dark corner of the room where a presence, a hulking man stood in the gloom visible only in outline. The face of a man with dead-fish eyes under heavy brows and a mouth full of blocky teeth shimmered into view then receded. As quickly as the apparition appeared, it was gone.

"Ggorchik," Duane said. "That's the…"

Both of the men covered their faces with their elbows as a rancid, rotten odor washed into the room.

"God. What is that?" Ron asked.

A searing porcine squeal ricocheted across the stone walls and trailed off to hyena cackles. From deeper in the gloom where the man had appeared, hulking, ape-like forms began to materialize.

Suddenly Ron was jerked forcefully backward, as if a rope encircled his chest. Duane reached for him, but it was too late. Flailing and breathless, Ron was yanked back through the door, along the damp hallways, back through the greasy darkness and up the steps, accelerating all the while. In a blur, he was pulled back through the lobby, out of the lodge, across the beach and aloft, disappearing upward into the hazy blue.

Chapter 11

Salvi Lopez

IT HAD ALL HAPPENED so fast. And then they were gone.

Salvi had met Angeline and Alisa in their first year at Metropolitan State University in Denver. Now in their third year, they had set off on what they called the *dumbest spring break* trip ever. Anyway, this year was important, and they wanted to finish with few distractions. So, they decided to visit Angeline's family in Rapid City, and on the way they would circle around to see some of the sights and play tourist.

They took a day to wind through Pine Ridge Reservation where Angeline had lived as a child before she moved with her mom to Rapid City. After the reservation, the girls tracked north through the Badlands.

Boyfriend problems were also at the root of their spring break plans. Salvi's mom and new boyfriend were going to Corpus Christi for a few days, so they wouldn't be around during break. Salvi didn't like her mom's guy and did not really want to go home to Las Cruces anyway. And Alisa had recently broken up with her boyfriend, so she was in the mood to get away, forget about him, and maybe spend at least a couple of nights partying her troubles away at a number of Rapid City's clubs, taverns, or whatever they could find.

None of the girls partied much, but being away from Denver, dancing with a different crowd, and listening to some different music appealed to all of them. They just loved being together and laughing out loud.

Salvi tended to be a loner, and Angeline and Alisa had been friends, but they discovered Salvi as kindred, and quickly included her in their circle. They could have been three sisters, carefree, and they seemed to turn heads wherever they went.

They took a winding route through the Badlands, stopping a couple of times. When they needed a bathroom break they pulled into a souvenir shop. Leaving the shop, Salvi noticed a woman setting up a stand. The woman waved to Salvi and motioned her over. Curious and needing a little more time out of the car, she wandered over. The vendor wore a long ribbon dress and a ball cap pulled tight over her head, with the brim drawn down partially hiding her face. One arm bent, she held a cigarette casually above her shoulder. The other arm crossed in front of her, tucked under the arm holding the cigarette. The woman wore mirrored sunglasses that gave the appearance of wide, reptilian eyes that Salvi could sense were following her. The woman had laid an old door across two sawhorses and set out a small selection of earrings and bead work. There was a wooden box strewn with polished stones and crystals.

Salvi's grandmother had been a curandero who gathered herbs and plants to use for healing. Salvi had learned little of the healing skills but shared her grandmother's interest in crystals and precious stones. She paused to look at a set of earrings and slid over to look at the crystals, touching a blue stone that reminded her of one that her grandmother kept on her mantel. It was deeper blue than turquoise, almost purple, and was crisscrossed with veins of cream and black.

Truth is the key. The Truth will make you free, her grandmother—her abuela—would say. At that moment, Abuela's voice could not have been clearer if she had been standing right beside Salvi.

Startled, Salvi looked around. In her mind, she recited to herself the rest of her abuela's saying.

"But even a little lie may cause the child to die," the vendor said. Her voice was heavy and raspy from tobacco. She pulled on the cigarette and blew a long stream of smoke.

"How did you know...?" Salvi asked reaching behind and flipping her long hair, then she swept a finger across bangs that she kept cut straight above her brow. Women in her family had worn their hair similarly as long as she could remember.

The woman ignored her question. "That stone is Sodalite: the truth stone." The woman said. "And if you carry that stone and get lost, someone will find you. Like radar."

It took a second for Salvi to gather her thoughts. "My abuela used to say that. About the little lie. And she had one of these stones."

"And I bet she never got lost." The woman smiled sideways.

The woman's hidden gaze was making Salvi feel uncomfortable and she nervously turned the silver and turquoise bracelet on her wrist. She was not shy about wearing a good deal of the turquoise and other jewelry her abuela had given her before she died. Her belt buckle was an eagle figure and she had replaced the buttons on her denim jacket with silver.

"That belt buckle is lapis. I bet it's from the Incas."

"Yeah, you're right. My ancestors. It's from Peru," Salvi said.

The woman offered a trade or discount if Salvi wanted to part with the turquoise bracelet. But to Salvi it was too precious, so the woman was not persistent.

"You were looking at that blue stone," the vendor said. "What do you think?"

Salvi had not really planned on buying anything and the stone was priced about forty dollars more than she could afford to pay.

"Sorry, not today," Salvi said.

The woman picked up the stone and rolled it in her fingers a moment. It seemed to catch the sun just right and a light roiled deep within. Finally, she flipped it up, caught it, and extended her arm toward Salvi.

"It's yours," she said.

"Ha! What do you mean?" Salvi asked.

"Your grandma, your abuela would want you to have it."

"I can give you at least *something* for it. I like it, but it's just not in my budget."

"No. Take it. I've had it for a long time, and it seems no one is buying Sodalite." She dropped the stone in Salvi's hand.

"Thank you. I don't know what to say. I will treasure it, for sure."

The woman waved her off.

The other girls had drifted back to the car and Salvi took a moment to at least buy the earrings she'd been eyeing, then scampered to catch up. But as Salvi turned to wave, she was rivetted. The woman had already picked up her phone and was busy texting. The glint off her phone flashed in the woman's face and for an instant the creases at the corners of her mouth appeared like serpent's fangs shimmering with droplets of blood. Slowly the reptilian sunglasses lifted from the phone and stared at Salvi, and she rushed to catch up to her friends.

She didn't say anything to Angeline and Alisa, convinced her strange vision was only the result of fatigue and a trick of the fickle light.

The girls arrived in Rapid City that evening hungry and tired with a load of dirty clothes from school. Angeline's mother was generous with her home and with her washer and dryer, and the girls were eager to take advantage of her charity.

Standing on a postage stamp lot, the small, gray house was wedged between two similar homes in an older part of town. Angeline's tiny bedroom was built into a half-story created by pushing a sole dormer out one side of the roof. The other half of the upstairs was attic.

Angeline's mother worked nights, but the girls were ready to wind down anyway, and they had gone to bed before she left for work. Salvi knew that Angeline and Alisa liked to talk more than she did, so she was glad to take the room in the basement. The space had been divided between storage and a corner with a lamp on a table next to a foldout couch that had been opened up and made into a bed. The clothes dryer at the other end was rumbling and ticking with the last load of wash. Most of the basement was built of block walls, but the corner had been paneled with knotty pine planks. The glossy varnish had aged beyond yellow to a sickly orange. It was cozy, like a cabin, she thought. She found the blue stone in her jacket pocket and, with a smile, laid it on the table beside the bed.

She thought that she would drift off to sleep without a problem, but she had never slept in a basement, and in the dark she felt the press of the underground walls. What might burrow and skulk in the tunnels and rat holes right on the other side of the walls? How like a grave it was.

Eventually, she dozed.

Like the ant farm in grade school, giant ants peered at her with their blank insect eyes, meticulously cleaning their antennae and rubbing together their thorny front legs. Soon, they scuttled away at the advance of the carrion beetles, their creamy heads searching for death, and the burying beetles carrying their putrid treasures deeper and deeper underground. The floor shuddered as a larger specimen tunneled near. A mucoid squelching sound came from every side and hemmed the small room. A gray flank large as a barrel, but long and writhing, pressed inward on the walls until its length encircled the room, squeezing until the walls cracked. Salvi tried to scream but could not.

Gradually a seam gave way and a massive serpent bobbed into the room with the face and mirror eyes of the jewelry vendor with fangs dripping blood.

Salvi thrashed awake and swept at the lamp, catching it before it launched from the table. In the light, she found the stone and held it close. But she slept little the rest of the night.

The next night, they went downtown and hit a couple of the taverns along Main and Sixth streets. They hung out with a few of Angeline's friends, sang karaoke, danced with a couple of cowboys, and laughed a lot.

Wrapping up the night they cut through an alley toward the parking lot. The area was poorly lit and as they walked behind a black van someone spoke. "Hermanas. The sisters."

The hairs stood up on Salvi's arms.

"Are you taking care of that truth stone?" the voice said.

Salvi stopped. With her hands in her jacket pocket, she instinctively clutched the stone nestled there and determined that she would not let go of it.

Wearing a black hoodie and jeans, the woman had blended into the side of the dark van. She still wore the cap pulled down over her forehead above the dark sunglasses. Salvi paused while Angeline and Alisa went a few steps ahead.

The woman came nearer. "So sorry. I did not mean to frighten you. So, all of us is stayin' in Rapid City, I guess."

Salvi did not know what to say.

"Come here. I have something you might be interested in." She slid the van door open.

Salvi did not want to be rude. She stepped nearer and shrugged and showed the woman her palms. "I uh...we are all tired out and we are headed home. Thanks anyway."

It all happened so fast.

A man reached out of the open door and grasped Salvi's wrist. Before she could pull back, the woman had wrapped her arms around Salvi's legs and while the man slapped a wide piece of tape over her mouth and pulled, the woman hefted her into the van.

In seconds, two other men were wrestling Angeline and Alisa. The young women whined and tried to scream through the tape. Dragging them inside, the woman slammed the van door shut.

By the time Angeline's mother returned from work that morning, the van was already somewhere outside Omaha.

It had all happened so fast. And then they were gone.

Chapter 12

Awakening

"Where'd you go? We lost you for a while," Gracie said.

To Ron, the voice was incoherent for a moment as it seemed to reverberate off the walls of a deep well.

"Where were you?" she repeated.

He saw Gracie. But it was as if from the bottom of a deep shaft; he was peering upward at her face framed far away and above. The face and the voice lowered nearer. Ron tried to respond, but his tongue was thick and the pain in his head felt like a spike had been driven through his forehead. He had left home to seek his newfound daughter and here again she drifted over him. But distant, like an entity, like a moon floating right there above him.

He had imagined that when he met her, there would be all those awkward hugs and stumbling phrases to be spoken one over the other. There was none of that.

She was just there.

It took a few fuzzy moments for Ron to become aware of his surroundings amid the stuffy medical scents, the purr of blinking equipment, and the concerned faces on the two apparitions hovering nearby.

He fumbled with words and felt like an infant making nonsense vocalizations until he was able to put together two words, "What happened?" His voice felt like vomiting chalk.

Adam's face floated into view like a huge parade balloon. "You're in the hospital. In Green Bay."

Ron made a slightly sozzled grin to see Adam bobbing above him with his narrow features, black glasses, perpetually tousled hair, and short mustache and goatee. Ron thought Adam could look a little comical even in a normal situation, but as a parade balloon…?

But Adam was also the man who had been a faithful friend through so many years and many ups and downs. Adam had tragically lost his first wife while employed by Ron and he had fled for years only to return to work with Ron. Where he eventually had to face a harsher truth concerning his wife and how she died. But through all the pain there had been one very bright light: Adam had met Gracie.

"In the hospital? Green Bay?" Ron flicked his fingers at his mouth, motioning for water. "Go…Packers," he whispered. "Why? Green…Bay?"

Gracie brought the straw to his lips. He took a sip, paused, and took another sip.

"Thanks, Gracie," he said, his voice still hoarse. "Much better."

"You got really sick while you were on the ferry. The cleaning staff found you in your cabin and by the time you were transported here, you were in a coma," Gracie said, looking up at Adam then back at Ron. "A few days ago, you started to come out of it. But then your heart stopped, you coded. They revived you, and…"

Ron took another sip. His brain still hummed, and when he blinked, he saw flashes. "Where was I, again?"

"On the ferry from Ludington."

"No, I mean now." Ron squeezed his eyes shut, then opened them wide. He still spoke slowly. "It was like a dream," he said slowly. "Adam, I thought you were supposed to be the dreamer."

"Thank God, I don't do that anymore. At least not since Lake Superior turned over and I moved over here to Keshena."

"This was so real. It was just a minute ago. Duane. He has long hair…and a ponytail, now?"

Gracie flashed a look toward Adam again. "You saw Duane? In this…dream?"

"Yeah. So strange." Ron's tongue circled his lips, and he took another sip. "I saw him run into a big lodge." He spoke slowly. "I followed him down into a cave or an old cellar where there was a room with girls and young women laying on stone slabs. So weird."

"Yes. Duane's hair is long. Now that he is no longer on regular duty," Gracie said thoughtfully while looking at Adam. She laid a hand on Ron's shoulder. "What else do you remember? Duane has talked about a lodge from a dream world for as long as I can remember. It's always been part of his past when he was a kid. And a couple of months ago Maura, his wife, asked me about it. But I didn't know why he was thinking about it again."

"We were winding through moldy hallways, down dark steps, through passageways." He paused and Gracie helped with another sip. "Someone was peering out of the dark: a big man. Those dead, blue eyes, bushy brows and—so much hate." Ron winced. "Ugh. Then the awful smell. Some kind of apes or monsters came for us just as I was jerked away and woke up."

"Yeah. That sounds like a fever dream," Adam said.

"No. I'm not so sure," Gracie said. "It sounds just like something Duane would've said. Those creatures, they are the Manabai'wok," Gracie said. "The giants. They exist in that space between this life and the next. Whenever he talked about it, Duane mentioned seeing them in that weird underworld lodge. As a kid, I thought he was just trying to scare me. But now I have to wonder."

"It had to be a dream." Ron massaged his eyes with a hand and looked from Adam to Gracie. "Wasn't it?"

"Who knows. But this sounds too familiar. These are things you would not have known about." She looked at Adam. Worried. "Things from the past."

"There was one last thing," Ron said. "Something one of the women on the slabs said. It sounded so cryptic. Like some kind of nonsense riddle. But I knew I was supposed to remember it." Ron took another sip and wiped his mouth with a shaky hand. "'Find the key, Truth is the key. The truth will set them free.' I am certain that is what she said."

He ran his tongue over his lips again. "And I know that what she said was important to Duane."

Gracie bit the corner of her lip and looked at Adam.

"Weird. Sounds like an explorer show that I saw as a kid." Adam smiled and eased his arm around her and pulled her near.

She rested a hand on his chest and said as if to herself, "We have to contact Duane. I am not sure what he's up to. I am afraid he might be in danger."

"Of course," Adam said. "But Duane's like you. He knows how to take care of himself."

"I've learned that doesn't always work." She looked up at him. "Sometimes you have to rely on others."

Through the haze, Ron looked from Gracie to Adam while in his fuzzy mind he stitched together the threads of their lives and how they had passed through his. This caused something new to stir inside him. Contentment was dissolving away the anxiety he'd carried for days. Contentment like he had not known before.

THE THREADS OF GRACIE and Adam's life had wound together a couple of years before. A month or more after she left Sault Saint Marie, Adam's mind was still brooding on this enigmatic woman. It was not only her whimsical beauty and quick humor that had captivated him. It was realizing how much he was intrigued by her strength and stability.

It was after the cataclysmic events that had occurred in Lake Superior. Adam was still working at the counselling center in Sault Sainte Marie, where Ron was his supervisor. Ron called him into his office, scrolled through his phone, and showed the screen to Adam.

"Read this," Ron said. "If you won't take it from me, maybe you will pay attention to her."

Adam scanned up and down until Ron pointed to a one-line message bubble:

BTW I think of Adam often.

Adam felt a tingle up the back of his neck. But he knit his brow in confusion, looked at Ron, and shrugged.

"It's Gracie Bird. And it's not the first time she has asked about you," Ron said.

Adam fidgeted with his glasses and scratched the black stubble on his chin. "What should I do?"

"Ha! Ya big oaf. You know me, and I don't think I am someone who should be counselling you on matters of the heart," Ron said.

Many things came clear to Adam in an instant, and a possibility arose that he had diligently tried to suppress. Then a lonely widower's whim became not only a possibility, but suddenly an overwhelming and urgent need.

"I've promised not to give out her number, but she can reach out to you if you want her to…"

Eyes wide, Adam nodded rapidly.

It was only days later that he drove across the Upper Peninsula into Wisconsin. His boyish excitement matched the fruit candy colors of autumn, and the five-hour trip flew by. Soon he was parked outside the café in Shawano where they had arranged to meet. He waited, running his fingers over the steering wheel, gathering his courage until he took a breath, held it, and got out of the car. Feeling awkward, his head swiveled, looking for that familiar face.

There was a flurry, a giggle, and he spun in time to see a commotion of long black hair above a broad grin framed by red lips, the same lovely lips he recalled the first time he saw her behind the desk at the casino where she was working undercover as a desk clerk. She slammed into him and hugged him closely—for a long time. He did not expect this small person would be capable of a full-on bear hug. But she was.

Even as she held him, the thought flashed in his head, *what am I to a woman like this?*

There was no memory of lunch, or even if they had eaten. He only remembered talking while at another table sat the Ogichi-daa, her big bodyguards Donnie and Leo.

When they got to the park, she finally had to tell the two men to wait in the car. They shuffled off, but they were probably never out of sight. Adam and Gracie walked along a short trail in the forest. It was bright and unusually warm that day. Maple and birch leaned over the river, the tree's reflections bleeding color into the black water while their leaves unfurled like maypoles and settled onto the surface. Along the path, the branches cast dappled patterns on her white T-shirt.

"You've always been such a good listener. Like my brother, Duane. I miss him when we are apart like this." Glancing back toward the parking lot and her bodyguards, she told him about forces that might be pursuing her and her brother. Forces they were only beginning to understand. But she could not say more.

As they walked he realized that they had been holding hands. Her small hand seemed so natural in his. He walked off to one side of the path so she could walk on the path. And she did the same. The path ran on between them.

There was much for Gracie to consider, too. Yes, Adam was a good listener. But was that enough to build a life around, start a family—grow old together? And Adam's previous marriage was still difficult for him to overcome. Would the imposition of bodyguards and the threats faced by her and Duane derail their budding relationship?

Adam returned to Michigan, but it did not take long to resolve any worries she had.

Because then there was the card. He sent her a card. It was *so* Adam.

The image on the front was an entirely culturally-appropriated caricature of a little Indian girl with big cartoon eyes, braids, and a short buckskin dress. And she held some feathers, of course.

Gracie covered her mouth to suppress the laughter, unfolded the card, and read what he had written inside.

Regardless of my past and the hurt that love brought to me, you have shown me that I don't want to sit in the shadows. I don't want to live life without passion—or pain. I want to cleave to someone who will complete me, so that I do not live life by half. I do not want to live as a parcel or remnant.

She melted. It was as if he had spoken her mind—with her own words. Her heart that had been tempered brittle soon quickened, turned within her chest, and beat again.

Chapter 13

Home Is a Compound

THE CHIMING OF THE car door awoke Ron in the backseat, and he looked up to see Adam's eyes smiling in the rear-view mirror.

"How're you doing?" Adam asked.

Ron rubbed his face, raising his brow. "I can't stay awake."

"It's only about half an hour until we're home. We needed to get some bread, and Gracie had to pee—of course."

"Is this Keshena?"

"No. We're just outside Shawano," Adam said.

Gracie departed the convenience store and strode across the lot. Despite her sizable stomach she stepped confidently, eyes level, scanning. Pregnancy had not changed her coiled readiness, and she was not one to waddle and brace her stomach between her hands.

Ron yawned. "She's not in any danger? I mean, with all that's happened in the past around her and Duane?"

Adam huffed. "Gracie? I worry about her more than I am allowed to say. But I've learned it's fruitless to say anything." He stared at her as she approached. Even in the rearview mirror, Ron could see Adam's admiration. "Freedom means more to her than anything and she will not allow fear or anything else to control her. Never."

Ron watched her. Even in his hazy awareness, he was amazed that this creature could be *his* daughter.

"And how do you feel about that? As a husband, I mean—with a woman like Gracie. How do you manage your feelings for her freedom and safety?" Ron was speaking to Adam, but he was also thinking to himself.

"Well, that's kinda heavy. Isn't it? I wasn't prepared for therapy from a psychologist in an addled state of mind." Adam smiled and was silent for a beat while looking at his wife. "I think that she taught me that there is no other way to live. We can talk philosophically about liberty until it is stolen from us. Then you'd cut your own leg off to be free. So, if you have it, you relish it. She relishes her freedom more than anything."

The car door opened. "Well, there he is. Are you back from dream land again?" she said. "I've got some jerky...and some more jerky." She fanned the flat packets toward the back seat. "Elk, venison, or beef? We girls need us some protein." She patted her stomach. "Adam?"

Ron pursed his lips and made a quick denial with his head. "No thanks, I think I'll wait."

"Are you car sick? Do you want to switch places?" she said.

"No, I'm fine. Just...not hungry."

She tore open a packet and handed it to Adam. "That's the venison. They just got a fresh shipment from Carl's place." She swiveled toward Ron. "Our favorite is the elk."

"I'm not sure I got to congratulate you," Ron said. "You said *we girls*. So, you're having a girl?"

"Yeah. I can't wait. She's a cutey on ultrasound. And everything's great. I'll show you the pics when we get home."

Heading north, white pines lined the highway like guardian giants. They wound through the village of Keshena that seemed to spread through the forest like a Native village of centuries past. Shops and neat homes emerged here and there to dot the highway. After twenty minutes, they turned off the highway through an alley of trees and followed a chewed-up black top road thin as burnt toast. Around a bend, they crossed a narrow bridge spanning a glistening river scattered with sandy shoals and riffling rapids. They slowed at a dirt road marked only with a faded sign not much larger than a clipboard: *Bear Paw Lodge*. A few twists and turns down the rutted road and a long two-story lodge loomed out of the woods. Faded white, it hulked far from its glory days.

A broad porch at the back overlooked a clearing that opened to the river.

"This is yours?" Ron asked incredulously.

"Well. Technically, it belongs to The Council. Wait till you see our place." Gracie said.

They slid past the inn and Ron gaped at its sagging eaves scarcely supported by the corbels and flourishes that braced against the walls. He scanned the elaborately corniced windows with listing shutters. It was all in need of repair and three coats of paint.

Past a leaning wooden fence and a collapsing garage, the two-track folded through a row of cedars.

Adam pulled up to a double-wide trailer that slumped into brush. The front of the trailer was scattered with a rusty motorcycle, rotting planks, an upturned toilet, and a trash heap of old toys and other nameless garbage. Two or three rusty metal sheds were entombed in tag alder. One of them had been cleaved and collapsed by a red pine trunk.

Gracie watched Ron's face and laughed out loud. Adam joined with a chuckle.

"There's a surprise inside," Adam offered.

"You mean it gets better?" Ron said, suspecting something was up.

"You don't like it? I am so hurt." Gracie smiled.

They grabbed Ron's sparse luggage and navigated the rickety metal-grate steps that led up to the rusting metal door of the mobile home. There was no keyhole or latch, only a small black square on the door frame. Gracie tapped the screen and a numerical keypad appeared with a gray rectangle above it. She pressed her thumb to the screen and tapped in four numbers. There was a mechanical drone from the door frame as deadbolts retracted.

"Shuffle back a step, the door opens outward," Adam said.

Gracie went in first and they stood in the gray and yellow living room. There was a sagging couch, a dim lamp, and a few magazines and dishes scattered over a linoleum floor that was lifting at the seams. It was dark, musty, and foreboding on this warm summer day.

"Right out of a magazine," Adam said.

"They still publish *True Crime Magazine*?" Ron retorted. "This looks like a set from a horror movie."

"We'll have to work on that. Make it look a bit cozier, more lived-in. I think I have a box with some leftover pizza in the refrigerator," Adam said.

They crossed the narrow room and Gracie stepped to another door with a similar security pad. This door opened inward. As the door swung wider, the scene was like stepping from frankly awful into Frank Lloyd Wright.

Gracie snatched a remote from the wall inside the door and pointed it across the room. There was a clatter of corrugated metal panels and light began to stream from clerestory windows that lined the top of the great room. She aimed the remote nearer the floor and there was more clattering and a thin metallic squeal as panels slid back, and one by one, tall windows were exposed and encircled the space.

"We have to get those metal shutters oiled, I think," Grace said.

There was a sunken sitting area laid in sandstone. Couches were thrown with tan pillows on peacock blue cushions. A fireplace was set with two gold-colored overstuffed chairs each with a heavy bronze floor lamp. Riverstone walls climbed to the ceiling. On the opposite side of the room were towering bookshelves loaded with volumes and scattered with rocks, pottery, model ships, and carvings. Throughout the room, the heavy trim and wooden floor were a redwood hue.

At the center of the sunken seating area, a bulky coffee table was set with a bouquet overflowing with sunflowers, ferns, and daises set in a blue porcelain camp kettle. It was one of the few things Gracie had inherited from her mother. Duane had given it to her and told her that their mother used it to collect berries.

"This is amazing," Ron remarked. "The council built all this behind a crappy old mobile home just for security?"

"Actually, the house was already here, and they moved in the trailer, dumped some trash, and put up the corrugated siding to look like an old garage or warehouse from the outside." Adam said. "If anyone wanders down that road they'd never know we were here."

"Well, that would lower your taxes, I suppose."

"It's still on tribal land, so they take care of the road back here for us."

The tall windows opened to a back yard that meandered to the river through ferns, pink forest phlox, and a trio of sprawling maple trees.

"The landscaping and the architecture make it almost impossible to see the house from the river even with the windows uncovered. There is a tint on the windows. They thought of everything," Gracie said as she walked to the windows and looked across the yard.. "And there is rarely any traffic up here on this stretch of the river. Especially in this section, where it is rocky and shallow. Plus, there are signs along the shore posted *Keep Out*."

"What about the inn? How do you hide something like that?" Ron walked to the big windows, standing away from Gracie. He still felt awkward beside her.

"It's been there forever, so most people think the lodge is just some kind of tribal enterprise or housing. We keep a listing on a vacation rental site in case we need some legitimacy—but ironically, the availability says it is always full." She smiled. "Covertly, we use the vacation site to coordinate visits by Lake Council members or Ogichi-daa training."

"The Ogichi are *warriors*, right?"

"Yep, Leo and Donnie are the best guys. Nice condos have been remodeled on the second floor of the inn for them, and they stay with their wives—who are also trained. And Leo has two kids. That's another reason we display it like a vacation rental. Anyone who is curious would see kids and families running around.

"But this is essentially a compound." She pointed in the direction of the lodge. "There are also rooms when other Ogichi come for practice.

Two cadets are staying there now for training: Eddie and Tony. You might run into them. At least Eddie. He likes to repair stuff and does some of the maintenance."

Still a little hazy, he looked at her in wonder and could only admire her. He watched her but paid little attention to what she was saying. *If I'd ever imagined having a daughter, this would be her.* He looked away and fumbled with a question to counter his embarrassment. "And you're still training and working out?" He knew immediately it was a dumb question. "Um, I think Adam wrote something to me."

"Of course." She laid a hand on her stomach. "This little babe is going to pop out, put feet to the floor, knees bent, waist hinged, hands poised, eyes forward, and challenge *Whatchu lookin' at?*"

They laughed as Adam stepped behind her and crossed his hands on her stomach. "I don't think this is how I imagined raising a family," he said. "But for now, we are managing well." He grinned at Ron. "And it is great to have an old friend to visit us—despite all you went through."

"It has all come together," Gracie said. "There was a time in my life when the last thing I wanted was to be a mother. But when I met Adam, it was like the universe had other plans in mind. Big plans."

"It certainly did," Adam agreed.

Ron couldn't take his eyes off of them.

They ate a small lunch while seated around the big coffee table in the sunken area of the main room. Like the old friends they were, they shared small talk while catching up on Gracie and Adam's plans.

There was a long silence.

"Do you need to lay down, Ron?" Adam sat on the couch next to Gracie. "You've had quite a week, and you look exhausted."

Ron did not answer for a while, then sighed and rubbed his forehead. "I should be able to discuss this stuff. But when it is affecting your own life, I don't know if anyone gets good at this. But I suppose we're going to have to address the mastodon in the room. Better sooner than later."

"Always the psychologist." Gracie smiled.

"Well, I—" Ron began.

Gracie held up her hand. "I can make all of this easy for you. And it is quite simple." She dabbed her mouth with a napkin and slid her plate onto the coffee table, laced her fingers over her stomach. "Adam and I have talked about this, and I will be brief—or I will cry," she said, slipping her hand in Adam's.

Ron felt nervous and faltered. "I just want to say I am very—"

"No. I don't want to hear it. As I have told Adam many times since I learned that you were my...dad." She took a breath. "All my life I wondered who my father was, and I always figured he was probably some guy my mom met in a bar, someone who had probably abused her, then threw her away. But as a little girl, I always pretended that he was something special: a nice guy, a tribal leader, maybe an explorer, or the captain of a ship who had valiantly gone down in the lake." She suppressed a smile with her hand. "I made up all sorts of stuff."

She paused again, catching her composure. Sitting on the couch, looking across the room and out the windows, she dabbed the napkin to the corner of her eye and sniffled. Adam leaned toward her, but she waved her hand quickly in front of her face.

"I'm sorry," Ron said flatly.

"No. Do not be sorry." She chuckled. "You're here. You're the guy who showed up—for me." She looked at him. "And I could have never imagined that my father would be someone as wonderful as you." She sniffed, folded her hands in her lap, and sighed. "There, I said it." Her lower lip was thrust upward, and she had regained control.

Ron sniffled, leaned forward hid his mouth behind a fist and his shoulders trembled. Gracie slid beside him. The rest of the long afternoon, they talked. Shafts of sun streaked through the upper windows and tiptoed around the room as Ron, Gracie, and Adam built a family.

Chapter 14

Dinner Meeting

THE FAMILY SAT FOR a few moments, preoccupied by nothing more than silent contentment. The metal skin of the house ticked and settled in the changing light.

"You really look like you could use a nap before dinner." Gracie smiled at Ron. "Leo and Donnie will be walking over for dinner, so you can expect some commotion with the kids and everybody. I think the guys are putting something on the grill."

"That's right. Now would be a good time to rest if you need it," Adam said.

"There is going to be a lot for all of us to go over," Gracie said. "Before everyone comes over, I might have to take a little nap myself."

Ron rubbed his beard. "Yeah. I might take a snooze. But before I lay down, can I tell you something else that has been on my mind?"

Adam and Gracie nodded.

"It was a dream or something. It must have happened when I was fading away on the ferry." He rotated to Adam. "I am so sorry that I have stolen your mantel as the Great Dreamer."

"Oh, a few years ago, I would have handed it to you in a second," Adam said. "I have had no use for it. And I am grateful to give it up."

"So, I get sick, I have some kind of near-death experience, and so from now on I will be saddled with prescient dreams? That hardly seems fair." Ron grinned.

"So, tell us the dream." Gracie shrugged. "My in-house dream interpreter has given up, I guess. You told us about that other dream, or whatever, the one with Duane. If this one is anything like that, then we have to know." Gracie looked at Ron intently. "Every part of the puzzle is important, now. No matter where it comes from."

Ron shifted and leaned back. "This one really *did* seem more like a fever dream. And the reason I think it happened on the *SS Badger* is because in the dream or whatever I imagined that the ferry was alone and frozen in the middle of Lake Michigan. And I was alone—I mean really alone. Other than some ghouls, it was only me."

Gracie raised her eyebrows.

"That part was not so important. But I climbed off the ferry and was walking across the ice with the snow devils whirling past, when all of a sudden the ice broke, great slabs pushed upward, and Mishipezhu crawled out and stepped right onto the ice."

Gracie leaned in.

"But soon the beast turned into something that was the size of a regular lynx and curled around my feet—purring." Ron raised his eyebrows, grinning.

"It seems like you were being told that Lake Superior is settled. Nothing to fear anymore. The dream is telling you that you can move on. Maybe it was a special message for someone with your attachment to the big lake," Gracie said. "I don't know. That would just be my take."

"So now you sound like a pretty good dream interpreter yourself," Adam said.

Gracie raised her palms. "Well, isn't that obvious?"

"Right. Obvious," Adam said flatly.

"Go ahead," Gracie said to Ron.

"But you're right. I *did* sense that there was nothing to fear anymore. But the next part of the dream I thought was more, um…cryptic." Ron looked at Gracie. "And I think it has more to do with you than anyone else."

Gracie did not shift her gaze.

"A white doe and its fawn were walking on the ice and came into view around the stern of the frozen vessel."

Her eyes widened.

Ron continued. "But working its way along the rail of the ship above, an enormous coyote seemed to be stalking them."

"Of course..." Gracie said slowly. She had the trace of a knowing smile.

"What do you mean *of course*?" Adam asked.

"The white deer makes sense. Because Ron knows about me and my mom. But my intuition should have told me that the coyote had to show up in all of this somewhere. With all the confusion and stuff coming at us from different sides."

"What do you mean?" Adam asked.

"Coyote is just about the most familiar spirit across all of Native lore," she said. "Tribes across the continent have held a special place for the coyote. Sometimes he's considered the chief spirit and often a secondary spirit. But he is always capricious, unpredictable—and dangerous."

"Why didn't I think of the coyote spirit? I've read about him," Ron said. He hesitated. He wanted to say something about shared interests, but he was not sure if they were there yet.

He continued. "And do you remember a few years ago when Lake Superior turned? Every continent has a great lake that is like a repository of evil that eventually fills to capacity and overflows. Some also believe that every continent has its own chief spirit and its gods. I won't go into all of it now, but the coyote is like that. All across this continent, and even in South America and all the way to the Arctic Circle, the coyote is known."

"Exactly," Gracie said.

Ron paused, thinking, then said to Gracie, "Could this be related to that group that tried to use that fake shaman James Graves? They used him to try and conjure Mishipezhu. Do you think they have something up their sleeve with the coyote spirit? Or are we just being crazy."

"That would fit, wouldn't it? We can't be too careful, realizing the forces we are dealing with." She took Adam's hand. "If we are not using the insight given to us, we may not be prepared."

"We have to think of everything if we want to stay ahead," Adam said.

"But let's wait for Donnie and Leo. I need to see if they've contacted Duane. We need some answers." She bit her lip. "Soon."

It was late afternoon when Ron awoke to laughter and voices down the hall. He stepped into the bathroom, looked into the mirror, and decided he needed to take a quick shower and he would change into a T-shirt and jeans.

"There he is," Gracie said when he walked through the living room toward the broad kitchen. "The guys are outside. This is Lelah and Nessa, Leo and Donnie's better halves—*much* better halves. And the kids tearing around are the responsibility of Lelah and Leo."

"Oh, I hope they didn't wake you up," Lelah said. Her green hair fell about her shoulders in curls and ringlets. She was tall, and with her lean coiled vigor, she reminded Ron of a Kenyan marathon runner.

"I slept great. Much better. And a real shower away from a hospital was wonderful," Ron said.

Lelah offered her hand, smiling, but Donnie's wife was furtive, leaning back in a corner next to the refrigerator. She looked away quickly when their eyes met. Ron sensed a cold vibe, but there was also a familiarity about her that he could not pinpoint.

"Nessa is my aunt. Well, more like my big sister when I was growing up. She met Donnie one day when we were hanging around, and the rest is history, as they say." Gracie pulled a sarcastic smile into her cheek. "Though I do not know what she sees in that big guy."

As is often true, time and patience had healed the wounds in Gracie's family and had healed her disheveled young life. In later years, Nessa rebuilt her relationship with her parents and gradually, she and Gracie built a bond as strong as sisters.

Nessa covered her smile with her hand and looked at the floor.

Ron felt awkward. He had not expected to meet Gracie's family—especially not Dee's sister.

Nessa cleared her throat and regarded Ron. "You're family here, Ron. One big happy family." Her words seemed insincere as she motioned around the room with her beer. "This is a place where we should just leave the past behind and forget." She looked at the other women, but they seemed to be measuring her remarks. "We all have some things to leave behind."

Ron nodded in agreement. She did not make eye contact again but pushed away from the kitchen counter and walked toward the dining room. The edge of insincerity wrangled him and there was a chill as she brushed past.

Lelah looked at Gracie and hitched a shoulder.

The patio door slid open, and the aroma of smoke and barbeque wafted into the kitchen. Adam, Leo, and Donnie toppled in carrying platters of meat, corn, and foil packs.

"The dreamer arises," Adam said.

"Nope. No dreams this time. I slept like a rock."

"Let's rock n' roll!" Leo said. "I need to turn on some tunes."

"No. C'mon, we're gonna talk," Gracie said.

Leo tilted his head in resignation.

The men laid the food on the table and Donnie and Leo wiped their hands and introduced themselves to Ron.

"You are the legends," Ron said. "For years I've heard about you guys, but I don't remember if we ever met."

"Oh yeah. We met, but I think you were in limbo land. Coma city." Leo grinned.

"Well, uh...great," Ron said. "Those days are all a fog."

Ron reached to shake Donnie's hand and he extended it shyly, looking down at the floor and offering a limp handshake.

"This is Donnie." Gracie stepped up. "He is only quiet until you challenge him on the mats."

"Then he screams like a banshee as he rips out your throat," Leo added. He gripped Donnie's shoulder. "Or he will talk your head off if you ask him about his damn antiques."

Donnie's eyes brightened as he looked up at Ron. "You like antiques?" Donnie said hopefully.

"Oh, lord. Here we go," Leo said. "He used to scavenge through the furniture donated to the rez when he lived at Red Lake. He would find the antiques an' him and his dad would load up the pickup and go down to Bemidji and sell it."

"Ignore him," Ron said. "I like antiques. I'm sure I have some questions."

"Ah, geez," Leo said. "Well, there ya go, Ron. You just met the only Native guy on earth who wants to talk about old furniture."

"Let's eat," Adam said. "We hope you like fish. We have a mess of perch and walleye from one of the fishermen. And genuine Wisconsin bratwurst, of course."

"No cheese? I thought you guys were all cheese heads," Ron said, his eyes moving over the feast. "I am so hungry."

"Right here," Lelah hoisted the cheese and fruit platter from the kitchen. "But Gracie's crazy pregnancy cravings have changed to fish, of all things."

"Oh my god. And fry bread," Gracie said, lifting the cover of a big plastic bowl and extracting a thick, brown chunk of bread. She closed her eyes, sniffing, then savoring a bite. Still chewing, she said, "I swear, this kid is going to be born wrapped up like an Indian taco."

Adam broke through the laughter, "Father Jarvin, do you want to say grace?"

Ron pointed a finger at Adam. "You, young man, are the only person who gets by with calling me that."

The large dining room sat in a cove off of the kitchen. Built on the river side of the house, it had six high transom windows near the ceiling, but only a single tall window that was similar to those in the living room. It was separated from the living room by two folding Japanese-styled panels that swirled with koi, lily pads, and water plants: *carp and cattails,* Leo called them.

The meal proceeded with enthusiasm and playfulness more like an off-duty battalion than dinner guests. Leo's kids, Lucie and Lance, joined the adults at the big table and watched with a mixture of curiosity and tolerant humor while the adults pitched their miserable wit. Lance, the older one, grinned through the gap left from his decommissioned front teeth.

"I saw one of the cadets here on the roof today. Was that training or did he just get lost again?" Adam said.

"No, that was Eddie. He volunteered to lubricate the tracks that those squeaky metal shutters run along," Donnie said. "Just a little silicone grease usually fixes it."

When there was a pause, Gracie faced Ron. "Well, I hate to interrupt all the fun, but we have some things to talk about." Motioning around the table, Gracie made a quick circle with her hand. "We have boring things to talk about like building maintenance, Ron. You're welcome to hang out. But we definitely want you here when we discuss some of the chatter we're hearing about other stuff."

"I'm going to take a break for a few minutes and then I will loop back, if you don't mind," Ron said.

"Lance and Lucie, you guys can play in Gracie's spare room or go outside," Lelah said.

"Can we get a popsicle?" Lucie asked.

"You know where they are," Gracie said to their bolting backs.

Ron stepped down the hallway toward the bedrooms. There was a glass door at the end of the hall, and he leaned in to take a view from a side of the house he had not yet seen. He glanced left where some of the faux trash trailed away into the underbrush, then he turned right to peer through spruce and birch toward the river.

Not expecting to see anyone near the house, he was startled for a moment when he saw someone emerge from next to a large spruce trunk and stand looking over the back of the house. A heavy-set man in a tan shirt and floppy fishing hat swiveled to face Ron. The man looked surprised at first, then caught himself, smiled warmly, waved, and came toward the house. Ron lifted his hand, waving cautiously.

Still grinning, the man approached, signaling for Ron to open the door. Ron looked back down the hallway. Ron thought the man might be a local, or possibly the cadet, Eddie, who was supposed to fix the shutters. Or he could have been other staff that he had not heard about. But when the guy approached he did not look Native, and he was too old and out of shape to be a cadet. His hair was light brown, gray-streaked, and pulled back in a short ponytail. He wore one of those wide-brimmed, floppy outdoorsy hats: hallmark of the urban adventurer. A flannel shirt was stuffed into cargo pants and cinched with a narrow belt. His 20th century hiking boots and aviator glasses would have taken it far enough, but he had to complete his woodsy ensemble with a fanny pack and a dream catcher earring dangling from one lobe. The guy seemed harmless enough and was probably lost.

Ron unlatched the door and eased it open a crack. "Can I help you? I don't believe we've met."

"Oh, man. I am so sorry. This is stupid. I'm such a dumbass." The guy looked mortified. "First I run out of gas then I run aground here in the shallows trying to float back to town. And my damn phone is dead," he said holding up the supposedly useless device.

"I'm really sorry, but I can't let you in. Go around to the side and the owners might let you in that way." Ron made a swirling motion with his finger and pointed around the corner of the house.

"Nah. I don't want to bother anybody. Can I just use your phone for ten seconds to text my brother-in-law?"

Ron dragged his phone out of his back pocket and handed it to him. "Reception is not great back here, but it seems to get through."

The man swiped up and across then appeared to key off a couple of quick messages and handed the phone back to Ron. It took no longer than twenty seconds.

"I am so sorry. I can't thank you enough. I'm going to go and wait by my boat. I feel like such an idiot."

"No worries. I hope everything works out."

"You are an angel," the man said, waving as he walked away.

Ron went to the bathroom and then unpacked a few things in his room. He set up his laptop on the big oak desk with the matching antique office chair that was charmingly similar to the one he worked at in his apartment in Sault Sainte Marie. He would not put it past Adam and Gracie to have furnished the bedroom with this detail. And maybe Donnie helped with acquiring the furniture.

Whether it was merely the distractions or the fog that remained from his ordeal and hospitalization, Ron soon forgot his encounter with the fisherman.

Chapter 15

The Dark Council

By the time Ron rejoined the group, the dining room was cleared, Adam and Leo were returning through the patio door after putting away the grill, and Donnie and the women were seated along the cushions in the sunken area of the living room, sipping coffee.

"Well, I could not have timed that better," Ron said.

"Yeah. Everything is cleaned up," Adam said as he circled into the kitchen. He held up the coffee pot to Ron. "Coffee?"

"Yes. Great. Anything to help clear a few more cobwebs."

The small talk grew thinner until it drifted away like the steam rising from their cups.

Gracie set her cup down and looked toward Ron. "You must have a ton of questions. Duane has fed us bits and pieces and we are getting more chatter from members of the Lake Council. We'll try to fill you in as best as we can about what we're dealing with."

"That would be great," Ron said. "But I know you have lots to discuss, so I don't want to take up all your time together."

"It won't hurt any of us to review a few things," Donnie said. He ran his fingers through his hair, removed his black-framed glasses, and cleaned them on his T-shirt.

"Agreed," Leo added.

"The first thing we need to do is clear the air," Gracie said.

"What did I do?" Ron smiled.

"Oh, nothing. It's what *we* did." Gracie continued. "You're here because of what might have been a mistake on the part of the Lake Council."

"I know *about* the Lake Council, but I actually *know* little," Ron said. "And of course, most of it remains secret. Has their mission changed or anything?"

"Not really. They have always been this ancient Lake Council of Keepers that is intended to surround and protect Lake Superior. They have this sort of spiritual connection to Gitchi Gami. It's a connection that they think may even precede many of the tribes that currently live along the lake and precede the Midewiwin religion of those tribes. That connection will never change."

"You mentioned a mistake?" Ron said.

"You probably know a little about this other group: The ones who killed my mother and tried to hijack events when the big lake turned over and James Graves went...missing." Gracie made a wry smile.

"The Dark Council, some call it," Donnie added.

"That's generous," Leo said.

Donnie nodded. "Yeah, I know. I don't really think that they are smart enough or organized enough to be called a council."

"We can't underestimate them. We never seem to know what they are capable of," Gracie said.

"I have never learned much about them. But in the past, it was not clear whether they were Native. Right?" Ron said.

Nessa had been sitting quietly on an end of the couch with her knees folded under her. "The ones who killed my sister are not Native," she said. "They pretend to be Native. Wannabes. They counterfeit and steal Native culture and ceremony, because they want to gain some kind of magical power. But no tribe would have anything to do with them."

"That is all true. But the mistake that we made was when we tried to flush them out by using the DNA ancestry site," Gracie said. "We knew that they were looking for other male relatives in order to build some kind of family tree or to discern heredity, because they were stupid enough to think that the succession passed through male lineage. But they didn't focus on Duane because they determined he had somehow been *passed over.*" She rolled her eyes. "As a child, Duane would have been present at that critical ceremony when my mother was charged with her authority and conferred with her title as the White Doe. He was not honored, so they assumed that he was of the wrong lineage or something. They have no clue how any of this works. But Duane still went into hiding. Partly so he could protect his family and do his work, but also because he was my mother's son and he knew too much." She shook her head. "It is all so stupid and disgusting. They know absolutely nothing about us."

"But they are not stupid," Adam said.

"No. They nearly hijacked the catastrophic events on Lake Superior with that sham shaman, James Graves, and now we think they are up to something even more sinister," Gracie said.

"What are they up to?" Ron asked.

"Like I said, Duane is in hiding, but he has let us know that he has good sources that say they might have something to do with abducting and trafficking women—especially Native women, and some kind of drug trade," Gracie said.

"Human trafficking and drugs? Seriously?" Ron said.

Gracie tilted toward Lelah.

"I know some of this stuff and still have contacts because I was working out west with two of the reservations," Lelah said. "I came back here to pursue a lead. Long-story-short, that's how I met this big guy." Lelah reached over and squeezed Leo's arm. "I was with the FBI's special unit on missing Native women."

Ron raised his eyebrows.

Lelah smiled. "I know. It never ends, right?" She shook her head. "So, in the past year I've been following suspicions that this Dark Council has been trafficking and are into drugs. But it's not just about regular drugs and not just regular trafficking."

"Right," Gracie said. "This is some crazy shit. They have come up with this concoction of sedatives and psychedelics that puts people into a near-death coma condition. Ketamine and ayahuasca. They pursue women. They don't just pick off the drug-addled or helpless girls. They are *selecting* and pursuing women for something unique."

"What? I've heard of these drugs," Ron said. "Ketamine was used in anesthesia and can induce a dissociative state and ayahuasca is being experimented on for depression and PTSD—and abuse and..." Ron paused with a blank stare as remnants of a vivid memory played in his mind. *I saw Duane among those women,* he almost said.

"What is it?" Adam asked.

Ron waved him off. *I need to think about it.* He did not want to blurt out nonsense about dreams and underworld lodges to this seasoned group of professionals. Not yet. He needed to digest this. The group thought he was just having a moment of cloudy recall.

He continued to ponder, debating whether to say anything. It was so vivid: Too obvious to be a coincidence. But he did not want to talk about it now, he did not want to deal with weird dreams, or whatever they were, and he certainly did not want anyone to perceive him as some kind of *seer* or *clairvoyant*. That would be completely out of character for him. He had been a failed activist, a defrocked priest, nearly killed in a futile attempt to stop a twisted shaman, now he would be some kind of twenty first century Padre Pio. What would be next? Stigmata?

Gracie pressed ahead shifting the group's attention from Ron. "You're right about those drugs," she said. "So, we have a ton of threads to tie together, and Duane is doing all he can to snuff this group out. For good."

"For Dee," Nessa said, but she was casting a look at Ron.

There was a gravid silence and Leo cleared his throat. Donnie scrunched his lips thoughtfully, rubbed his hands together, and looked at his wife.

"Well." Ron finally looked up and uncomfortably broke the silence. "I think I'll settle in for the evening. It's been quite a week."

There was awkward muttering as the group dispersed.

Chapter 16

Corporeal Demons

A MORNING SO DRIZZLING and gray that several streetlights still mirrored the lot behind an abandoned strip mall just outside of Omaha. Four or five vans were parked in a row, and there were masked and hooded figures quickly shuttling between the vehicles. Occasionally, a stuporous woman would be led stumbling from one van to the next, and some were being carried.

Her hands in her pockets, the vendor woman from the Badlands wore her reflective glasses despite the gloom, and she tilted her head while she spoke to a man in a floppy hat with a dream catcher earing dangling from one ear.

"After we picked up those three in Rapid City, we were handed four more for ya outside the Rosebud reservation. Young'uns. And I think they will suit your requirements. I don't know what's in that concoction that you had us inject, but it worked like a charm. They slept like babies, and we never heard a peep out of them," she said.

The brim of his hat dripped. He scratched his nose and leaned near her, conspiring. "And you don't have to monitor their pulse and blood pressure because it is much safer than fentanyl or any of those horse sedatives that they used to use."

"What's in it?" she asked.

"It's our special sauce." He grinned.

"So, you'll sell some…to your favorite supplier?" she said.

"We'll market it soon enough." He grinned. "And you'll be first to know. Right now, we plan to use it at our new enterprise way up in Michigan's Upper Peninsula. We might just keep our girls sedated all the time. Those girls will be our product line. It will be a unique experience for our very unique clientele."

"Sounds devilish." There were spaces in her teeth when she smiled.

Salvi lay jumbled in the back of the van amid six other women. Two were barely in their teens. She groaned while propped against the wall, drugged and paralyzed into dead silence.

"Salvia, my dear one. Truth is the key. The Truth will make you free."

Suddenly her abuela's voice was beside her. And soon Salvi felt herself lifted from the fetid van to stand in sunshine next to Abuela. They stood at the edge of a mesa, and in a dark valley far below lay the damp parking lot, the vans, and the scurrying traffickers. Salvi recognized the vendor, who was talking to the man with the floppy wilderness hat.

Salvi turned to see her abuela's bright face. Her smile deepened the web of wrinkles on her face, and she wore a blue bandana. She pulled her shawl over her head the way she would do when preparing to do a healing ceremony.

"Do you have the stone that I sent to you?" Her abuela asked, bending to pluck a few twigs of sage. She rubbed the leaves between her palms and scattered the powder to the wind and watched it sift toward the valley below.

Salvi opened her hand to see the blue truth stone in her palm.

"I will not allow those human demons to harm you. The truth will make you free. And if you hold onto that stone with all your will, you will never be lost," Abuela said.

Salvi felt her feet lift from amid the sage and the ground-hugging cactus. Her spirit lifted above the pinyon pine and followed the sage into the valley, returning to her body in the van.

Chapter 17

A Vision of Ancients

THE GUESTS HAD LEFT, the house was quiet. Ron bid Gracie and Adam *good night* and he headed toward his room. Dim lights set close to the floor splashed a warm pattern leading down the tile hallway. Set on a dresser were matching rectangular art deco lamps lit with square amber panels on top. Through the base of the lamp, fingers of light splayed across the surface of the dresser. A bedside lamp with a pyramid shade sat next to the bed. Cherry-paneled walls glowed in the low light. He cranked open a window to allow in the dense night air and, one by one, lowered slatted wooden shades over the wide windows. He changed out of his clothes, crawled into bed, and turned off the lights.

Enfolded in the soft bed, he stared at the ceiling and felt the embrace of domestic tranquility that settled on the home of his new-found daughter and his long-time friend. As he lay there, it was hard to clear his mind of all that had happened and all that he had heard in the few days since he had left his small second-story apartment overlooking the tourist strip in the Soo.

A draft crept through the open window and across the room, prompting him to click the light on again and slip out of bed to search for a spare blanket. He rummaged through the closet and the dresser, but only found a set of sheets and some pillowcases. Not wanting to bother Adam and Gracie, he pushed further into the closet, where a few boxes were stored on one side and a squat cedar chest on the other. The chest seemed the best bet for a blanket or quilt. Feeling a bit like a nosey intruder, he slid the chest out of the closet so he could open the lid.

There were no blankets stored on top of the remnants of material stacked in the chest. It was mostly old cloth and some scraps, so he did not want to snoop any further. He began to lower the lid when an item caught his attention: the hem of a garment made from white buckskin and patterned with coarse thread and beads. It had been carefully folded and laid to one side. He hesitated, knelt beside the chest, and lifted the item out. It fell open as he held it up. It was obviously a long ceremonial dress that probably belonged to Gracie. *I shouldn't,* he thought, and began to fold it again, but something about the garment caught his attention, spoke to him. He lifted it into the light and the beads and shells sparkled in the low light. But something more attracted him. Off to one side was a brown splatter and four parallel smears that dropped to the hem.

Ron jolted as flares and flickers of memory blasted his vision and flung him away from the chest. The windswept Agawa rock invaded his senses. Pain seared in his right hand, injured in that showdown with the bogus shaman James Graves during the climax of the catastrophic rising of spirits and the overturning of Lake Superior. Miraculously, the fingers had been reattached and healed. He also felt the pain in the scar on his arm and he touched the arrow wound at the back of his skull. In strobes of lightning, he saw James Graves' nephew, Harley, blood streaming down the spear shaft that jutted from his mouth. A small woman in white buckskin dashed behind Graves, slit his throat, and pushed him over the cliff. As Ron lay mortally wounded, he heard above the howling storm, "I'm here, Ron. I'm here."

Gracie. On Agawa Rock. It was Gracie.

He found himself back on the bed, staring up at the ceiling. The light next to the bed was still lit. While on his back, he braced up on his elbows, lifted his shoulders off the bed, and looked at the buckskin dress laying across the open chest. Scrambling, he got up, folded the dress, and returned everything to the closet.

Turning off the lights and laying back in bed, his mind relived the events of the Rising; all that he had experienced in those agitated anxious days, and all the wounds delivered by that shaman and his worthless nephew. He rubbed the fingers that had been gravely injured in the attack. He did not think he would sleep, but his unraveling thoughts became a tangled ball as threads from his fever dreams and strings from his visions wound together: the *SS Badger* frozen in the ice, the sinister coyote stalking the white doe, and horrors from that dark place where he encountered Duane and the mysterious shrouded women laying on stone slabs. It had been hard not speaking to the rest of them about all he'd seen, trying to decipher his place in all this. He didn't *want* to have a place in all this. He had not even come to grips with finding out that Gracie was his daughter, yet.

Through the open window, forest sounds trilled and wavered with insect and amphibian harmonies. A whip-poor-will, clear and strident, echoed across the river and through the woods. It repeated.

A serene and primeval spell was cast.

He opened his eyes, surprised to see that the room shown in a low light. Moonlight cut through the horizontal wooden blinds and painted bright zebra stripes over the furniture and across the bed.

Surrendering to sleeplessness, he rubbed his face, threw back the covers, and swung his feet over the edge of the bed. Approaching the window, he saw the slatted orb of the full moon. He raised the blinds. Hoary moonlight washed the clearing with an inviting glow while long fingers of fog kneaded the fronds of bracken and slithered across the grass.

Unable to resist the seduction of the evening, he pulled on a hoodie and slipped into his shoes. Silently, he stepped to the door at the end of the hall. He had been given a rundown of the security system and he hoped he did not trigger any alarms.

Slowly, he turned the deadbolt and eased down on the lever-style door handle, hearing the smooth metallic hiss as the hardware disengaged he stepped into the liquid night.

Dense and fluid like blood, the night was without a breeze and the insects were hushed, yet the leaves rushed and whispered. There were skitterings and tiny ticks and taps. He felt the magic of a forest beneath the moon's enchantment.

By increments, his eyesight adjusted. The clearing bloomed from creamy and gray to drab blue and olive as the moon lavished its light and hurled its silver spears far into the forest. He inhaled. The liquid air was like pond water as he drowned in the depths of a nocturnal wonderland. With the night pulsing, he trod slowly on sacred ground, crossing the clearing to draw near the river.

Far away, a single coyote yammered at the moon.

Beneath the sad smile of the moon the outlines of scrub brush, broom grass, and ferns layered one over the other like paper cutouts.

Something moved. At first blending with the boundaries shifting in shadow, as if it were melded to the undergrowth, a small figure divided from slate-green foliage. In silhouette against the moonlight, it flowed into the clearing. Or had the vegetation simply receded? For a moment, Ron thought the children must have been drawn outside to revel in the seductive night. But this was too small for one of Leo's kids. And this was not a child.

A spray of feathers fanned from the head and the figure resolved into the frame of a small muscular man. He held a staff or spear and wore a loin cloth that hung beyond his knees. Beads spangled against white buckskin. Soon, three similar figures escaped from the shadows. Each with broad headdresses. Two were women, bare-chested, wearing long, white leather skirts that glinted with pieces of silver. The light danced on their jeweled collars and off a broad chest plate that swept from their shoulders and nearly to their breasts.

The long feathers wavered as if on a breeze. Noble and stately their forms stepped further into moonlight. Ron knew what he was seeing—or dreaming. The memory had recurred when he found the buckskin dress in Gracie's closet. And still vivid in his mind, he recalled his fingers being severed as that fake shaman slashed at him with his broad knife. The detached digits had hurled into the darkness, only later to be placed on his chest as he lay unconscious. When he had revived and lay in a daze, he had recalled the scuttling of tiny feet all around him that night, and those tiny hands so healing and comforting.

He continued to watch in disbelief as the small man who had first emerged held up his palm in salute to Ron. The man folded two of his long fingers into his palm leaving two fingers upright. He pointed at them with his other hand. Ron thought he could see the glint of a grin in the pale light.

Since they had been severed, Ron had lost all feeling in those fingers. Now a cold sensation began at the tips, he flicked them at his side as the sensation grew to a tingle. Then hot. He brought his hand up and blew on the wriggling digits as if to cool them. But the sensitivity bloomed to pain until it felt as if bees were trying to crawl out of his fingers.

"Ouch!" Ron flailed his hand, trying to make it stop. He stuffed the burning fingers under his arm, but the pain subsided as quickly as it had begun.

When he looked up again, a cloud had slipped over the moon.

And the little people were gone.

The chorus of night creatures grew, and a mild breeze rustled the ferns.

He pressed ahead. It was his compulsion to go forward into darkness. To embrace the fear and meet its source. Just like he had as a child and just like he had when he confronted James Graves, the sham medicine man on that stormy rock. Even though it had been a confrontation that had nearly killed him, there was a sort of dark pleasure in challenging an evil that lay hidden. He had become a priest to do no less.

One cautious step at a time, he ventured past where the little people had emerged and ventured to the edge of the river, where night sounds were swept away by the water. He made a slow circle around the clearing and heard another maniacal coyote call, closer and more threatening it approached the opposite bank of the river. Its mockery could have been intended for him.

Ron lifted his chin, listening more intently, trying to peer into the darkness on the other side of the river. There was crashing through the underbrush as though a creature much larger than a coyote were fleeing the riverbank.

Ron waited a moment in silence, watching, and retraced his steps back to the house.

When he awoke in the morning, he was in a fog, as if he had not slept. Forgetting most of the events from the night before, he ambled out to the kitchen, where Gracie was pouring coffee.

The windows were speckled with rain and muted light wrapped the home snugly like an old blanket.

"Coffee?" she asked, holding out the cup to him. "As much as I love my coffee, I just can't hold much of it with this baby competing for all the room I have. And, dang, I might have another UTI coming on again. Leo is taking me to the clinic."

Distracted, Ron took the coffee. "Thanks. Ooo, that's hot," he said shifting the cup to his other hand and shaking his fingers. Holding up his fingers, he wiggled them in front of his face. The scars from the reattachment were gone and he had full sensation in his fingers.

"Are you okay? Sorry. Too much information about the UTI?" Gracie said.

"Uh, no. No, of course not. I hope everything will be okay." He continued to stare at his fingers.

"I'll be fine. It happens at this stage. What about you? Are you okay?" she asked.

"Yeah. Yeah, sure. Um…did you see that amazing full moon last night?" he asked, still pondering his fingers.

"Really? I don't believe you could have seen a full moon last night. Strawberry moon this month." She smiled. "And it's not for a couple of weeks, I think," Gracie said. "Why? What did you see?"

"Long story. We sure have a lot of ground to cover, don't we? A lot to talk about."

She swept her hand toward the living room. "No time like the present, as my Pops would say."

They still kept a comfortable space between them as they sat on the couch. Ron slid his cup onto the coffee table. He was trying to muster his best therapeutic opening to a difficult conversation. He began to speak, then backed up and started over.

She sat with her fingers tented over her stomach and their gaze met. "Is it about Agawa Rock?" she said.

Right to the heart. She should be the therapist.

"Well, yes," he stammered. "I was looking for an extra blanket last night—"

"The chest with the buckskin."

He inhaled. Held his breath for a moment. "Yep. I feel like a...I don't know."

Her fingers folded, she nodded thoughtfully, and watched him with her lips scrunched to one side. But she did not have to speak.

"You realize how this has stayed with me," he said. "It was something I suspected, of course, but it was never confirmed," he said as he sipped his coffee and stared into its black depths. "As hard as it may be for us to talk about—I mean that horrific night on Agawa Rock. And now it just seems like a debt I have to recognize."

Gracie lifted her chin and gazed out the window. "I thought that chapter would recede into the distance." She shook her head. "But it never does. Warrior dreams are the worst." She turned to Ron again. "But here we are. Two lives were taken that night. I did that. And I am trained to leave the past behind; to regret nothing. But that is one skill I just have not been able to master. I never talk about it. Not even with Adam."

She continued to brood, looking into the yard. But the scene she was watching played behind her eyes. Ron let the silence settle for a while.

"There's more," he said. "About last night."

She closed the scene in her mind with a flickering smile and pivoted. "And what did you see in that impossible full moon that never was?"

He told her about the night, the appearance of the little people, and his fingers.

"Here? Really. Right here?" She swept her hand toward the window. "The Puckwudgies." She laughed softly. "Well, I'll be damned."

"Yeah. That's what I saw." Ron took another sip and turned the mug in his hands. "But thank you. For everything. No good deed should be received without gratitude. Just thanks for saving my life."

She ran a finger under her nose, started to speak, stopped, took a breath.

He waited.

"What if I had not found you? What if you had been lost on that rock with that damn shaman? What if we had never discovered that you were my...dad." Her voice hitched. "You saved *my* life. I am so much more, now." She slid a hand across her stomach. "I feel complete. Like a real family."

Through the clerestory windows, the misty gray morning intruded their silence until chiming came from the front door.

"That must be Leo. I have to run to the clinic," she said. She reached over and squeezed his knee. "And you're welcome. I am glad you're here."

Chapter 18

Tribal Clinic

Gray clouds and a cold spittling mist followed Gracie and Leo as they left the resort, veered onto the highway, and drove into town. She wished that she could have spent more time with Ron, and she hated the intrusive, dehumanizing boredom of medical appointments. This was probably the third infection that she'd had during her pregnancy, so she knew what to expect when they got to the tribal clinic. The wipers dragged intermittently.

"Hey, buddy, ya think you could step on it? All this water everywhere is not helping my bladder," she said. Her urgency was another reason she didn't want to go all the way to Shawano to see her OBGYN. The tribal clinic was much closer. One of the Nurse Practitioners at the tribal clinic had become a friend.

"Ah, geez. I was going to stop at Drake's and get a breakfast burrito and a large coffee. You want one?" Leo snickered.

"You mention coffee one more time and I'll chop off your…braids," she replied.

"Yeah, when Lelah was pregnant with Lucie, we could hardly leave the house for the last month because that baby was just squeezin' down. I mean really sque-e-zing. Hard. Right on her bladder." He threw a stealthy smile her way. "I mean—"

"Shut. Up." Gracie huffed, then grinned. "Did I hear Lelah say that Lucie was going into pre-school next fall? Really?"

"Yep. Just waiting for that empty nest phase." He grinned.

"Well, I wasn't sure if I should be sharing Ron's dreams, visions, or whatever, but I think we might want to start listening to Lucie's fantastic imagination a little closer," Gracie said.

"What do you mean?"

"Her imaginary friends may not be so imaginary."

"You mean the imps, the Puckwudgies? Those little people that she pretends to see at night? She loves them."

"Well, Ron had a dream or an encounter or something last night. He described them perfectly." Gracie described to him what Ron had said.

"No way." Leo paused. "And we thought we were just playing along with her. We should have known better." He glanced quickly at Gracie. "What do you think it means?"

"There is no way to interpret what it means or what they want. It's certainly not my specialty, but I know that they are not always...safe, they *are* impish."

"We'll need to have a serious sit down with Lucie and Lance," Leo said.

"I'm afraid we will all have to be paying closer attention. It might be that things are about to get very interesting."

They rode in silence for several minutes until Gracie interrupted. "Thanks for the lift. Are you a cop today?"

"Nope. It's cop city for Donnie today. But he just checked in with me before we left and he hoped to be back to cover the inn. We're each just subbing two shifts a week at the tribal office. It's been pretty quiet, thank God. He might get off early."

"Yes. Thank God. No chatter? Nothing new?"

"Nope."

"Adam texted and said he'll be back from Neopit mid-afternoon. He only had a half dozen clients or so. Not too many crazy people 'round these parts."

"I know. I think he's already texted me three times to be sure I picked you up on time and to be sure that you would be okay." He smiled. "I don't know what you did to make him so nuts about you. I sure as hell never saw it."

Holding her stomach, she let loose with a single loud *Ha!* followed by her spritely giggle. "Well, I never had to smack Adam around the way I have you and Donnie."

The clinic was just off the highway down a side street. A wide avenue curved past the police station and tribal offices. Leo slowed to a stop under the stone and timber canopy at the front of a sprawling building that looked more like a wilderness lodge than a clinic. Shrouded in drizzling haze a lawn unfurled behind the building, spreading to the Wolf River.

"I'll see you inside," Leo said as Gracie eased herself out of the car.

"No, I'll be fine. I can text you when I'm done."

"I'll see you inside." He faked a stern look.

She only smiled and waved as she turned to enter the clinic.

While she registered at the desk, she asked if she could leave a urine sample right away before the dam broke.

By the time she was done in the lab, they were ready to put her in a room.

She knew much of the staff, but the sullen nursing assistant that took her vitals and led her to an exam room was new.

"I don't think I've met you before, I'm Gracie," she said extending her hand.

The assistant looked up at her for a brief second, brushed a loop of dirty blond hair out of her eyes and jostled Gracie's fingers. "Melanie." She waved toward the exam table.

"Is Jill here today? I usually see her," Gracie said, trying to remain pleasant.

"Oh, uh...Jill is running late. Doctor, um...Peters is going to check your sample and then he should be in pretty soon."

"I don't think I met her. Is she new?"

"*He*. It's a guy."

It didn't really matter to Gracie if her provider was male or female, especially for something simple as a UTI. But this assistant's attitude was terrible, so Gracie did not want to ask any more questions or keep the assistant in the room any longer than necessary.

Gracie swiped her phone and texted Leo: *Shouldn't be long. In the exam room.*

Leo: *In the waiting room.*

After ten minutes the door opened abruptly, and the grim assistant was back.

"He wants you in a gown, 'cause there was something in the urine sample and he's going to need to do an…exam—to be sure the baby will be okay." The last was tossed in as an afterthought, as if to bolster the case for a more invasive exam.

Gracie felt a lump in her throat that quickly sank to her heart. "Explain, please," she said.

"Oh, I don't think it's anything serious. He will explain. Take everything off except your top and your socks and he'll be in." She tossed a gown and sheet onto the exam table and hustled out the door.

Gracie hurried into the gown and sat on the end of the table with the sheet over her lap. Not knowing what else to do, she texted Leo.

Gracie: *Might be longer. Need an exam.*

Leo: *Going nowhere. They have…* was followed by donut and thumbs-up emojis.

She grinned, rolled her eyes. Setting her phone beside her she hesitated, bit her lip, and scratched her head. Something was not quite right and nagged at her thoughts, causing her to wrestle with a host of instincts from martial arts to motherhood. She stared at her phone for a moment, then picked it up again and texted Leo two emojis: a question mark followed by a yellow flag.

Leo: *??*

Gracie: *Just cautious.*

Leo texted a thumbs up.

Outside the door she heard a brief, hushed conversation between the nursing assistant and a male voice. The door opened and a tall man in scrubs entered, followed by the nursing assistant. She shuffled in, looking at the floor. The scrubs seemed a size too small on the man. They were tight across his shoulders and the sleeves rode high on his muscled biceps. He was wearing a mask which always elicited a sort of instant aversion and affected caution for someone like Gracie, who was trained to read faces. His eyes were pale blue and arresting beneath his black brows. Two braids, thin as yarn, trailed to his shoulders. He wore a surgeon's cap, even though he was only in the clinic, which informed Gracie that he was either self-consciously balding, had something to hide, or both.

"I am Dr. Peters. We are so sorry that Jill the Nurse Practitioner will not be available for you today, Mrs. Knowles." He spoke with an Eastern European accent while holding out his hand. Gracie noted that he wore surgical gloves on both hands. He had a firm handshake that he held for a beat too long as he locked eyes with her. In several years of marriage, she could not recall anyone calling her *Mrs. Knowles*. How quaint.

"What did you find?" she asked.

He held up a finger for her to wait.

Jerk, she thought.

"Nurse, could you help our patient to get ready for the exam." He looked at Gracie, "Oh. I'm sorry. It is only a minor infection. We just need to take a quick swab to check. It will be just a moment."

Too formal. Like someone from a medical drama. But he seemed efficient.

The assistant did not make eye contact or speak as she motioned for Gracie to ease back on the table, unfolded the stirrups from the table, and guided her feet into position. Gracie clutched the sheet across her lap, keeping her knees together and legs covered.

The doctor was edging his stool near the end of the exam table and maneuvering a stainless-steel tray spread with instruments. *Too many instruments, sharp instruments.* There were probes, scalpels, scissors, and biopsy punches. And a big syringe and needle. He took another pair of gloves from the tray and slipped them over the ones he had. *Strange. At least he's being sterile.*

Gracie cleared her throat. "So, it was just some kind of infection. What did you find in the urine? Can you tell me what you plan to do..."

"Oh, yeah. Just an infection. No problem." He waved a hand, but his voice was not reassuring. "I just need to get a quick sample to look under the microscope, and we will be all set."

"What kind of infection?" she asked.

"Oh nurse, I don't see a tube for the culture. Could you just scoot out the door and grab a test tube?"

"Well, I thought I laid everything out, and..." the assistant began.

"Nope. I don't see one." His brows raised, and he tipped his head toward the door.

She scurried out.

"I'll just get the first sample and she will be back with the tube, and we can be on our merry way," he said while taking the hem of the sheet and lifting it toward Gracie's knees.

Gracie pulled the sheet down. "I, um...I'm kind of shy. I'd like to wait until she gets back. Okay?"

His brows knit and he looked down at the instrument tray, back toward Gracie, and rubbed the back of his neck. "Okay, we wait."

"Can you tell me more? About the infection?" she asked to break the uncomfortable moment.

"Um, well, it was an infection of the vagina, I think. Something in your vagina." He rubbed his temple with a knuckle, like he was trying to recall something. "It was probably just a little trichinosis or something."

"You mean Trichomonas?" she said. "I think you get trichinosis from eating raw pork or something, right?" She laughed nervously.

"Yes, yes of course," he chuckled coldly. "I got them all mixed up. Such a busy day." He looked at the door and back at Gracie's knees. "Where is that darn nurse?" He shrugged.

After a stretch of awkward silence, he ran the back of his gloved hand across his forehead and without looking up, he rolled the chair nearer to the end of the table again.

"We'll just get a quick sample and no problem." He took the edge of the sheet again and began to lift it.

"No. We will wait."

He reached up and clutched the inside of her right thigh, squeezing. "I said, it's a busy day!" His voice was as cold as his blue eyes.

"Oh, hell no," Gracie said. Taking her left foot out of the stirrup, she cocked her leg and thrust her heel at his face, making a crackling thump as it connected with his nose. His mask was ripped from his face, but his features were already distorted by a wash of blood. For an instant, she flailed like a turtle on its back trying to get up, until she caught him on the side of the chin with her right foot. She thrust her hands on the table and bolted upright. As he rose from the stool, he seized the large needle and syringe from the table. She realized that he was about to inject her with whatever was in that syringe. She swept with her left foot and struck at the syringe. An arc of liquid sprayed around the room and sent the syringe spinning out of his hand. Her foot followed through, past his hand, and struck the stainless table, launching the tray and instruments across the room with a deafening clatter.

He was standing, dazed, blood pouring down his scrubs. She launched off the end of the table and for an instant stood perched on one foot with her right knee cocked. Before he could react, her foot had connected twice to his groin. He made a godawful groan like a calving heifer.

Bleeding and clutching his crotch, he bent forward. She was bringing her knee up when he dodged left and brought his hands up, grasping for her throat. She shoved both her hands between his forearms, spread his arms, and like pistons delivered one-two thrusts to his jaw. He stumbled backward, fell into the hallway, scrambled up, and reeled away.

Gracie reached for her phone and began to text, but in seconds Leo burst into the room, gun in hand. He scanned the room to see the scattered instruments and the blood on the floor. "What the hell?"

Gracie held her phone in one hand and clutched the back of her open gown with the other. "Do you mind?"

Leo turned around while she whipped the sheet around her. "Where'd they go?" he asked.

"Didn't you see him? He tore out of here." She smiled wryly. "At least you didn't lose your damn donut."

Leo held up the half-eaten pastry in his other hand and smiled sheepishly.

A blood trail led to an exit five steps from the exam room. Out the door, the broad lawn stretched to the river. Empty.

To one side and away from the clinic, a narrow stand of trees lined the river, and from behind the cover came the roar of a large boat engine.

Chapter 19

More Revelations

"I SAW THAT NURSING assistant hightailing it through the lobby. She looked like she was going to have a heart attack. I thought maybe she was just leaving because there was a family emergency. I asked the desk if she was okay and they just shrugged," Leo said. "'Who knows. 'She's new,' is all they said."

The clouds had thinned enough to allow peeks of sun to dapple the highway.

"Everything was chaos. I was able to talk with Jill for a little while," Gracie said. "She told me that the nursing assistant had only been there a week or so and had already been written up. I don't know if she was planted there or just some poor girl desperate for a bribe."

"Donnie and I will check into it at the station. This could be attempted murder, so I imagine the FBI will be called on to the rez."

"I don't know if calling in the FBI will be good or bad. Did you pick up that syringe?"

"Yeah. Be careful." He handed her a plastic bag with the large syringe and needle.

"Leo, you're shaking. Are you okay?"

He looked at her quickly, then out the window. "This was too close. This is the stuff we spend thousands of hours training to prevent." He inhaled, clenched his jaw. "And I was not there. I'm pissed."

"I take the blame. I have been way too careless lately."

They rode in silence for a mile until she interrupted. "He discharged the syringe when I hit him. Is there enough to get a sample?"

"You only need a drop, and there will be some left in the needle even if it was all discharged."

"The rez cops were there. Did they see it? That syringe?"

"I don't think so. It was still on the floor. They must have thought it was normal medical stuff, but I'll show Donnie. He knows more about testing and handling evidence. It wouldn't hurt to have another toxicology run. Even if the FBI or the cops were to run it, I think we would want to use our own resources so that we can know for ourselves. They might not be looking for the same things that we are." He held up his hand and wiggled his fingers. "There might not be any prints on the syringe because you said he was wearing gloves. Donnie and I are fully deputized on the rez force, so we can work with them. The FBI won't interfere if the rez cops are in the lead."

"Yeah. I told the cops as much as I could. You and Donnie can work with them at the station to figure it out."

"Yep. We will come up with something." Leo looked in the rear-view mirror and scanned the edges of the forest. "Donnie texted that he'd heard that they had already found the raft. It was a big one. Powerful. They would have brought it in from somewhere."

"That figures. It was stolen, right?"

He nodded. "They'd headed east, pulled in just before the bridge, and someone picked them up long before anyone could get there."

"Unbelievable. It's happening."

It was quiet again until Leo sighed, ran his hands around the steering wheel.

"What's the matter?" Gracie asked.

"Ah, geez. I wanted to wait until we were all together so we could talk about it."

"What is it?" she said sternly.

"While you were getting your prescription, there was another text."

"From Donnie?"

"Nope."

"Well?"

He sighed. "It was from The Lake Council."

"Oh man," she whispered.

"Actually, it was the chairman, Virgil Clement."

"How'd they find out? Do they think they want to convene a council? God, I don't want to go all the way to the Soo." She rubbed her face with both hands.

"No. They didn't know about it, yet. It's not about you." He gave her a quick look then back at the road. "It's worse."

She stared at him, wide-eyed.

"They found big Wally Anemki from Red Rock."

"Oh no."

"The hospital said he had a heart attack, but Virgil is insisting that they do a drug screen," he said.

"This is too bizarre. I'm glad Virgil is on it."

"It's worse," Leo said.

She waited.

"Carl Odjig from Batchewana got hit by a truck on the Trans Canada and is in a coma in Soo, Ontario and Dr. Kakegamic is missing on her trip to somewhere in South America."

"Lord. Half the Lake Council has nearly been wiped out." She stared ahead, shaking her head slowly until she snapped her head toward Leo. "Oh no. Tell me Jacob Payment is okay."

"He's been in the hospital a week or two for something else. But I talked with his wife, Ginny, and she said he's home and doing pretty good. All the rest of the council has either gone to ground or have a pair of Ogichi-daa."

"Has anyone tried to reach Duane?"

Chapter 20

The Inn Has a Guest

BEFORE THEY HAD LEFT for the clinic, Leo had a short conversation with Ron. Nothing important. Then they left. Adam had already gone to work. Now alone in the sprawling house with the gray day misting the windows, Ron felt restless. He quickly got bored checking his mail and scanning the internet. He folded his reading glasses and slipped them in their case.

Taking care of the kitchen and pouring the last of the coffee, he tucked his laptop under his arm and padded down the hall to his room. He pulled on the hoodie and found his shoes. The old inn next door with its history and architecture interested him, and Adam had urged Ron to check it out. The quarters for the Ogichi-daa took up a wing on the second floor, but the rest of the inn would be vacant. Gracie said she had seen her aunt Nessa slip away early and Donnie was at the police station for a while. Leo's wife Lelah and the kids would be away at a summer day camp. It was unusual to have everyone away, but security could be monitored remotely.

Even the cadets were gone. Eddie said his grandmother was ill and the other cadet had decided to take some time off, too.

He stepped down the rickety steps of the trailer house and crossed the yard toward the inn, pausing to scan the front of the grand old building. In a previous renovation, the broad porch across the front had been demolished and still visible was the outline where the old porch would have been attached to the side of the inn. The only other evidence of the porch was a long deck built of treated lumber and composites. A narrow awning had been built over the front entry, and the original double doors still remained with frosted glass etched with woodland settings.

About to take the three steps up to the deck, he swiveled. Behind him, he'd heard rapid footfalls and the distinct *huff* from a large animal. Just off the deck, standing at the corner of the inn, a large coyote was watching him. Its curious demeanor resembled a wise German Shepherd rather than a wild animal.

"Hey boy," Ron whispered. There was the briefest wince of proud indignation on the animal's brow. There was little to fear from a coyote in the wild, but this animal was big. It could have been mistaken for a wolf or some type of crossbreed. Though wolves and coyotes were skittish and afraid of humans, its proximity gave him pause. Frequently he had seen coyotes in the wild, but he had seen wolves only twice. Wolves seemed huge, hulking, whereas a coyote had the demeanor of a large fox with a rounder face. Wolves were also more uniformly gray or even black, compared with this animal that had the reddish-gray bushiness of a coyote.

At the corner of the inn, the animal continued to regard him. The reddish and slate hues of its fur were vivid against the gray greens of the forest. It raised its snout to regard the human scent, blinked slowly in bored affirmation, and slipped around the corner of the inn.

Ron bounded up the steps and across the deck toward the double doors. He grabbed the bronze handle on the left door, but it didn't budge. Neither door moved. He was about to leave when there was a bare click from the left door. He tried it again and it opened silently a few inches, then made one squeal like a baby's cry as he opened it further. The sound carried across a broad lobby. He was about to thank whoever had opened the door, but the expanse stood empty as a mausoleum. The automatic door lock must have been another security measure—had to be.

A span of dull blue threadbare carpet sprawled before him. Along the walls, sky-blue paint peeled away from an older green coat, leaving every wall with patterns like the maps of ancient worlds. All the broad trim had been cream-white at one time, but had faded to mottled gray on panel moldings, wainscoting, cornices, casings, and beading. A flight of steps with carved railings swept up each side of the room to a lavish landing overlooking the main lobby. To complete the classical baroque architecture, three tall pilasters supported the landing and three murky windows cast a seamless dim light across the room, viscous and changing. On each end of the room stood fireplaces tall enough to walk into, with hearths as large as a stage.

There was no furniture except for a dusty baby grand piano that tilted precariously on a broken leg. Like spaces long vacant of humanity, the room was heavy with an aroma of old rags, tobacco, and aged perfume. It seemed utterly abandoned. How did it manage to stay like this if there were occasional guests and with the families living upstairs?

On his left at the end of the great lobby was a wide doorway trimmed similar to the rest of the room with a tall entablature, floral corner blocks, and dental cornice. This opened to a side room with more windows and another fireplace. Surprisingly the fireplace was ablaze and unattended—he thought. He saw the arm of a couch; a winged, pleated Victorian couch with spotless red velvet upholstery. It was a dramatic contrast to the decaying surroundings. It seemed as out of place as if someone had just plunked it there right off the moving van.

As he entered the room, he stopped and almost pivoted to leave—or run. The entire inn had been dead silent. No one could have entered, left, or hardly breathed without being heard. Yet, at the center of the couch sat a man. A very strange man. Ron had no way of knowing what sort of guests or consultants might find their way to this hidden retreat, but he had expected no one. Certainly no one like this.

The man shifted his position. He had a narrow face with a long nose, and his small mouth and narrow chin jutted forward, giving him a chiseled, almost canine countenance. Amused, the man regarded Ron. A mane of dusky gray streaked with red swept to his shoulders. With a flip, he vainly tossed his hair. His moustache and narrow goatee were similarly hued. He wore a white shirt billowy to the cuffs with a sharp collar. Not quite Shakespearian, but oddly incongruent with the present century, though not entirely inconsistent with the setting. Crossing his legs, he flicked at the knee of his crisp brown and gray serge pants. Ron stared at the man's bare feet.

"I hate shoes." The man grinned slyly. Not unfriendly. He could have been from anywhere on the globe. In the dull, changing light, Ron could not be certain that the man's visage itself was not actually in flux. "I cannot fathom why you wear those damn things on your feet when it is not cold."

His accent was hard to fathom. Southwestern, maybe Navajo or Hopi.

Ron began to feel a crushing sense of confinement and stepped back. There was a scent like steam: hot, ferrous, and alkaline. Pressure built against the sides of his skull and across his chest as though the room were filling with the depth and presence of something as abysmal, vast, and dark as the bottom of Lake Superior. As if fighting a gale, he struggled to remain standing, or to raise his head to make eye contact. Though he had shifted from where he stood, yet the inn, the room, and the man seemed to be streaming past in a blur, a smearing distortion. Trying to focus, he whipped his head back and forth. But it was not coming from his head or from the room.

It was the man.

His very presence. Too great, too large, too crushingly substantial for the inn—for the world. Ron felt he was in the presence of an entity that defied the confines of this meager reality. A creature whose heart was beating from a schematic that earthly science would not fathom.

If the sensation had lasted another instant, he would have expired, as if crushed between the gravitational forces of two colliding planets. Yet the feeling was also irresistible and awe-inspiring like the halls of a great cathedral. Reverent. It was as if the being was so nearly perfect, that its very presence should demand awe—worship.

Nearly perfect. But not perfect.

Ron knew. He pressed his fists to his temples and stifled the need to weep. "No. I will not acknowledge you."

"Would I ask you to...worship me?" The man grinned and waved a hand in front of his face as if annoyed by a fly.

The churning forces and throbbing pressure subsided.

"Who are you? Tell me. You are compelled to tell me. I am—" Ron said.

"Silence, friend. I know who you are. And, no, we have not met. Not formally. But we have seen one another. And you know *of* me." He preened.

"How? A client? Friend of the family? Help me remember," Ron said.

The man burst into a cascade of laughter, rich and full that rang through the empty rooms.

"Indeed. A client." He wiped his brow. "Oh, dear man, I do like that." Smiling, he met Ron's eyes. "I like you, you know?" He gestured toward a winged chair with matching red velvet that Ron had not seen a moment before. "Sit. We must talk."

As one drawn to approach the tantalizing darkness, to approach the alluring fear and fright, Ron sat.

RETURNING FROM THE CLINIC, Gracie and Leo drove past the inn. Leo walked Gracie to the door. For a long time, she had wanted the freedom to walk around without a bodyguard in tow, but her gentle giants had worn down her resistance and she allowed them to protect her. And now, with this attack at the clinic and possibly on other members of the Lake Council, her protection was not only to be permitted, but imperative. Her daughter's future and possibly the future of a land and its people depended on it.

Leo entered the house ahead of her, walked room to room while Gracie put away her things, then nodded once on the way out and said, "Be safe."

"Of course," she said, waving off Leo and smiling as she pressed the remote control to rattle open the metal shutters covering the clerestory windows. Again, there was an annoying metallic squeal. She shook her head. *I thought Eddie lubricated those.* Gray light billowed into the room like old sheets.

In the kitchen, she opened the small white bag that contained her antibiotics that Jill had prescribed for her. While drawing water from the tap, she read the label on the bottle, then tilted her head back and downed two of the white tablets.

On the wall near the sink was a classic mid-century wall phone. Harvest gold, it was an authentic addition to the home. She rested her hand on the handset for a moment, then took it off the hook, putting it to her ear. The line was dead until she clicked the hanger twice, paused, then once more. She put a finger to the rotary and dialed 0-1-0-1 to the comforting whir-click, whir-click of each digit. A steady buzz, then a number was automatically dialed: *beep-bop, beep-bop.* Then came the old World Wide Web refrain that whirred like a sick bird trapped in a sewer pipe interspersed with *twang-twang.* She smiled to herself at the ingenuity.

A recorded voice, precious and familiar, greeted Gracie. "Please leave your message and get the heck off this line."

"Hi, Duane. I think it's time," Gracie said.

Chapter 21

Coyote

THE MAN ON THE red velvet couch sat with his fingertips pressed to each other and measured the former priest with one eye until Ron felt compelled to speak.

"This doesn't feel like a dream. Too real," Ron said.

"Tell me what you are thinking. I'd like to hear it in your words." The man grinned.

With his fingertips touching, Ron tactfully mirrored the man. "I don't believe this is real. It must be a dream. Or will you just tell me that dreams are real?"

"I will answer any question you have. And no. Dreams are not real."

"Who are you, then?" Ron asked.

"If I spoke it, you would not understand it."

"If you are Lucifer, you must reveal yourself," Ron said.

"Oh, stop." The man snickered. "That megalomaniac? Should I be flattered or insulted? I think I would be insulted. He gets all the press despite how utterly vain and corrupt he may be. He is beyond the pale. I imagine I would fall more appropriately under the label of principality. Yes. I like that. But it will suffice to call me Roamer, or Ma'ii or Koyotl." He hesitated. "Today I like Ma'ii. Sounds tropical, exotic." He lifted his shoulders for effect.

"Coyote. I should have known: The trickster," Ron said.

"In the flesh." A brown hand swept in front of his white shirt and along his body. "Well, shapeshifting is not one of my strengths, but I did not think you would walk into a room with a wild animal sitting on the couch."

When entering seminary as a younger man, Ron had been distracted, too enthralled by his own spirituality. He imagined casting himself into the supernatural, performing miracles, and seeing into other realms. Now he did not seek it or relish it. It was unsettling, overwhelming, and disorienting. Though trembling inside, he instinctively shifted his demeanor to manage the encounter like any other tense or treacherous counseling session.

"Can I call you Mr. Ma'ii, then, or do you prefer Coyote—or another name?" Ron needed to assert some control. He knew well the tales of Coyote: A joker, not entirely corrupt, but not often good. He plays the game for his own entertainment. Ron would need to play well.

Ma'ii shrugged a shoulder. "Suit yourself."

"Okay, Mr. Ma'ii. Is this a comfortable form for you or can I expect you to morph into something hideous and unrecognizable?"

"No, sir. And no, don't call me Mr. Ma'ii. Ridiculous. Ma'ii is fine. As I said, shapeshifting is not my forte. It is either this form or the furry one. This is how we look. All of us. Remember, you were made in our image."

"No demonic or godly countenance?" Ron smiled nervously.

"No. I just told you. This is how I've always looked." He lowered his gaze. "You don't know who we really are, do you? Despite all your theological pursuits, you know nothing."

"Tell me, then." Ron clung to his psychologist mode.

Ma'ii smiled. "Okay, I'll play along. You are interesting enough to me." He inhaled, exasperated. "Even in your Catholic Bible, you must have studied *'God takes a stand in the divine counsel, gives judgement in the midst of the gods.'* El in the midst of his elohim. Who do you think those elohim were?"

"I suppose you want me to believe you were there? Now I know I am dreaming."

"Like all humanity, you will believe whatever you want. No matter how implausible." He tugged on the cuff of his shirt. "How else would there be atheists unless humans were willing to believe the impossible."

He met Ron's gaze. "Again, you are not dreaming. And you are not listening. I imagined that you would serve as a better counterpoint, Father Jarvin." He tossed his hair. "To repeat: Dreams are not real. But what you consider *real* is but a fraction of all that is reality. There is reality more fantastic than dreams." His head tilted. "But I will let you draw your own conclusions about this moment."

"The Jesuits thought those words from the Psalm pertained to the dispensing of human justice." Ron tried to refocus, trained enough to ignore the banter.

"Of course, they would. In order to justify their activist distractions, your order thought everything revolved around them and their Church."

Ignoring the taunt, Ron pressed on. "And since leaving the Church, I've learned that those words were probably talking about principalities in the heavenly realms, not human affairs."

"Correct."

"'It says something like *'you are gods, all of you are children of the most high.'* But the Psalm says much more, doesn't it? It says that the gods screwed up, and now *'like any mortal you shall die, like any prince you shall fall.'* That must hurt." Ron smiled, outwardly calm, inwardly flailing.

"The curtain has not fallen—yet. Not by a long shot. It is amazing how a million years or so can distract you. A sort of sclerosis settles into your anxieties and fears. Even humans learn this in their eyeblink of a life." Ma'ii's face was grave. "But I've seen the glaciers come and go like waves on the shore. I was on the coast to receive the first family sent by the Dragon from Asia across the straits, that brief bridge between continents created for migration. When Anansi the African spider god's people landed in the south, I lured them north with displays of the Aurora.

"And I will be here, when soon, the next glacier slides south. Unless humanity is able to *save the planet*." He circled his hand beside his head and let out a yelp of laughter that rang in the empty inn. "The pride of your kind knows no bounds. With discerning human intent you always start with pride and work backwards. You are worse than Lucifer. You have no more ability to force the orbit or mar the face of a planet than a flock of locusts or a herd of swine. A planet! The audacity. Such hubris. Where is the fulcrum that your species would use to tip the planet? The physics don't add up for creatures to bury their planet." It took a moment for him to regain his composure. "But that's not why you stumbled in here."

"So, I can leave, or do I have to listen to another tirade?" Trying to keep the unstable entity off guard, Ron wanted to push the small wedge further beneath this formidable creature.

"You are free to leave any time. But you won't have the answers you want. As I said: I like you. Each person is equally positioned to speak for all of humanity. But you are slightly *more* equal, I suppose, because of your heritage.

"You humans think that your chosen officials, or your dictators, or even your priests and shamans speak for you. But those leaders are nothing to us. Those in our realm would have no interest in speaking with them. We choose with whom we will speak. Each of you is equally positioned to speak for all of humanity before El or before the elohim."

He paused and Ron felt a writhing sensation within, as if the entity were probing his soul.

"When the vine master tests the fruit, he selects a grape at random to see if the crop is ready for the wine press. He does not wait for a certain grape to volunteer itself. He chooses. The Harvester chooses the grain he will roll in his hand to see if the seed is ready for harvest. The grain does not decide this."

He rested an arm on the couch and tapped his fingers, weighing his next words.

"You deposited your seed and produced a child, so you think your job is done. But no, you had to waste my time and cross over when you briefly died in that hospital, so now you serve as my messenger. Like an angel." The coyote god laughed. "All your life, you wanted to be like one of those lowly functionaries. Angel is just a job description, the guy who works in the mailroom. Any entity can apply for the job. But why humans should want to take a demotion is beyond me."

"You are confusing me." Ron leaned forward. "Tell me what you wanted to say to me."

"I have a bad reputation. They say I am capricious. That is my fault. I've not been always a good shepherd of my territory."

Risking a tempest, Ron held his ground. "That would be an understatement, considering the past millennia or two on this continent."

"Well played." Ma'ii smiled. "I care more than I let on." He gathered himself modestly.

"I believe you," Ron felt compelled to say. "And I'm still listening."

"Let me lay the foundation." He made a circling motion with his palm down. "Where we are now, where you live, is the *Inside* world. I come from the *Outside*. Here on the Inside, you may be in wonder of some of the things that you see, but when you inhabit the Outside, you will not be in wonder. I come from a place where there is no wonder because everything is revealed. Reality is instant, pervasive, and substantial. To see is to know. Whether it's the fabric of the universe or whether it is grasping the intricacies of a universe of other creatures. Creatures like you could never imagine. There are creatures on the Outside that range from insect-like sprites and the winged beasts all the way to the seraphim." Ma'ii grinned. "Then throw in the gods and an extra dimension here and there. To see is to know. There is no wonder."

There was really no way to reply. Ron spoke the only thing he could think of. "So, from your position in the *Outside*, you believe that you are omnipotent?"

"Of course not. I have not seen everything. Because in this era I have been compressed, condensed, you might say. I have been injected into this little boil, this abscess of existence, and have been permanently merged with this continent. This is the principality assigned to me. Though the tribes that have inhabited this continent for millennia claim me, I am not their god. My charge was over the land, not the people. Humans come and go like a seasonal pestilence."

He laid a hand on his crossed knee and gestured with the other hand, smiling. "Yet any humans who have tread on this broad expanse have come under my purview. As I said, first from the African continent, the people sailed west. Anansi was their god. From the Asian continent, the people of the Dragon migrated east over the land bridge. Then your people were blown across the seas by Odin and Zeus. Now humanity has encircled the globe, having met on the east coast of my continent. But I belong to no people."

Ron began to speak, but Ma'ii held up a hand. He squinted as if looking far into the distance, then pursed his lips thoughtfully, nodding to himself. "And I have seen this certain pattern. It has been shown to me over and over. It is hard to give it credence, but there is a vision of a time of deep frost and ice, where many civilizations come to ruin and the Inuit leave the north and the Amazonians leave their jungle home and overspread and repopulate this continent." He waved his hand. "But that is of no consequence to you."

"No, I uh..." Ron stumbled.

Ma'ii pointed at Ron. "But here is something that concerns you: I have kept in touch from time to time with some of the humans who are the main players, like your ancestors. And now you. You had a primal connection to that Great Lake since before your people even sailed from Odin's shores. You wouldn't understand the machinations between my compatriots and the humans or all that we contrived on the Outside. But suffice it to say that you are the son of a long line of failed priests of your religion. Your name is so cryptic. Ronald Jarvin. Of course, you know that it could be construed as *King of the Lake*. You were granted a royalty of sorts in relation to the grand lakes of this continent, and your paramour—"

Ron braced in protest and Ma'ii flipped his hand. "Have it your way. Your partner, then. And your *partner* was the descendant of a similarly long line that originated in the region known to you as Asia, which is within the principality of the Dragon. The woman Gracie was the result." He grinned. "Didn't you call it a—what was the word? *Dalliance?* That is so human. But you had so little to do with it. We tried to arrange it with your father and grandfather, but they must have had a bit more moral rectitude than you. They could control themselves." He cackled.

"You're disgusting," Ron said. "It was my mistake. You had nothing to do with it."

"I *love* this stuff. You are absolutely wrong. This is all that brings the elohim joy. The foibles and machinations of humanity. Yet in this present age the passion and the drama fade for us. It's like Sodom and Gomorrah all over again. We all yawned at their debauchery. So boring. All perversion is the same. Simply narcissistic violence. Two humans of similar proclivities pleasuring one another. Ugh." Ma'ii shuddered. "No. Give me a fiery woman in a sweat of estrus and the ravenous man ignoring a host of temptations in order to impregnate her with child. They live a committed life no matter the temptations and the testing we throw at them." He smiled wanly. "Then there is the passion of betrayal. These are mortal cravings that will launch armies. Not the feckless foibles of a few erotically twisted folk."

Ma'ii made an exaggerated sigh. "In declining generations like this one, we see none of the raw theatre. The tragedy and the comedy. There is none of the passion of humanity. It was the reason for the fall, the reason sin entered the world: So that humans could demonstrate to the cosmos those attributes that would have been otherwise undiscoverable. Courage, remorse, defiance, excellence, beauty, justice, nobility, sacrifice..." He looked at the floor and shook his head. "Now we get only pride. Boring. It never ends." The god looked at the ceiling and spread his arms. "All the cosmos is leaning in to see what is happening here, on this tiny orb, this little speck of dust."

He sat back and folded his hands in his lap. The old building ticked and settled in the dusty quiet.

Finally, Ron ventured, "Do you have something more to tell me?"

Ma'ii leaned forward. "There are powers aligned against your daughter and her child. Your daughter is married to someone who is the descendant of those Natives who arrived from the south. His line emerges through Anansi and hers from the Dragon. Your line arrived from the east." He waved his hand. "You wouldn't understand. But there is much riding on this one and forces beyond your comprehension. I can't control everything, because humans are guaranteed their prerogatives—for good or evil. And the people that challenge your daughter, the ones who want to destroy her, are only humans. They are mere tools of something larger. But they are only human. But powerful, wicked humans who are desperate to develop skills from beyond the veil, and they will stop at nothing. They already have assistance from lesser beings. But I can say no more. And if I did, you would understand none of it."

They were silent again for a moment. Ma'ii held a straight smile. "I have something to show you."

LEO APPROACHED THE FRONT door of the inn. Opening the right double door, he entered a drab lobby. It was cramped and set about with brown second-hand stuffed chairs and hotel pictures on the walls. Ron would not have recognized this as the same inn he had entered—and it was not.

Sensing something had changed, Leo walked around the desk and checked the old mail slots and swept the cobwebs from the key rack. The door to their apartments led away to the left of the lobby and the door to the few visitor rooms to the right.

He took the door to the left. The old spacious lobby and banquet room had been remodeled into a training space and the steps to the apartments had been refashioned from the old double staircase that used to lead to a balcony. Cast iron railings from a retail lumber store led upward. Most of the old elaborate trim had been removed or painted over many times. The balcony had long ago been remodeled into a meeting area with a long table and wooden chairs.

On the other side of the training room was a side room that served as a small dining room now. The fireplace was dark and no longer worked. But they had always wanted to restore it because Donnie, Leo, and Gracie used the area for lunches and meetings and as a classroom for their cadets. Leo stopped a moment to look at the picture that hung over the mantel in the dining room. In the photo, the three of them were wearing black Jiu-Jitsu gis. The uniforms had been purchased by Gracie as a sort of joke because she was tired of them training in sweats. Often they trained in street clothes so they would be comfortable using their skills in any setting. Gracie was in the middle, arms folded, smiling broadly while Donnie and Leo, faces set in mock seriousness, stretched their arms above her head and around each other's shoulders. In his mind, it is how he would always think of her and his duty to shield her from the world.

"What the hell...?" A tattered red couch and chair sat against one wall. A leg on the couch was broken, a corner of the chair was torn, and the legs were dog-chewed. Leo snatched his phone.

"Hey Donnie. No, I'm right downstairs. When did you get back?" He paused. "Okay. Hey. It's Antique City down here. What the hell is with this shitty, piece of crap, spring-shot couch? It's covered with dog hair. But it...Yeah. It's covered with it." Another pause. "Why don't we move it into the basement if you want to fix it?" He listened. "Okay. Sure, I'll help."

Leo hung up and sighed. "Ah, geez." He muttered while brushing red and gray hairs from the velvet couch.

Chapter 22

Beneath the Inn

MA'II SWIFTLY STOOD AND with a tilt of his head summoned Ron to follow. They had been sitting in the side room and in the corner a narrow addition with a door jutted into the room.

In these old houses, it could have been a pantry or a closet, but most often it would be a stairway to servants' quarters or to the basement.

Ma'ii swept the door open, and a mist of dank air rolled into the room. He offered Ron through with a little bow and an outstretched hand. "After you," he said.

Ron leaned in and looked into darkness. "Nope."

"Coward." Ma'ii's laugh was a coyote's yip. "You should've seen the look on your face. Precious." He beckoned with a finger. "Follow." Stepping into shadows, he whipped his hand in front of his face, snapping his fingers twice. A marbled green glow spread along the walls and flowed downward. Waving away cobwebs, he turned, looking up at Ron with a grin.

The steps were wet, and Ron lifted a hand to the wall, steadying himself, but quickly withdrew it and looked at his palm covered in glowing goo. "Ugh." The front of his hoodie glowed where he wiped the slime.

"It's quite harmless." The coyote's voice reverberated on the narrow walls. "Or don't trust me."

"Should I?" Ron asked.

"Probably not. But you won't find the way through unless you sleep and unless I introduce you to a friend."

"Sleep? Do you think you're going to get me to stay down here overnight? I don't think…"

But Ma'ii ignored him, the creature's bare feet padding silently leading deeper down steps carved of stone. Ron continued to follow along the chiseled stairway farther and farther: long after there should have been a basement.

Downward the stairway twisted with glowing walls receding far into the distance.

Where the walls met the steps there were occasionally gaps, as if something had burrowed into the stone and hid in the dark at the side of the steps, lying in wait. Ron hugged the opposite wall whenever he approached these hollows. Ma'ii seemed to ignore them.

Before Ron could question, a tongue that was as large as a python and sticky with ooze lashed from one of the holes, flailing across the steps, hunting.

Ron jumped and plastered himself to the slimy wall opposite the lolling tongue. "It's, it's—"

"Just a Gunge Toad. Be sharp. But don't worry, they're slow. And the slime will only cause a nasty burn. It can't kill you."

"What the…?" Ron shot at Ma'ii.

"They don't live any deeper. Further down, you have to watch for the crack spiders." The coyote yapped. "And they are not named after cocaine or after rock crevices."

Further on and deeper down, it became utterly silent so that the moist walls seemed to absorb the sounds of their steps. But watching every dark gap and slimy opening, Ron thought he could hear his thumping heart. *No, not my heart.* Another rhythm pulsed from far below.

As they descended further, he recognized timpani, deep and steady.

Ron craned his neck to see further into the gloom as the relentless rhythm was joined by a flourish of higher percussion like small skin drums and congas, a tinkling like tiny cymbals, a hoarse flute, and a droning string that echoed along the cavern steps.

Ron was about to ask the coyote god where the music was coming from when the old wound at the back of his skull became crawling and prickly. In fear of crack spiders, he swatted at the back of his head, but a similar throbbing had grown in the fingers that previously had been severed. Shaking his hand, he muttered to himself, trying to settle his guts.

"Everything okay back there?" Ma'ii asked.

But Ron was too distracted to answer as the passageway began to brighten and grow larger. The pulsing percussion became a din as the steps opened onto a great cavern larger than the banquet room of a castle.

They stood exposed on the stone stairway that continued downward along a wall of the great room. And Ron paused to take in the spectacle. From their perch on the steps, they surveyed a bustling expanse.

Ma'ii held a finger to his lips in silence as they edged further down the steps.

The glowing walls faded amid torches and sconces that lit a hive of activity. The dewy cavern was heavy with the scent of blood, smoke, and carrion. Many small beings sat cross-legged on the floor, the sprays of their feather headdresses streaming together like a breeze through a wheat field. In coves notched into stone walls the drummers and other musicians were arrayed.

They all moved in pulsing pace to the tempo. Logs were set on stone slabs and small arms, muscled and gleaming, wielded machetes that glinted and stabbed as they hacked and sliced furred and feathered carcasses. Bare-breasted women wove rushes and strips of bark or suckled impossibly tiny infants naked and plump.

"Puckwudgies," Ron whispered. "I am dreaming."

"The Pucks are real. Dreams are not real," Ma'ii hissed, flapping his hand to hush Ron. But too late.

In an instant all movement stopped, and the music and bustle fell silent except for one infant at its mother's breast, whose wailing was no more than the mew of an ornery kitten.

The people stared up blankly at the pair edging down the steps. Ron turned and raised a brow to ask, *What should we do?* But ahead of him there was no longer a man. A large coyote crept ahead silently, its muscled shoulders rolling from step to step. Ears perked, the animal's tongue lolled from grinning jaws.

The tiny people merely watched as though seeing a portent in the weather, a red sky in the morning, or the shape of a passing cloud. The coyote looked back at Ron; its eyes widened, encouraging him to pick up the pace.

Ron scurried behind. At the bottom of the steps, he followed the animal as it disappeared around a corner and into shadow.

In darkness Ron edged along patting the walls, and stopped, afraid to get near the god creature. The drums and music abruptly resumed. Ron swiveled back and forth, trying to see until his eyes adjusted to the dim light trailing from the cavern. When he looked back, the coyote was biped and human-like again.

With a snap, Ma'ii lit the glowing walls. Sconces and crumbling doorways revealed that they were in deep stone hallways: the passageways where he had followed Duane. Each vacant archway loomed black and menacing.

"When I was here with Duane," Ron said quietly, "I thought that maybe this was just a dream. But I already know what you are going to show me," Ron said.

"This is not a dream. Damn it. Listen when I speak to you." Ma'ii snarled.

"I've died after all?"

Exasperated, Ma'ii stopped and turned. "Priest, will you never learn?" He folded his arms and stared at Ron. "Where do your prayers go? You still pray, don't you? I know that you do. I've heard you."

Ron nodded.

"Then where do your prayers go?"

"To the mind of God? Carried by messengers?" Ron shrugged. "I don't know."

"Typical." Ma'ii tapped his temple. "It's all in your head."

"I don't believe that. I've seen—"

"No, I mean it's in the mind. Yet you believe the mind is not real. The mind is great at weaving nonsense, but it is also *real*. It is the conduit, the bond, the bridge between your world and ours. There is no *afterlife*, there is only life—and death, of course. The life in your world and the life in this world are two sides to the same coin. Actually, there are more sides, but you're not ready to understand that yet."

"Is this the *Outside* that you were talking about?" Ron scratched air quotes.

"Actually, you might say this is in between the Outside and the Inside. The *Outside*," he mocked Ron's air quotes, "is far more interesting than here and more interesting than your life on the Inside. Even this place has some fascinating fauna and foliage that your best artists could not fathom."

Ron looked around nervously.

"But wait until you see beyond here: Beyond the in between," Ma'ii said.

"We are going to the Outside? How?" Ron scratched his arm, skeptical.

The god pressed the heels of his hands into his temples. "You might awaken in the Outside. But, ugh, I get tired of explaining this stuff." He tipped his head. "C'mon."

They passed a few doorways and were soon at the broken door with the stained-glass serpent.

"This is it. The room that I entered with Duane. What is this? This place is some place bac—twisted."

"There is more," Ma'ii said, pushing into the room.

Nothing had changed. In silence, all the girls and young women slept on their stone slabs, each covered by a heavy sheet. From the hallway, a retching scent of musk and death drifted into the room. And from the dark corners of the room came a snuffing and growling.

Ron whirled around as a broad face slid around the doorway to look into the room with large slate-black eyes dead as a shark.

Wide as the doorway, the tall creature bowed to enter. Ron paced backward, his head swiveling, and he nearly tripped over one of the slabs. More creatures emerged from dark corners. They hunkered, teeth bared, while their heads bobbed and long arms swayed.

"What. Are. They?" Ron whispered.

Ma'ii had raised both hands, restraining them. "Oh, they come by many names; here the Menominee may call them manabai'wok, ye'iitsoh to the Navajo. But you know them best as yetis, sasquatch, or just plain old bigfoot."

"I don't believe in bigfoot. Err...at least—" Ron said.

"Doesn't matter a whit what you believe in. Angels, yetis, and those little pucks are about the only creatures that pass freely back and forth through the veil. The manabai'wok exist between the worlds, but unlike angels, they are not messengers. They are there to guard and heal rips in the fabric of the veil. And this room is a tear in the fabric. Yetis are sort of like platelets and blood cells in the flesh, I suppose." He grinned. "But they like to pass through and raise hell sometimes. And sometimes they like to bring other things with them to manifest when they are around."

Ma'ii waved a hand in front of his face. "And it's not just their smell that they like to bring with them. They smell like shit—even to a coyote!"

The yetis slumped to their haunches, resting their enormous hands on their knees, their big eyes shiny like black beetles.

"They will be fine," Ma'ii said. "But now it's time for your journey."

"Wait, I don't want—"

Beside an empty slab, Ma'ii laid two fingers on Ron's shoulder. "Lie down," he commanded.

Ron felt every muscle twitch and tremble, then a wave of calm and weakness washed over him, drawing him to sit on the slab and lie back.

He drowsily rolled his head to look across the rows of silent women. At the last moment, something out of place caught his attention.

A small woman with long black hair to her shoulders lay flat. The only interruption on the smooth sheet that covered her was her large, protruding abdomen.

"Oh no! Oh no! Stop. You can't take her…"

" Into dead silence…" The coyote's voice trailed off.

Chapter 23
Dead Silence

THIS WAS NOT A dream.

This was not thought, or memory, or conscience.

This was not existence or being: Only seamless black silence. His eyes were open, but it was as though light had never existed. Not even the little ticks of light and color behind closed lids.

His ears could hear, but nothing in the universe vibrated or trembled enough to be heard. There was not even a quiet ringing in the ears or his own pulse: All the universe frozen at absolute zero.

Existence without prospect or potential. He had never been born, never lived, and had no future.

For eons, he slipped from nothingness to nothing, like a brainless worm wallowing mud-deep within an endless primordial night. A night without stars or ever the hope of light. Ever.

All knowledge of light escaped him. Suspended in a lake of tar, a deep ocean, without arms or legs, without body, brain, mind, or senses. Nothing drifting through nothingness.

Not the slightest flicker of cognition and only the barest remnant of self-awareness.

His mere dot of consciousness was microscopic as the very tip of the sharpest needle, yet it was as torturous as if that needle, searing hot, were thrust into an eye.

Endless, rancid boredom devolved into an eternity of pain. That final speck of awareness must also be terminated. Or he would writhe alone enduring an infinity of soundless agony.

Kill it. A million years it had taken to muster the intent to murder the last cell of his existence. He possessed nothing but a singular focus: To find this last iota of sentience and snuff out all existence.

Another century of grinding torture passed. Nothingness to nothing. All the while, he strained to focus on that single, tiny flicker. And extinguish it. He would glimpse it a moment like the faintest star that can be seen only at the corner of an eye. Pursuing it for eons, it would escape again into the bottomless night.

Then one time, he held it. One time. But only for a quavering moment, like an ephemera bobbing on night breezes or a firefly far ahead along a darkened jungle path as it stitches in and around the trunks of ebony trees.

The effort of observance left him in delirious mental exhaustion until he would collapse in fatigue for millennia.

Paleozoic, Mesozoic millions he had floated in dark slime.

Again, he held the vision: a tiny dancing green comet, much closer than before. If he had hands, he would pull himself, straining, his muscles shaking hand over hand along a bristled rope to draw nearer. But alas, even the wisp of green comet guttered and died.

But this time he laid only a century until he was awakened by a single shooting star, thin as a strand of a girl's hair, white in the moonlight.

Until, where there had not been sound or words: A voice. A single syllable. "La." Flat without timber or character, inhuman and disconnected.

"La."

For a year, that flat syllable lay. Like the word that brought creation into existence. Fading with the thin timbre of a pure brass bell.

Then another.

"Laz-ar." Two syllables in the firmament, as complex to his mind as every word of holy writ, every word spoken since the dawn of humankind.

For a brief moment he recalled a history, no more than a few Latin letters scratched on crumbling papyrus. But it was *his* history. A shred of seminary life, but he could not have known what it was. To him, it was merely something other and far away. A moment set before another moment, creating for him an entire dimension. He strained with all that he possessed in this non-existence to grasp one moment, to hold onto two consecutive thoughts.

"Laz-ar-re." A whole word: A concept, a name, a universe. Neurons sizzled and synapsed with spits of electric life. He strained, tugging together sinewy bits of memory that amounted to almost nothing. A hummingbird's nest of forgotten threads.

Then a great thunder ripped his black world asunder and divided the dam that restrained the lake of tar. The black sludge poured forth, leaving him flailing on a charcoal shoal.

"Laz-a-re. Ve-ni. For-as!"

"Lazare veni foras." *Lazarus, come forth!*

Lazarus had always haunted him. Wrapped in putrid grave clothes, the saint's zombie-like resurrection had always triggered more fear than reverence.

A spider silk of memory connected him back to his childhood and through his seminary days when he'd learned much more about the man who'd risen from the grave.

Now he understood.

More days—months passed recovering his existence. Until one moment, he beheld a vision wavering above him like a forest canopy of greens, blues, and golden light. Occasionally a voice soothed and cajoled him again. *Come away, son.* A hand loosely gripped his shoulder. *Ronald, wake up.*

He awoke from a dream of someone washing his feet. It was a dream about a humble king and a banquet of betrayal. He realized that his back was damp, his feet lay in the water caressed by gentle waves, and the first rays of a new sun slanted across a broad beach. The sky above was sapphire fading to powder blue and pink. Each wave whispered and was joined by the gentle murmur and cluck of aquatic birds and the scent of roses and the sea.

"I think our man needs a strong cup o' joe," a familiar voice said.

"I do not believe I have tasted that in a very long time. I believe my dad would sometimes offer a sip," another replied. A younger man.

"Oh, I had a cup on that day I met him in the restaurant before he boarded the ferry. It was to die for, as they say."

Both laughed.

"Will he be all right now, Malachy?" the younger man said.

"I believe he will. Providence led you to help us find him, Scott," Malachy said, addressing the younger man.

"It was a long way back. But this stage of the conflict is crucial. It needed our intervention. When Dee sent a messenger, I was happy to receive the command and return. By helping Ron, we help her son and my old friend, Duane." Scott said.

Ron turned his head, his vision blurring for a moment, then clearing enough to see two men sitting near him on the beach. One was immediately familiar: The guy he met in the restaurant in Cadillac. Wearing a robe and looking years younger he sat cross-legged on the sand. Ron did not recognize the other man, though. He was barely out of his teens, with longer auburn hair and a round face. Their smiles beamed at him.

Ron tried to speak, but his mouth felt as though it were stuffed with spider webs.

"Drink this," Malachy said, holding a small cup.

Ron sipped. "That's not coffee," he said.

They laughed. "Sadly, no. But the fruit of the vine is what you need to get you back on your feet, son," Malachy said.

Ron took another sip and looked at Scott.

The man lifted his chin. "I'm Scott. I used to be a friend of Duane—when we were kids."

"Duane Bird, Gracie's brother?" Ron said hoarsely, memory returning in flashes.

Scott affirmed with a smile. "You will be fine now. We will help you to go back through."

Each man took a side and helped Ron to his feet. Taking a moment to steady himself, he gazed across the serene and lovely coast. "Where was I?"

The men looked at each other and Scott spoke. "You were left in another plane. A place in between, you might say. In the Deep Silence."

"Am I supposed to know what that means?"

Malachy grinned and gave a quick shake of the head. "Well, no. But many never find their way out. You were lucky. It is not often the elohim intervene here, but he virtually dropped you at our feet. They do not do that often. Almost never. But that is a capricious one, indeed. He took a risk knowing that passing you through Deep Silence would be the only way to open a celestial portal to us in hopes of saving your daughter."

A memory returned to Ron. "Gracie! I saw Gracie there. I am sure it was her. Laying on a slab. She's pregnant. My daughter." Emotion welled inside him, and he put a hand to his mouth. "My daughter."

"Yes, son. She is there," Malachy said seriously.

"We have to go back!" Ron said.

"Those women were laid there by others, using other means. They can only be pulled back by using their methods," Scott said. "That is what Duane is trying to do. Because long ago he and I were there. He knows how to find them, now."

"The sooner we get you back home, the sooner Duane can help them. He might have a plan," Malachy said. "And all hell is breakin' loose back there," he said with a straight smile. "All of hell. You will not see us again, but we will be near. All the way through."

Ron rubbed his face and looked far along the beach. In the distance, a woman moved along the beach, her feet at the water's edge, her arms moving gracefully at her sides as she walked. Because of the distance and morning haze, she was only a silhouette.

"Is that her?" Ron pointed. "Is that Gracie?"

"No." Scott's smile grew. "That is her mother."

The woman lifted a delicate hand, waved to Ron. He smiled. She paused a moment, nodded, and turned, the hem of her thin gown sweeping the sand.

Ron felt himself lowering, his consciousness fading, but not back into the horror of dead silence, but into a profound and restful sleep.

Chapter 24

Raid

Eddie sat within a nest of emotions that felt as maddening and annoying as the mosquitoes and deerflies that buzzed around, needling his flesh and sucking his blood. He brushed greasy black hair off his forehead, nervous about whether Donnie or Leo would figure out that he had pried loose one of the clerestory windows while the security system was off and he was supposed to be lubricating the track for the metal shields.

There had been a moment, back when he had volunteered to be an Ogichi-daa cadet, that he imagined that he had become something like a Ninja. That was until he had pulled on his camo to discover it was too big. He used a knife to poke another hole in his belt, so he didn't have to walk around like a skinny dumbass clutching his waist and hitching up his pants. He thought his life would finally be exciting: the girls would take notice, he'd smash some noses, fire off some heavy-duty weaponry, and carry a piece just like the bad guys do. None of that became reality. Instead, he got yelled at by two old Ogichi-daa who imagined they were Dwayne "The Rock" Johnson, and he got slapped around by a little pregnant chick: no guns and no girls.

Eddie tugged at his body armor where it chafed his side.

"You're not going to shit your pants, are you, Rookie?" The guy in the floppy hat and cargo pants hustled next to him. Eddie turned away so he didn't have to look at the man's dream catcher earring that wiggled below his fat lobe like a minnow on a hook.

"You hired me because I was trained." Eddie's Adam's apple rose and fell as he clenched his jaw. He hissed. "I will be fine."

"Bullshit. We gave you that roll of cash because you could get on the roof and jimmy that damn window behind the metal shutters. And because you could give us phone numbers and draw a floor plan. We had to show you how to rewire the cameras. Don't get a big head."

"Not exactly a roll of cash." Eddie huffed.

The man cuffed Eddie. "You'll need to prove yourself. Then you can try to be greedy. Maybe we'll listen." Floppy Hat sneered. "Otherwise, you will soon be just a body laying over there after we get in that house."

Eddie was just about to grumble and remind the guy that it was not his fault that they had to resort to a fallback plan after the botched extraction at the clinic. But a big man pulled aside the ferns and joined them. He was also dressed in camo and body armor and his stringy braids swayed as he crab-walked to their position. Under his breath, he spoke in an Eastern European accent. "Schmidt, we're just about set. What's your name, again, Rookie?"

"Eddie."

"Okay, Rookie. Stay with us." The big man looked at Schmidt. "The three are in position in the woods on the other side. They'll cut down anything that comes out of the inn, and they'll cover the van when it pulls in." His black brows were level above severe blue eyes. With the broad bandage covering his nose, the gauze stuffed in his nostrils, and his horse teeth he looked like an insane clown. But Ggorchik always scared Eddie.

Ggorchik pressed his collar and leaned his head slightly to speak, the frenzy of words becoming more intense until he was nearly spitting into his tiny microphone. "Five minutes. Again, remember line of fire when that van gets here. She will be most vulnerable during extraction and there could be lead flying everywhere. She cannot get a scratch. She is mine!" He pointed at his partner. "Send the texts, Schmidt."

The guy in the floppy hat bobbed his head once and brought up his phone, and with a swipe and a couple of taps, he sent a flurry of texts to all the phone numbers he had gathered when Ron had foolishly handed him his phone.

Adam's phone was the first to receive a text. But he was with a client so he wouldn't see the fake text from Gracie assuring him that everything at the clinic went fine and that she would be napping. Lelah received one of the texts, and it was from Leo telling her he would see her when she got back with the kids and to swing around to the grocery store for a few things. Everyone was being steered away, but only Gracie's phone went unanswered. It vibrated unnoticed next to her bed, where she was slipping deeper under the influence of the drugs dispensed to her as a prescription for a simple urinary tract infection.

And Leo would not see the text that was supposedly from Lelah. The text was supposed to tell him that her car broke down and she and the kids needed him urgently. But his phone buzzed while he was standing behind two of the three men who crouched in the brush across from Gracie and Adam's junk-filled yard. The moment they reacted to the buzz of Leo's phone, a third man who lay on his stomach concealed behind a rotting woodpile pulled the trigger. A bullet punched into the side of Leo's head, twisting him onto the trunk of a big poplar. His eyes crossed as he slid down the tree until he was seated on the ground, his mouth contorted in a frown.

"Shots fired!" Ggorchik spat. "Move." Ggorchik pressed the bud in his ear, then spoke into the mic. "Okay. Good shot. Hold your positions and watch for any others until you see us come out of the house."

Schmidt pulled Eddie by the shoulder and the three men scuttled along the edge of the clearing toward the house. Dashing across the patch of lawn one by one, they scaled the ladder that Eddie had left in place after sabotaging the window. Ggorchik held a device to the security sensor on the window. A green light blinked twice. He pried the window out of its frame.

From a pack Schmidt withdrew a telescoping rod, opened it, looped a rope around, and braced the rod across the window frame to serve as an anchor. He unfurled the rope into the room. Ggorchik was inside and had dropped to the floor in a second, clearing the room. Schmidt followed and Eddie was last to hit the floor, a black cylinder dangling from a strap on his shoulder. The device was the size of a fire extinguisher, with two handles, a metal square on one end, and a keypad on the side.

In a few more seconds, Ggorchik was beside Gracie's bed. He felt the side of her neck for a pulse, but her legs shuffled beneath the blanket. From his vest he withdrew a tourniquet and syringe and deftly wrapped the tourniquet, slid the needle in a vein, loosened the band, and injected. He was proficient, having injected the solution many times. Lifting her limp body, he tramped through the kitchen and up short steps toward the door that led from the house to the trailer. Ggorchik clutched her tightly as he leaned backward and kicked twice at the metal door. It did not give way. He lifted his chin toward Schmidt, who took the cylinder off Eddie's shoulder, slammed the square end against the door above the handle. There was a high-pitched whirring sound like a drill. He stepped away. "Get back!" Schmidt yelled. The device hummed, accelerated, and delivered two deafening, concussive thuds. The whirring sound recurred, and the device dropped off the door and lay smoking on the floor. Schmidt shoved Eddie and the cadet picked up the cylinder by the handle, Ggorchik kicked the door, and it banged open.

They capered through the scattered junk on the lawn as a white van roared past the inn and slid sideways, stopping in front of the mobile home. The three men in camo broke from the woods on the other side and jogged toward the van, spraying the front of the inn with gun fire.

The side door of the van slid back, and the back doors spread open. Ggorchik clumsily chucked Gracie into the van, pushed her to the other side, and hopped in. Schmidt followed. Eddie grabbed the side of the door and looked back to see Donnie crouch-stepping around the corner of the inn, his 9mm rapid-firing until he paused to throw a clip. Then Eddie whirled to pull himself into the van but suddenly he thought he had been punched just below the collar bone. He pivoted back again and saw a dot flare above Donnie's eye. Time slowed. Donnie's glasses creased in the middle and exploded, his hair puffed straight back, and a red cloud billowed from the back of his head. And before Donnie went down, a trail of red rosettes bloomed one by one from his right shoulder to his left side.

The three men breaking clear of the woods bounded the last steps and jumped into the back of the van.

As the van revved, men were yelling, and Eddie saw Donnie crumpled in front of the inn. He looked down at Gracie lying helplessly on the floor of the van. No longer the threatening woman warrior, she looked like a little girl. She could have been his little sister. The hair lay across her forehead, tangled with sweat. Her small hand lay on her stomach as if unconsciously protecting her daughter. Emotion welled up in Eddie.

As the van readied to pull away, Eddie looked forward through the windshield. Like a wounded Goliath, Leo pushed through branches and stumbled into the clearing. There was a ragged wound near his temple and his eyeball bulged hideously. Blood obscured his face as blindly he outstretched a hand and trudged step by step, mouthing *Gracie, Gracie,* until he stumbled over a rusty truck fender and collapsed.

Eddie stared at Gracie. The men were jostling her. Covering her with a dirty blanket and securing her with straps. When the van accelerated his fading vision met Ggorchik's cold blue eyes for one second before Eddie leaned back against the doors and fell out as the van accelerated.

"No." Ggorchik shouted. "Grab that son of a bitch!" He flailed, trying to grab Eddie. "Too late. Kill him."

Eddie was feeling weak as he thrust both legs to push himself out of the van and he used his final effort to tumble clear of the van. Nearly every shot from the back of the van missed him, except one that connected and penetrated through the side of his heel. The pain brought down the curtain.

Chapter 25

Emerging

From a placid beach Ron felt as though he had been pulled far offshore and lowered into the deepest trenches of Lake Superior. With arms outstretched he had sunk into bracingly cold darkness, the air crushed from his lungs. A tiny circle of light seemed a mile away as slowly, he began to rise. Accelerating upward, his body planed back and forth, his throat burned, and his head pounded. But the light was too far, and he would soon expire. The glimmer expanded to a ceiling of green light and just as he was certain he would drown, he bobbed to the surface like a cork.

He lay there a long while, feeling the waters recede.

The sound of hammering awoke him: Sharp, forceful, and rapid. Who was he? Where had he been? He opened his eyes. He was laying on a ratty red velvet couch. He scanned the room. A table was set around with folding chairs and above a cold fireplace hung a photo of three people dressed in martial arts uniforms. After a long while, like faces emerging from water, he recognized them as Leo, Donnie, and Gracie. The events of the past weeks filtered back in bits and pixels until the concussive hammering repeated.

Gunshots. Many gunshots.

Prying himself off the couch, he braced himself against the table a moment and steadied. Stumbling out of the room and into the larger training room, his foggy mind reeled with confusion as he registered that this was no longer the shambling inn he had entered before he met the coyote. The elaborate trim was gone, the walls had been stripped, and the musty ancient scents had been replaced by fresh paint. The

Victorian staircase had been replaced by functional steps with factory railings.

The peeling paint and dank carpet were gone. He walked through a tiny lobby and past a desk that had not been there when he had entered the empty expanse of the room. His head buzzing, he was trying to remember a vital forgotten dream, to stitch together all that had happened since he had entered the vacant inn that morning.

Pushing through the double doors and onto the deck, he felt that he had walked onto a movie set where the entire scene had gone south, the actors had all missed their cues, and the director and crew had abandoned the actors where they lay. The scene was silent except for one young man who lay on his side whimpering. His leg was drawn up, his shoulder was bleeding, and he clutched his heel with one hand. Scanning to his right, Ron noticed a large man lying face down, bloodied and unmoving, while across the clearing, the feet of another man protruded from behind a rusty fender. As if on signal from the director, the man behind the fender moaned, and his feet shuffled as if he were trying to stand.

Ron slowly stepped across the deck as more players came on set and action resumed.

Lelah tore down the drive in her SUV and skidded to a stop in front of the inn. She opened her door and with a gun in one hand, she motioned with the other for the kids to stay down in the back seat. Without a word, they obeyed. She crouched low and swept quickly with her hand, signaling Ron to get off the deck and behind the SUV.

Across the yard, Leo moaned again, and Lelah darted toward him, looking down once at Eddie, who clutched his heel. She knelt beside him a moment and realized something more than his wounds was not right. The camo uniform and body armor were not like anything they would have used.

"Are they gone?" He whined and looked around warily.

She grabbed his shoulder and yanked. "Who? Tell me. Where are they?"

He gave a sharp cry and said, "They took her. The van is gone, dammit. So, they're all gone."

"Don't you dare move, or I swear I will finish you off," she said, quickly patting him down.

Eddie would not move. He cared little about his life at that moment, but would not risk more pain.

Adam was next to arrive on scene and stopped his pickup behind the SUV and saw Ron crouching wide-eyed and confused. Lelah waved to Adam frantically and he dashed to where she stooped beside Leo. He had begun to thrash, his head and shoulders covered in torrents of blood.

"Call 911," she said. "Then take this and get in your house." She handed him Leo's gun. "I saw that the door on your house is open, and Eddie said everyone's cleared out. He's desperate so I have to believe him." She grabbed his arm. "I don't know what the hell this is. Be strong," she said, kneeling beside her mortally wounded husband. She looked into Adam's worried face. "It's Gracie. I'm afraid they took Gracie."

Crouched beside Leo, Adam began to rise.

"Wait," Lelah said.

She pivoted toward her SUV and called. "Ron! Check on the kids in the back. Don't let them come out. Then get over here."

Lelah examined her husband, trying to calm him, and she looked at Adam. "You have to be careful. Something is wrong with Ron," she said. "He came out of the inn in a daze. I don't know what he saw in there. I have not seen Nessa." She pointed with her chin. "I think that's Donnie over there. Check on him before you go in your house, but from what I saw when I pulled up, I'm sure he's gone."

Standing, Adam fumbled his phone out of his pocket. His fingers shaking, it took three tries to dial. He shouted into the phone while sprinting toward Donnie. The man lay sprawled, one arm extended, another twisted around his back. The back of his shirt was ripped and pocked with glistening exit wounds. An entry wound above his left eye matched a bowl of blood, brain, and skull at the back of his head. His half-open glassy eyes stared at infinity and his bloody tongue lolled.

Trying to martial every resource and calm every nerve, Adam lifted his elbow and swept it across his forehead, stuffed his phone in his pocket, and sprinted toward the mobile home. The door yawned black and ominous, and like the echo of a malicious mantra, a memory from several years prior burst upon his vision: In sunshine he was standing on a sparkling beach, the driven sands biting his ankles, crashing waves of Lake Superior were drubbing the shores, and the whitecaps far out in the bay leapt like lambs and pounded the shore like rams. His first wife Julie was lost to the waves, and he would never see her again...

Like in a nightmare, the quicker his steps pounded, the further the door receded from his grasp.

Through his jumbled mind he recalled countless facets of Gracie's life that she had revealed to him about herself.

***

Gracie. A few years ago, in that time of overwhelming confusion, when the parameters of his world—of reality itself had been destroyed, Gracie became the beacon; a lighthouse built of stone shining through terror and chaos. Then abruptly she left and returned to Keshena. After using her skills and prowess to destroy a bogus shaman and the sinister schemes of the Dark Council that had supported that fraud, she left the shores of Lake Superior and returned to her home. It had been her brother, the Lake Council of the Keepers, and her Ogichi-daa that had helped her to build a fortress to hide from forces that could destroy her.

Then Gracie opened up and shared a life with Adam. And she had made herself vulnerable. Towers are lonely places. And even a young woman with a ceramic veneer and an iron core is still a woman.

She had known and trained with many good men, but most had been like her. They were men who possessed the same edge and intensity. But from the first time she met Adam standing at that casino desk, she saw someone with a honed intensity that had not been stropped into severity. He was someone with vulnerability yet without weakness. Someone who possessed the classic definition of meekness: open to reason, without gullibility or cowardice. And that intrigued her. But more than intrigued her, it gratified her, opened her heart, and melted her carefully constructed exterior. He made her feel understood without having to speak a word.

She had never known her mother. But Duane and her grandparents had described Dee as a person who was flawed but rectified; redeemed, and by her strength, triumphant. Gracie had felt triumphant but had never been vulnerable enough to allow anyone to see her flaws. Adam allowed that. He encouraged that. And unlike many of her coaches and trainers, he did it without judgement or reprimand.

"Didn't you love anything?" he asked one day. And compulsively, she just began to cry. *No*, she thought, *she had loved greatly*. She loved her grandparents, her brother, even her mother whom she never knew.

She knew what he meant. She had not loved anything as it related to her or simply *because* it related to her. She had not taken her love to heart. Had not internalized it in the way or brought it inside her and allowed it to affect her in the way he meant. *How could he have known that?*

After months of a long-distance relationship, he had taken a job with the tribe and moved to Keshena. It was a big step and one that they were not entirely sure they were prepared for. Adam was shy and chose his words carefully. But in his fascination, he did not let his intimidation show. He was uniquely sensitive—aware. Sometimes he may feel inside like he was losing all control, his heart thumping, his palms sweating, but his training as a counselor, like hers as a fighter, had taught him how to maintain that steely exterior. And that got them through the first months until they gained confidence, a sweet certain cadence, and their lives entwined around trust. All she felt for him, he also felt for her.

Adam flew up the rickety steps of the mobile home and crashed into the house, tearing from room to room shouting for Gracie.

In the midst of the carnage at the inn, another player arrived on scene. A tall Native man furtively edged near the brush that lined the driveway. His hair was tied in a ponytail and his movement and dress enabled him to nearly blend into his surroundings. He came to the corner of the inn and paused just as Ron was shuffling around the SUV. Ron saw the man as if in a dream.

"Duane?" Ron said.

Chapter 26

Gracie Dead Silence

GRACIE LAY AT THE bottom of a black lake, a million feet of crushing depth compressed all her life, all of her thoughts until only a kernel of her existence remained like a bird embryo turning slower and slower in an unbreakable shell, until frozen she existed like a fossil in stone for one hundred million years.

Yet inside her was another seed intent on liberation, driven by forces ancient but fresh as a quickening soul. This new spirit whispered to her in words more elemental than speech and spoke to her with the riveting passion that only a mother and child can bear; a language of song not syllables.

This buoyant conversation lifted her from repose, up through the depths; from shadow to shimmering light that wavered through layers of clear water until she lay on the surface in her body again: naked, gravid, and bathed in warmth and life.

From the waters onto the sands, her body no less cradled, she lay groggy a long while, her eyes closed, relishing the air she breathed that was heavy with the moist scents of life and healing.

"Yet a girl with imagination lives a life not quite her own. I will love you forever and ever," a woman said.

"She is lovely, Grandmother. Is she whole?" a young girl asked.

"She is whole." There was a smile in the woman's voice. "And she will be well enough to return when needed."

Upon fully awakening, Gracie's first instinct was to reach for her abdomen and was assured as she ran the tips of her fingers over the swollen contours. She realized she was covered, now, in a white, downy gown.

"Oh. She moves," the girl said.

Each time the girl spoke, Gracie felt the infant stir within her.

Fully awake, she sat suddenly upright and turned. Beneath a seamless pink sky that betrayed neither morning nor evening, a woman and a girl stood. Though the beach was as still as the inside of a crystal, their hair flowed to their waist as if nuzzled by a breeze. The woman's hair glistened black, and the girl's dark face was framed by a snow drift of white hair. In the yellow light, they stood clothed in long white dresses adorned with intricate and interlaced patterns of beadwork, shells, and pieces of silver.

If the world were cloaked in unreality, they would be truth.

"Ah. You are awake, my child," the woman said. "My girl."

The words drew Gracie to ponder the woman's face. She inhaled with recognition: a face she'd only seen in old photographs, but a face that would be infinitely recognizable to her. "Mother?" Gracie stood with fluid ease. The woman smiled, extending her arms. They embraced and Gracie breathed in a scent of ferns, smoke, and freshwater seas, a scent only a daughter of Rose Delight Bird could recognize.

They parted. The other girl stood silent, pondering, her brow knit in a wisp of confusion. Dee extended her hand to rest on the girl's shoulder.

"You know her, Gracie," Dee said.

The infant stirred inside her again and the girl smiled.

"She longs to be born into your world. Her name will be Aaida, after the one who rescued me and the messenger who rescued your brother while in the lower realms." Dee stroked the girl's white hair. "She wants to be there, with you, and you are the vessel of her transition."

There was familiarity in the child's elegant features and willowy form. Gracie stared at the girl, trying to discern the face, narrow and sculpted. Like Adam's.

The curtain of unfamiliarity fell away, and Gracie groped toward the child, but Dee put a gentle hand to restrain her.

"Not yet. Soon. But not now." Dee nodded at the girl. "This child needs you to return. And you will return. You will survive." She waved a hand across the sky. "The realms are watching and will assure it."

Hot tears ran down Gracie's cheeks, looking from Dee to the girl, then to Dee again.

"Lie down, daughter. You are growing tired, and you have much to do," Dee said. "You have been drawn from the dead silence and you will only sleep, now."

Gracie felt herself suddenly beset by weariness again. She hungered for sleep and could not resist lying again on the soft sands. Embraced by the warmth of the sand and the opulence of the day, she rested a hand on her stomach and deep sleep enfolded her.

Chapter 27

Aftermath

FROM THE BACK SEAT of the SUV, the children had craned their necks to see the flashing lights of the ambulance as it crawled and swayed along the pitted dirt drive and drew into the yard. Ron sat in the back seat between them. He drew on his scant experience talking with traumatized children and knew a few words to say. They leaned against him: Lance wide-eyed and Lucie sniffling. Now and again, they would murmur a worried question about their father, or "What's the matter with Uncle Donnie?"

Lelah rested her hand on Leo as he was loaded into the ambulance. His hand slid to hers, grasped and released.

More police and authorities arrived.

Duane had made a sweep of the inn. On the deck in front of the double doors, two men in suits talked with him. One of them tilted his head toward Donnie, who lay covered with a black drape. They pointed toward the mobile home. A half dozen rez cops were spread out across the property and two women in crisp slacks and flak jackets were combing the grounds and taking photos. One of them held back the corner of the drape as more photos were taken of Donnie's ruined body.

Another ambulance left with Eddie and two police.

Lelah hastily retrieved a few items from their apartment, hugged Ron. "Take care of Adam," she said, then buckled up the kids, and followed Leo's ambulance to Green Bay.

Toward evening, authorities had wrapped up preliminary investigations and left. A sad stillness settled throughout the house. The stillness lay outside the tired mobile home, across the tattered inn, and through the forest to the river. It felt almost reverent, like a funeral wake. High in a tree a robin struck up its evening dirge, and the notes fell one over the other in wavering melody. A few peepers ventured a timid reply. Fireflies twinkled like bright souls departing earthly confines to float toward the heavens.

As dusk turned to darkness, the three men huddled on the couch in the sunken living room. Adam sat in the middle, bowing, his forehead pressed to his entwined fingers. Ron rested a hand on Adam's shoulder and Duane sat on the other side.

There was not much left to be said.

Ron looked at Duane and broke the silence. "I had a dream where you—"

"It was not a dream," Duane said.

"It was weird because the last time I saw you was years ago, and you looked—"

"It was not a dream," Duane repeated.

"I heard you." Ron leaned in. "But what do you mean?"

"I saw you too, and I thought you had died. You *did* die."

Ron gave Duane a dubious expression.

"I texted Gracie that day. I told her I saw you and I thought you had died. And she told me that you had coded at the hospital," Duane said. "That explained what you were doing there."

"What do you mean? What I was doing *where?*"

Ignoring their conversation, Adam pulled his legs under him on the couch and sat staring at his reflection in the darkened windows. When he tried to speak, his voice caught in his throat. He sighed and sat back. "Where is she? Who's looking for her?"

Duane squeezed Adam's knee, stood, and walked toward the windows. "I know we'll find her. They want both her and the baby alive. We have every available asset looking for her. We will find her, Adam." He turned back to the couch.

"That's right," Ron said. "Anything that can be done, is being done."

"Then how did this happen?" Adam asked.

Duane braced both hands on his knees and slumped back onto the couch. "We did not expect them to have these overwhelming capabilities. We thought they were just amateurs. From the time they tried to hijack that fake shaman, James Graves, we thought they were just hacks. They must have upped their game. These guys, Ggorchik and Schmidt, have added a new wrinkle to the Dark Council. I'm sorry. I wish I had more, but I don't know what else to say."

"Can you tell us anything else? Who the hell are these people?" Ron said.

"Remember that weird guy that sort of loomed in the darkness then disappeared when we were in the underworld?" Duane said.

Adam interrupted. "I don't know where this is going. But I need to be alone a bit. I'm going to get some water and wander down to the bedroom." He went to the kitchen and opened the refrigerator.

"Do you need anything else?" Duane asked.

"Just water," Adam said.

"So, what is this? What do you know?" Ron repeated.

"That weird guy that you saw in the shadows is Ggorchik. I'm not sure how far back he goes with the Dark Council, but we know that he's been in the country for a long time, and he's infatuated with Native culture. He probably moved here from Eastern Europe to *be with the Indians*."

"Huh?" Ron furrowed his brow.

"That's what someone told me." Duane pinched the air at the sides of his neck like he was tugging on braids. "Two skinny braids do not make an Indian—especially when you are white as November snow." He lifted his chin. "The other guy is Schmidt. He's another *wannabe* from the Chicago area. A real wilderness adventurer. He wouldn't be caught dead in anything that wasn't from The North Face or Patagonia. Classic. He wears one of those stupid floppy hats with the wide brim."

Ron did not smile but turned away from Duane and picked at the couch, remembering his encounter with the guy with the floppy hat.

"Did I say something wrong? What did I say? I think you know what I mean. Are you okay?" Duane said.

Ron just shook his head slowly.

"What is it?" Duane asked.

"I saw him. Schmidt."

"Where? In town? When did you leave the house?"

"Nope. I saw him right here. The night before last. After we had dinner I headed to my room, and he was outside. He said he was lost, and I gave him my phone to text."

"Oh shit." Duane put a hand to his forehead. "That's how they got all of our numbers—and probably everything else on your phone," Duane said.

"I am so sorry." Ron looked to the kitchen where Adam leaned against the counter with a glass in his hand.

"It's water under the bridge. Nothing we can do about it," said Duane.

"It was my fault."

"Nonsense. We have all screwed up. They would have got what they wanted anyway. Ggorchik is relentless."

"I feel horrible. I don't know what to say. What else can you tell me about them?" Ron asked.

"I thought that it was interesting that when we were in that room with the women in the underworld, Ggorchik faded and never actually entered into that room. I watched him. He did not seem like he even knew he was in the room."

"What does that mean?"

"He's trying to break through but he's not there, yet. The yetis were there. That tells us that there may be some kind of a breach in that room. Yetis are known to show up where there might be portals or where other strange things are happening."

"What else?" Ron asked.

"I believe the living bodies of those girls are really located somewhere else. They are like a collection. Hopefully, they are not dead yet, and what we saw in that room is only an extension of their existence. Somehow they are preserving them in a near death condition until they want to use them."

"Use them where? For what?"

"I hate to think, but we can guess. We have the names of at least a dozen girls that they might be holding. We saw Salvia Lopez there and I recognized a couple more. There might be twenty or thirty more that they have. We just don't have solid leads. We are getting tips, but we don't know all their names yet," Duane said.

Ron looked to the kitchen, where Adam was leaning against the counter, holding a water bottle, and looking blankly forward. He did not seem to be listening, so Ron leaned closer to Duane and asked quietly, "So, those were the missing girls? What do you really think? Are they dead or not?" He pressed his hand into the couch and leaned closer. "What in the hell was that, Duane? I mean literally, *what in hell?* You were there, does that mean you were dead or something, too? This is all so damn weird."

"No, I do not believe they are dead. Like I said: Ggorchik and the Dark Council have something going on here. I believe they have figured out a way of keeping them in some kind of a suspended state." He rubbed his chin. "It was not near-death for me," Duane said. "I was there because I had crossed over before, when I was a kid. Me and my friend Scotty. We got hit by a truck. He got killed and I nearly..." Duane walked to the window again and studied his face in the glass, remembering.

"Scotty...Scott?" Ron whispered.

"What?" Duane asked.

Ron placed a hand on his forehead. "Nothing. Just thinking. I need to stew on all this." Since he had emerged from the inn, it had all been such a jumble and so much to process that he had forgotten what he'd experienced with Ma'ii. He didn't want to talk about it now or take them down another rabbit hole. Add all the events of the day to everything else....

Things were piling up.

"What do you see out there?" Ron asked to change the subject.

"Oh, nothing—and everything." Duane sighed.

"I'm serious. What was that place where I met you? Where were we? I need to know." Ron said. *Because I was there again,* he almost blurted. But he did not. He had not figured out how to tell anyone something so fantastic as being led into the underworld past a bunch of little people by an ancient god, celestial elohim, or whatever... Not yet. All this dream world, this other fringe stuff was new to Ron, and he was skeptical—of his sanity. He was not ready. This was not like him. He had been the unruffled academic, the psychologist.

And there was the pregnant woman lying in that room. She had to be...That had to be...

Ron shot a glance at Adam standing in the kitchen. Ron did not want to say anything that would rile Adam more than he already was. It would have to wait. He had to trust that the right time to tell everything would present itself. Not now.

"People talk about the afterlife as if it is someplace you can go to." Duane walked back and sat. "As if you leave here and go somewhere else. But I always think of it differently." Duane smiled. "I grew up living next to Scotty's grandma: Shirley's cabins."

"Sure. I remember that place," Ron said.

"Here is the way I think of the afterlife. Shirley had a few of these aluminum row boats and canoes and she would let Scotty and me take them out along the shore. If we were swimming or hanging out in the water, we would take a canoe, roll it over and play underneath. Face to face, breathing the stuffy damp air, I remember the light filtering up through the water from beneath the canoe." He made a flickering motion with his fingers. "And Scotty's big round head and yellow hair. We'd laugh like herons." Duane stared at the floor. "All these years and I still miss that kid. I think he rescued me. I've never known anyone like him, and he still seems close sometimes."

They were silent.

Ron was still not prepared to mention the man he had seen with Malachy on the dreamworld beach. He tried to keep the conversation going. "Explain the overturned canoe and the afterlife."

Duane jiggled his head "Oh, yeah." He faced Ron, gesturing an arch with his hands. "Under the canoe is like where we live now. Outside the canoe—that is the afterlife, the real world. If one of us dunked under and came up on the other side we could see the big lake, the blue sky. We could see the birds and hear the world." He swept his hand across the ceiling. "While the other kid was still bobbing around under half of an old canoe that was about the same as a tin can. The only signs of something larger outside the canoe were the sway of the waves, the glow, and the warmth of the sun on the aluminum shell. Or if the kid on the outside would *tap tap* on the hull of the canoe."

"But that place where I saw you was hardly a swim in Lake Superior," said Ron. "That room was like the basement from a slasher movie—only worse. With those women, those monsters snuffling around. That weird stained-glass window with a serpent on it," Ron said. "What the hell was that?"

Adam was leaving the kitchen and heard the end of the conversation. "A window with a serpent on it? I didn't hear everything that you were talking about, but I remember a place with a stained-glass window that had a snake on it," Adam interrupted.

Duane and Ron turned.

"That window with the serpent. It's the Rod of Asclepius, a symbol for medical care. I remember seeing it in that old infirmary at Maggie's Sainte Marie Inn in the Soo."

Chapter 28

Road Trip North

Having been awake much of the night, the men were too distracted to put anything together for breakfast the next morning. They paced from the kitchen and around the living room with coffee cups in hand.

"No, we can't just barge in to Maggie's inn or sneak into that old infirmary. We don't even know if that's where they are. Maggie doesn't own it anymore," Duane said. "I'd heard that somebody bought it and made it into an exclusive place for high rollers. We've had a hell of a time keeping tabs on these guys, but I was not told that any of the characters from the Dark Council had anything to do with that place. But that doesn't mean anything. I'm not in touch with many people on the east end of the Upper Peninsula right now."

"If they are hiding people there, I'm sure they have tons of security," Ron added.

Duane agreed. "And after that raid yesterday, we know that anything is possible. If there is any chance of getting in there, it will take planning, coordination—and much more. It will take connections."

"What do you mean? Who else? What sort of connections?" Adam asked. He eased himself onto the couch.

"We were outgunned once, so we can't do anything to tip them off or mess this up. We get one shot, or they will take those women—and Gracie—deeper under cover," Duane said.

"Who else?" Adam repeated. "Gracie can't wait. I can't wait. We have to call the FBI. We have to take them down."

"Yes. Agents will be part of it." Duane motioned with his cup. "But there is a lot to do. We only have a hunch based on a premise. A premise that no one in law enforcement will believe: *It came from a vision.* It's pretty hard to get warrants with that."

"What's next, then?" Adam said.

"Today we have to get Adam and Gracie's house secured," Duane said. "Then we have to be sure Leo's family is okay and get the inn secured."

"Nessa," Adam said. "Where is she? She doesn't know her husband is dead."

"We still have not located Nessa. I talked to the rez cops again this morning."

"Seriously? We still don't know where she's at?" Adam said.

Duane looked at his phone. "No updates. We don't know if she was also taken or if she's traveling for work or something. I texted Lelah, but she has no clue."

"What are we going to do? Who are the other connections?" Adam asked.

Duane held up a hand as he moved into the kitchen and set down his cup. He rubbed his jaw. "The rez cops are working with the feds, and they can hold things down here for a while. We will also bring in at least a couple extra Ogichi-daa to stay here and some extra help in order to monitor chatter. And they will continue looking for Nessa. I am afraid of what might have happened to her."

"Where are you going?" Ron asked.

"When I said we need connections, I was thinking about more than agents or Ogichi-daa."

"What are you thinking? Where are you going?" Adam asked.

"*We.* I think we should all go. I can't go forward without talking to Jacob Payment. He's the connection. He's the head of the Lake Council of Keepers, and I've known him for years. He has powers and access to things we can't imagine. We have to meet with him first."

"We can't wait that long," Adam said.

"Trust me. We must talk with Jacob. We have to bring every resource we can into play. But we won't wait," Duane said. "I'm arranging to see Jacob tomorrow."

"Gracie. And the baby..." Adam covered his face with a hand. Ron sat next to him and rubbed his shoulder.

"Listen to Duane. He's right," Ron said. "I've seen..." He hesitated, wanting to say more, but he was afraid he might push Adam over the edge if he said another word about an underworld and all the other supernatural hocus pocus he'd been experiencing. And certainly, if he were to say anything about a coyote god or that he may have seen Gracie lying in that dungeon-like room...

"You've seen...what?" Adam looked at Ron.

Ron waved his hand. "Nothing. Later. The Dark Council thinks that Gracie is royalty. She's what they've wanted all along." Ron looked toward Duane for support.

Adam ran his arm under his nose and followed Ron's gaze toward Duane.

But Duane bit the corner of his lip, thinking. He hesitated, then bobbed his head in agreement. "No. You're right. They are not going to do anything to harm my sister. At least not for a long time. Just like us, they are also deciding their next move." Duane tugged at his ponytail. "Our next move—the right thing to do, is to involve the Lake Council."

"But other than Jacob, who's left? Gracie told me that the council has been..." Adam said.

"Jacob is out of the hospital and doing better. He is the only one who will be able to work both sides of this."

"Explain what you mean by *both sides*," Adam said.

"Like I said. There is no way we can break up something like this without...connections. Connections in our world, in the underworld, or any other world that a man like Jacob may be familiar with," Duane said.

"Can we phone them? Group chat? *Zoom*?" Adam asked.

Duane disagreed with a head shake and added, "If you go back centuries, the Lake Council of the Keepers have always met in person. Only in person. They can't trust doing anything online. Certainly not since the rise of this pack of dogs."

"We don't have time," Adam said.

"We only need to talk with Jacob for now. And time won't matter if we screw this up. We get one shot," Duane said. "I want to go back to my place up near L'Anse and then Ron and I can hop over to Thunder Bay and meet up with Jacob and any other council who can show up. I know a guy with a puddle jumper out of Hancock. We can be across the lake to Canada and back in a day and we won't miss a beat."

"What should I do?" Adam asked.

"How's your Spanish?" Duane smiled.

"I don't know any."

"Computer skills?"

"None, unless *Call to Valor* is considered a computer skill," Adam said.

"It's not. Just asking. Up there, my wife Maura and I are known as Juan and Rosaria. Our front is a computer shop. It's also a great way to track any threats in the area. It's an old rock shop, there is an abandoned train in the woods, and behind the shop is a very weird old mine shaft. But that's another story."

Ron knit his brow. "It all sounds like an Upper Peninsula Disney Land. But I just can't imagine taking a little plane across Lake Superior. You might have to take Adam if he doesn't mind."

Adam shook his head. "I want to meet Jacob."

"What's in the mine shaft?" Ron asked.

"It's hard to explain. Just wait till I show you."

THEY WERE ON THE road before noon. They rehashed the catastrophe of the previous day, revisited the loose ends, and calculated their rending losses. Donnie was dead and his wife, Nessa, was missing. She was Gracie's aunt and also Dee's sister, so it was likely they wanted her, too. The early report indicated Leo would survive, but his head was messed up and he'd probably lose an eye. The extent of his brain injury was unknown. Eddie, the cadet, remained in the hospital guarded by the feds. But the boy knew nothing about the whereabouts of the Dark Council, or anything more about them.

Duane filled them in on the threads of information that he had been fed: Before Ggorchik and Schmidt had abducted Gracie, they had staged the whole operation out of a roadside motel near Antigo. No one in or near that motel knew anything. The owners of that place just thought they were hunters or some of the weird militia that come up from the cities to play soldier in the woods.

They rode a long while in silence, following the winding and wooded highways toward Duane's home. Ron sat in the back of Duane's SUV and Adam in front. There was only occasional small talk and hollow questions that floated inside the truck, empty as bubbles. Each of the men tended their Gracie-wounds and their loss of wife, sister, and now daughter, until Ron broke the silence.

He teased Duane. "So, J and R Computer Repair? That's the best name the FBI could come up with for your computer repair?"

Duane looked in the rearview mirror at Ron sensing the awkward moment. "Sure. Juan and Rosaria. Up here, *Metropolitan Digital* or *City Electric* just didn't seem to click. Though I think *Packer Land Computers* would have been a winner," Duane said, looking over at Adam.

Adam was diverted from staring out the window and smiled. "Has your cover been convincing? I mean, has anybody tried to find you?"

"Spanish cultural appropriation aside, I think the cover has worked," Duane said. "Maura's grandparents are immigrants from Columbia, but neither of us would pass as natural Spanish speakers. So far it has not mattered around here. I still get called Ju-on, like that Japanese horror movie, instead of Juan. Anyway, our cover story says we're from Chicago, not Mexico or South America. And if someone who actually lives in Illinois shows up, we can deflect their curiosity because I spent two years in Chicago and Maura went to school at Northwestern. She knows her way around the city better than I do. That's where we met."

"Wait a sec." Duane held up a hand. "We're almost there and I want to pull down this road that runs below Worm Lake. I have something to show you. You might feel better after you see the big picture a little better."

After ten minutes, the two-track narrowed even more, and the SUV veered around a couple of large puddles and splashed through a few more. Duane cranked off the road and Adam braced because it looked like they were running straight into the brush.

"Sorry. It's right up here," Duane said as they broke into the open. "It's worth it."

Over the ruts they sloshed side to side inside the big vehicle.

"Is this the big picture that's supposed to make us feel better?" Ron asked.

"Hang on," Duane said.

Like many days in Michigan's Upper Peninsula, ragged buntings of gray cotton clouds floated above the forest. As if they were driving right through those low-hanging clouds, a dense, stationary mist hung in the air and painted everything with a sodden sheen. The SUV splashed through a shallow creek, branches slapping the window, and crossed into another clearing that lay deep in a mattress of reindeer moss and blueberry bushes. A great wall of rusty metal arose from the gloom.

"What is this? A lost ghost train?" Ron asked.

Train cars angled away in both directions. Small trees and brush had grown up through the tracks and surrounded the cars.

"Yeah. It could be," Duane said. "It's one of those weird hidden mysteries that are so common up here. There are hundreds, maybe thousands of cars abandoned on these old lines. I think lots of them were stashed here after a downturn in Detroit. The line goes on forever. And there are more on other side tracks."

"Do you own them?" Adam asked.

"Let's say we borrow a few. We control them so hunters and the homeless don't set up camp in the ones we want."

"Why?" Ron asked.

"I'll show you."

They flipped up their jacket hoods against the cold mist and stepped between a faded yellow boxcar and a tanker and walked beside the tracks to the next boxcar. There was a big combination padlock on the door, but Duane took out his phone and after a couple swipes, keyed in a few digits. "The padlock is just for looks," he said. There were two beeps, a pause, and another beep. A mechanical whirring led to a rattle and the big door trundled open a couple of feet. Duane reached in, pulled a ladder out of the interior, dropped it, and climbed in. Adam and Ron followed, their eyes adjusting to the dark.

"What the...?" Ron said.

"We have an array of PSCs—Polymer Solar Cells, and other photo voltaic cells spread over several of the cars. They're practically invisible. And we have battery storage capability, to back up the little bit of sunlight we get up here."

Duane flipped a switch and overhead lights blinked on to reveal several workstations lining the inside of the train car. The walls were finished with vinyl wall coverings and mounted with shelves and cabinets.

"It's insulated and we can heat it with electric if there is enough juice or we have alcohol burners to save electric and still avoid detection. It even has a compost toilet and sleeping quarters in case someone has to stay."

"Why are you showing us this? I would think you'd want it to remain completely unknown," Ron said.

"For some reason, I trust you guys." Duane grinned. "We use it, but it is more of a fallback plan. In case we have to make a run for it. But

I wanted you to see this." Duane bumped Adam's shoulder. "So, you know we have the resources. We will not lose Gracie."

Adam nodded thoughtfully. "But... I mean, this is cool and all. And I'm sure you have more resources than this high-tech box car with solar panels. But then...I mean, how did they...? If you had all these resources to keep ahead of them?"

Duane rotated from Adam while he scanned the inside of the boxcar. "I know. I know. They won this round. But we learned a lot and it will not happen again."

They were silent.

Duane broke into their thoughts. "Actually, Korey and Kyle, our two ITC guys, will be here tomorrow. I think we will have lots for them to do. But let's go to the house. You can see Maura and the kids." He smiled. "Then I have something else to show you."

Off the highway, marked only by a twenty-four by eighteen-inch sign, the home of *J & R's Computer Repair* was partially hidden by scrub brush and balsam. The old rock shop was a chipped and fading yellow that looked as if it had been painted with pancake batter and pelted with eggs. Above the enclosed porch, a faded old sign whispered *Lucky 41 Rock Shop*. The house slumped, as inconspicuous as all of the other thousands of failed shops, cafés, and motels being reclaimed by the forest and fading into the underbrush or buried in snow along empty highways throughout the U. P. Like rocks and ravens, they are so common they become invisible. Each miscarried enterprise was someone's dream for a season, a family's escape hatch from the dismal alternative of poverty. Every one of them opened with a glimmer of anticipation, purchased with cash borrowed by someone who couldn't afford it. Some enterprises hung on for a few years against a growing tide of sleepless nights, alcohol, and domestic strife until the last drop of blood was extracted, their families drifted away, and their financial futures evaporated. No realtor or land developer would touch this stuff and eventually the property was abandoned by exodus. Or death.

Like barren churches, only the taverns survive to offer a last chalice of misery.

Holding one of the twins, Maura greeted the men pleasantly but soberly. The round-faced child removed a finger from her mouth and pointed at the strangers nervously until she saw her dad. Then she squealed as he scooped her out of her mother's arms.

"This is Annabelle." Duane snuggled her neck and she giggled. He scanned the room. "And somewhere Aiden is hiding. This is how he greets me whenever I've been gone for a while."

"Over there," Annabelle said in her best two-year-old speech, pointing with the wet finger.

In gales of laughter, the boy burst from cover and gripped Duane's knees.

"He's not shy. Just stealthy." Duane bent and picked up the other grinning twin. "A perfect set. Right?"

Maura shook Ron's hand, gave him a quick embrace, then hugged Adam for a long while. "You okay?" She asked. Her black hair spilled out of a bandana. She wore a long skirt and one of Duane's cotton shirts, sleeves rolled up.

"I don't think any of us are okay," Adam said. "No one."

Chapter 29

A Void in the Rock

AT DINNER, THE TWINS sat wide-eyed and mechanically pinched food and hoisted it into their mouths. As if doing research, they studied the adults.

"When do you have to meet Stan?" Maura asked.

"He wants to be in the air tomorrow morning by eight o'clock," Duane said. "We should leave here by seven."

"Last chance to join us, Ron," Adam said.

"Even if they had a 747 from Hancock to Thunder Bay, you might have to lash me in my seat," Ron said. "I'll hang back with Maura and the kids. It's been too long since I've had a play date."

Like a pair of headlights, the smiles of the twins flashed at Ron.

The men cleaned up after dinner and Maura took care of the kids. "The kids can come along with us back to the cave. I wanted to show the guys before it gets dark," Duane said.

Maura inhaled a short hiss. "I don't want the twins to get used to going back there. We've talked about that. It's dangerous." Annabelle regarded her cautiously while Aiden grinned.

"I built that new gate to keep them out. It's sound. They won't get through it. Not for a few years anyway." He smiled.

"Okay. I'll go along and get a look at that *amazing* new gate," Maura said.

When they were ready, Duane lifted a key from a board next to the door. "There is even a new key," he said to Maura.

She rolled her eyes, smiled, and hoisted Annabelle. "Don't patronize me." After a moment's hesitation, Aiden extended his arms toward Ron and was lifted. "Well, someone made a new friend." Maura laughed.

"Good choice, Aiden. Ron will take good care of you." Adam patted Aiden's small hand where it rested on Ron's shoulder.

A narrow, overgrown lawn strewn with kid fodder created a collar between the house and scrubby forest. Pale poplar trunks were interspersed with a few stunted white pines and maple. A heavy extension cord snaked through the grass to a faded brown and white Prowler camper trailer standing on a gravel pad.

"It's a little cramped in the house right now, so you guys are welcome to use the camper. We've used this for a couple of camping trips, plus we keep it set up if our tech help needs a place to stay," Duane said. "I think Korey and Kyle are bringing sleeping bags and will stay at the train this time. They have a lot to do."

The mist had let up, but it left a heavy sheen on the briars and ferns that leaned into the path, winding through the trees. A makeshift power cable that had been strung through the trees followed the path and disappeared ahead. Aiden pointed at everything, and Ron gently told him the names of the plants that he knew and threw in a few adlibs for those he didn't. He stooped to pick up a snail shell and handed it to Aiden, who regarded it as if he had been handed the Holy Grail.

Ron was comfortable around the kids. His practice had never been geared toward children, but he had always had a few as clients. The successes were gratifying, and child problems were often more pliable, while adult problems could be intractable.

He had never made a decision *not* to marry and have a family. Few people do. Often it is only after a series of starts and finishes or other events that a person finally claims to have made that decision. His detour through priesthood had sidelined him during prime mate-seeking years and then his tryst with Dee had confused him—or shamed him for a few more years. He dated and even had a steady friend for a couple of years, but it never seemed very romantic—or permanent. She was a ranger with the Forest Service and got transferred out west. Of course, he intended to catch up with her, but never did. And he had always pondered parenthood; what it would be like to have children. Now the boy in his arms felt right. Most people spend twenty years parenting before they consider being a grandparent, and those highway signs had flashed by and were receding into the distance before he had learned that Gracie was his daughter.

It was a short walk from the house to where two outcroppings of rock, no larger than a pair of small houses, loomed out of the dense undergrowth. One stood slightly behind the other. Both were topped by moss and stunted spruce. But the entrance to the cave was not visible until they were ten feet away. The trail circled around the first hillock to a cleft that separated the two mounds. Two wooden four-by-four posts had been set into concrete to cover the mouth of the cave. A metal gate had been overlaid with planks and secured with a large padlock. Duane keyed the lock and lifted a hasp. The heavy J-bolt hinges squealed as the black-throated cavern yawned open and it breathed a soggy draft of wet rock moldering in unfathomed depths.

Annabelle whined and pulled at her mother. "No-o-o. Don't wanna. No." She started crying and became more agitated, pointing back toward the house. But pointing into the darkness with a half-smile, Aiden wanted to go forward.

"I'll take her back. I've been in there enough." Maura smiled tightly. "And the gate looks great. That will help. Thanks." She touched Duane's arm and left with the child in her arms.

Duane stepped inside, fumbled with a switch, and a string of Edison lights flickered overhead and trailed far downward until the lights disappeared around a slight curve. They had to stoop to enter but were able to walk upright through a small vestibule that quickly narrowed to little more than shoulder width.

"This does not look like it was ever a commercial mine," Ron said, touching the walls.

"Nope. Most of it was probably scratched out before Europeans ever got here," Duane answered. "It follows along this crevice a way, then angles into a really narrow vein for maybe a hundred feet or so. But I wanted to show you a chamber down here."

As they walked further down, the floor consisted of wet tailings that had been compacted with dust and was slippery wherever the rock was exposed or where puddles lay. His adventurous spirit silenced, Aiden hugged Ron's neck to avoid touching the walls.

The string of lights veered around the corner and ended in a wider chamber not much larger than a one-stall garage. Without the trail of the crevice overhead, the chamber was dry except for seepage that followed down a wall, skirted the floor in a trickling stream, and disappeared into an even narrower cave. This would have followed the old vein of ore and metals that may have been mined for centuries. In the center of the chamber was a plain cot and lawn chair. A plastic storage container sat on a small metal table.

"Is this where you go when you need to get away from the wife and kids?" Ron grinned.

"Ha. Not exactly," Duane said. "But this is where I was when I met you on the other side." Duane rested a hand on Ron's shoulder and pointed at Aiden. "Do you need me to carry that guy for a while?"

The child hugged Ron tighter and swung his head back and forth to answer his question.

"Guess not," Ron said. "What do you mean, *this is where you were*?"

"Yeah. I think I missed that part of your story," Adam added.

"After Maura and I moved here, I was just exploring down here with a flashlight. Something came into my head. Something sort of spoke to me. That's the only way I can describe it. It was such a riveting feeling. I just felt like I was close to that place where my friend Scotty and I had been taken long ago when we were kids." He looked at Aiden, then whispered to Adam with a hand to the side of his mouth. "When Scotty had, um...passed."

"Since that experience, I had never felt anything like that again—until I came down here. It was a weird feeling like I hadn't had in twenty years."

"Why here?" Adam asked. "I used to have those strange and vivid dreams, but it didn't matter where I was. And I never thought they were real. I was always sure that they were dreams—or at most some kind of vision or psychic weirdness."

"Yeah. I have no other context and I have no other way to describe the feeling. But I did not want to explore this alone. That's why I brought Maura. She was interested from the start because her Columbian grandparents had connections to that stuff. There was something about the water trickling through here. I don't know. It's as if water flowing underground makes connections to places in the underworld."

Duane noticed Ron's flat reaction and grinned. "I know. Maybe it's best not to draw conclusions about how this works."

"I'm sorry. I am not being skeptical. But..." Ron said. *It's all relevant to me*, he thought.

"What are you thinking?" Adam asked.

Ron paused. "Nothing. Maybe later. I've been through a lot since my trip across Lake Michigan. I need to sort some things out and decide what is reality and what is not."

"Are you sure?" Adam asked.

"Yeah. I want to tell you more. But first I have to get it straight in my own head."

Duane continued. "I'm happy Maura is on board with all this. She really tries to understand. I need her with me. It's easy enough to get lost anywhere, but down here... I remember it all too well from when I was a child—even after all this time."

Duane fell silent for a moment, stared at the floor, shook his shoulders, and continued. "So, the first time I tried to go under, we dropped the kids off at a sitter and Maura came down here with me because I wanted to see what would happen if I just fell asleep down here. And that was it. Boom. I was gone. It was so disorienting and weird, but I knew right away there was a reason. There were hints. We did it a few more times, each time going a little deeper. Then I ran into Ron."

"What kind of hints?" Adam asked.

"Some not so subtle: an arrow pointing in a certain direction scrawled on a wall, a number, a voice. But it's more than that."

"Like what?" Ron asked.

"We had been in contact with the agencies about missing women. Not only Native women, but others who had been missing throughout the region," Duane said.

"How did you know there was a connection?" Adam asked.

"Ron. You saw those weird carvings on the doors and throughout that lodge."

Ron nodded.

"There were signs, pictures, dropped clothing—a name. By the second time I crossed over, I knew there was a connection. But I had no idea why."

"It must have been specific," Ron said.

"It was. Anyway, it was specific by the time I saw you there. I had seen enough to make it be specific to those women. In fact, I knew that I would find the women in the fourth room from the corner. Even though I learned that things change down there, and even the hints would sometimes change—or be erased when I returned. Something or someone was at work to help me find that room."

"Yeah. That's pretty specific," Ron said.

"Yeah. And was it just a coincidence that you happened to be there when I found them? After I returned I would not have remembered the stained-glass door with the serpent. It's all very strange how it came together."

"Will you do it again? Will you go in?" Ron asked.

"I might have to. I don't know. I may be able to find my way without having to come down here. I'd like to learn how. I don't know how it works. Brain waves, Alpha waves, or something." He jerked a shoulder. "I don't know."

Chapter 30

Return to the Chamber

THAT NIGHT, RON VOLUNTEERED to stay in the camper trailer. He'd cranked open the aluminum window and inhaled the heavy night air. He awoke often, twice to hear nearby coyotes yammering and arguing under the three-quarter moon and once to hear the lone pleading of a wolf in prayer. He mulled the strange visitation from the coyote god and his return from dead silence. And his encounter on the beautiful beach with Malachy and Duane's childhood friend.

He had still not gathered the courage to tell anyone. Not yet. Not even a friend like Adam. It might only serve to mock Ron's faith and the complexity of his inner life. They had witnessed much in the preceding years, from ghosts to creatures born of Native lore. But an encounter with an elohim by a confused and ailing former priest—and all that followed—may be one specter too far.

He must have finally fallen asleep. Then early morning a coyote yammered right near the camper and woke him just in time to hear Duane's truck backing in the driveway. Taillights glowed into the yard behind the house. Duane and Adam were leaving for their flight to see Jacob Payment. The first light of dawn was seeping into the old camper. There was no hope of going back to sleep, so he decided a solitary walk might clear his brain. When he camped, he loved to awaken early in the forest, where he could venture out and be the first human to awaken those arboreal realms.

Rummaging through the camper, he found a plastic pullover and a pair of tall boots that had been stuffed in a closet by the door. He snatched a compass that lay on an upper shelf. Even though he had one on his phone, he just never got used to trusting it. And you must trust your compass. Snapping open the compass, he watched the arrow pivot north. Every time he did this, he could hear his dad: *The compass tells you the truth before you leave. Remember that, so when you think it is lying you will believe what you saw first.*

He was interested in checking out the rock mounds cleaved by the cavern, and to see if he could climb them. He also wanted to see if there was a path that continued further back toward one of the small lakes he'd seen on his phone. He checked the map on his phone once more and pushed open the aluminum door of the camper that creaked in the morning silence.

The sky was uniform pink in the east, blending to dusty blue above. The trail was dripping with dew and the air was as heavy and delicious as lake water.

Around a corner, the rock mounds were outlined against the sky. Circling the first mound and approaching the crevice where the cave had been carved, he was not surprised to see the gate to the mine standing open. *Of course.* His subconscious had fore-ordained it, and he knew that it was not merely the need for a morning walk that had drawn him to wander back here. And now, just as it had been when he was a boy, he relished the shudder it gave him to challenge the unknown.

The string of lights was lit and laced downward along the ceiling. He flipped them off. It was unlikely there would be an intruder at six in the morning. There was nothing to steal in the cave. But turning off the lights should at least have caused a stir if anyone was down there.

Of course, he still remembered the coyote god. But he had never come to fear him, and he was ready to consider that maybe it had all been a dream. One of those things to file away. *Good thing I hadn't told anyone.*

But his mind was persistent. Did he really want to stumble on a massive coyote in a dark cave? Or something worse?

The cave was silent, and the throat of the cavern exhaled cool and flat. He readied his phone, his thumb hovering over the flashlight icon. And he took one step into darkness. He stopped. His eyes closed, he smiled, and went another step, then another. Wraiths and phantoms of every decrepit stature burbled into his mind and he imagined them slipping past in the narrow passage.

Ten more steps, he told himself, then he would either retreat or turn on his phone light. He'd faced a deadly shaman on a cliff overlooking Lake Superior. He'd been in the company of *spiritual wickedness in high places*. What could be worse than that?

From seminary a scripture verse came back to him in its entirety: *For our struggle is not against flesh and blood, but against principalities and powers, against the directors of this world of darkness, against spirits of wickedness in high places.* The Bible verse gave assurance, if not a calm anticipation.

Eight steps, nine steps, ten. Stop. Take a breath. Further? Eleven, twelve, thirteen.

He pressed the icon with his thumb and the light glared into his face, blinding him. Squeezing his eyes shut he waited, turned the phone downward into the mine shaft, and waited a second for his eyes to adjust. In the beam of the blaring light, there was shadow and texture in sharp contrast that highlighted every primitive gouge and scratch that had chipped stone from these narrow walls for centuries—possibly millennia. Mines developed by Natives were usually pits or shallow caves, but a crevice like this could have served as a resource not only to mine metal—but also for vision quests.

At the bottom, he shined his light around the tiny chamber where Duane's cot and chair stood. He showed the light into the fissure where the vein continued. It may have been wide enough for a small person to sidle into. Ron cocked his head, looking further to where it appeared to widen again. *That would be a place to search for artifacts.*

The cot beckoned like the hundred-foot slide at the water park which was just twenty feet taller than a reasonable thrill yet just the right height for a juvenile-screaming adventure. Smiling to himself, he reclined, clicked off his phone, and closed his eyes.

Complete dead silence. Utter darkness. Only the ringing in his ears. He opened his eyes and waved a hand in front of his face. Nothing.

With intensity, the memory returned from the dead silence he had experienced. He was sliding over a cataract of tar swept from nothingness to nothing. In panic, he fumbled for his phone and turned the light on.

He gathered himself and trudged upward toward the fracture of daylight at the mouth of the cave. Ahead, just outside of the cave, he could see the dewy morning expanding toward sunrise. Birds were twittering, and a sandhill crane trumpeted in the distance.

From behind him an intense pressure seemed to flow upward toward him from deep in the cave. That crushing presence he had felt at the inn next to Gracie's house.

Behind him came a rush of scissoring paws across the scree on the floor of the cave, and tongue-lolling panting. He spun.

From the darkness below, "Leaving so soon?"

Chapter 31

Jacob Payment

"Jacob has a nice spot near Grand Portage," Duane shouted as the plane throttled up. Then remembering to press a finger to his headset, "It is right on the shore overlooking Lake Superior. You can see Isle Royale on a good day. Beautiful spot—until the wind roars out of the southeast."

Stan, the pilot, was scheduled to drop off a hiker on Isle Royal then hop over to Grand Portage to drop off Duane and Adam. Then he would return in a couple of hours, so they would have time to meet with Jacob and learn all they could.

It was mid-morning when the plane throttled down, kissed the water off Hat Point, and shuddered as it settled onto the pontoons. There was a light chop to the water as the plane turned parallel to the shore, taxied toward a slender pier, then veered into the breeze, and allowed the plane to ease back beside the dock.

"Curb service, buddy," Stan said.

Duane pushed open the door and they stepped off the plane and crouched, pulling their jackets close. They were a few steps up the dock when the props spun, and washed with propeller mist, they picked their way up the dock.

Duane wore a black sport coat and jeans with a dark blue shirt and a turquoise bolo tie.

"Maybe I should've worn something more professional." Adam tugged at his sweater.

Duane smiled. "I don't know. It comes with the job, I suppose. I have a lot of respect for this guy, and I know he notices details."

"I didn't get the memo."

"You will be fine."

On the back deck of the Payment home, the patio door reflected the lake. Like a ghost, Jacob's wife emerged from the reflection. She was a thick-set specter with a wide smile, possibly a generation younger than Jacob.

"The G-man arrives lofted on the wings of a goose." She giggled as she slid the door open. "It's been too long, Agent Bird."

"Hi Ginny. How are you?" Duane said.

"We are doing well. Much better. We just got back from a nice walk." She looked into the room, grinning. "I hope I didn't wear him out for you."

"Duane Bird. Get in here." A sturdy voice hailed from inside the home.

Ginny tilted her head and led into the living room. The odor of cigarette smoke with a touch of litter box smelled domestic, but not overbearing.

A small man with a long mane of white hair sat in a frayed chair. He offered a remote control to the TV and the gameshow winked out. He hefted a big yellow cat off his lap. With his long slender hands, too large for his body, he brushed cat hair off his flannel shirt and sweatpants. His bare feet were supported by a wicker stool.

He stood slowly and offered a hand. "Hell-o, Duane and Adam. Welcome to our little home on the big lake." He spoke with the carefully lilting, consonant-heavy inflection of a Canadian First Nations elder.

"Miigwech," Duane said.

Jacob eased back into the chair. The cat sat back on his lap in a huff and looked up at the elder with a disgusted expression, as if to say *what the hell was that all about?*

"Oh, my little Mishipezhu is such a spoiled little eunuch. He only *imagines* himself the Great Panther. A legend in his own mind, as they say."

Duane grinned. "You named your cat after the Great Lynx, Mishipezhu?"

The cat raised his head and considered him with arrogant disdain.

"No. He actually believes it. If we take him to the beach, he will pad around at the edge of the waves as if he owns the place," Jacob said.

"We have tea or coffee," Ginny said.

"Some coffee sounds really nice. We got an early start," Duane said and Adam smiled in agreement.

"Yes. We need something bracing to help us with the dark things we will discuss," Jacob said. He lifted a finger to ask Ginny for coffee.

"Are you sure?" she said. "Will it mess with your..."

He leveled big, sad eyes toward her and made an almost imperceptible nod.

She smiled wryly.

"As I said, dark things. Dark things require dark coffee." He flashed a conspiratorial grin and reached beside the chair for the blue can of Bugler tobacco and papers.

Duane held up a finger, reached into his jacket, and withdrew a blue foil packet that was labeled *Cherokee* and was printed with the icon of an Indian chief.

"Cher-o-kee Blue." Jacob smiled.

Duane bowed his head in a quick nod and offered the tobacco to Jacob. "I was in Green Bay, passed a smoke shop, and thought of you."

Jacob held up the packet and returned a nod to Duane and another to Adam. "Chi-miigwech travelers."

Ginny rounded the corner with coffee and cups and smiled indulgently as Jacob raised the prize tobacco. "I can only do so much," she said. "Next time you'll sit your skinny ass in that hospital alone."

Jacob laughed a deep *heh-heh* until he coughed.

"Are you okay?" Duane asked.

"He's fine. He doesn't get many visitors, so he milks it for all he can," she replied.

"Can you see how much she loves me?" He gave her an endearing stare. "And why I love her?"

"That shit will get you nowhere." She smiled and sat across the room.

In a show of disgust, the cat hoisted itself off the man's lap, thumped to the floor, and left the room dramatically plying its steps, tail in the air.

"He hates tobacco smoke. He's worse than Ginny. I can't get by with anything," Jacob said.

He gnawed at the corner of the packet, then spread the zip seal open and inhaled deeply. "Ah-h, delicious. Thank you Mr. Bird...and you, Mr. Knowles."

"I'm sorry. I guess you've never met," Duane said. "This is Adam."

Jacob was spreading tobacco in a paper, then meticulously rolled the cigarette and regarded Adam intently as he licked the seam and ran the finished cylinder across his lips. "Consort of the White Doe," he said. "That can't be easy." A tiny smile squirmed at the corner of his mouth.

Duane snatched the lighter off the side table and lit Jacob's cigarette.

"It is not easy. Not now," Adam said.

"Of course not." Jacob flashed an eye at Ginny, took a drag off his cigarette, then leaned forward to rest a hand on Adam's knee. "Your heart must break."

Adam lowered his chin and looked away.

"She will be found. And your wife and daughter will be well." He waved his cigarette.

"You know this?" Adam looked at Jacob skeptically.

"I believe it because I have some favors to call in." He blew smoke sideways and reached in his shirt pocket, withdrew a roll of birchbark the size of his thumb, and handed it to Adam. "Give this to your friend, Mr. Ron Jarvin. He will know what to do with this when the time comes."

Adam grasped the bark roll, but Jacob held on to it for a moment, saying, "There are, after all, some things only a father can provide for a daughter." He held his gaze and released the birchbark.

"Find the key. Truth is the key. The Truth will make them free," Duane said, looking at Adam.

"Who said that?" Jacob asked.

"A woman. Something Ron Jarvin saw in a dream or vision or—"

"Yes. The key may well be right." Jacob grinned. "But I have no way of knowing. Like all of us. I am only the messenger—an angel." He looked at Ginny. "I heard that preacher man on the TV the other day say that an angel was never an entity, it's merely a job description that could apply to any celestial being. Any entity can be an angel or messenger." He raised his eyebrows to make a point.

"If you're an angel, then we are all going straight to hell," Ginny said.

Jacob huffed a laugh and coughed.

"Okay. I have to put my wash in the dryer. I'm not going to sit around here just to watch you die," Ginny said.

They smiled in the brief silence while Ginny left the room.

Jacob watched out the window over the lake.

Adam bit his lip and slid to the edge of the couch. He spread his hands like holding a vase, shifted them up and down emphatically, and plunged ahead. "I am scared. It's all beyond me. I deeply appreciate your concern. And I am sure you understand how desperate I am. But do you have any idea where she is? I have to know."

"Faith and belief are hard to understand. For anyone. I know that you came to this late in life. You were adopted. Isn't that right?" Jacob looked down while he picked at a piece of tobacco on his lip, *pfft*.

"Yeah. I was always told I was Mediterranean or something. It wasn't until I did that DNA test after I met Gracie. Then I confronted my parents. I'm sure my parents never wanted to have kids. But it seems you are not the only one who had some favors to call in. It turns out my adopted mom was half Paiute, so they were allowed to adopt me from an agency out west. I hardly ever talk to my parents, and my mother still refuses to tell me the whole story. But Gracie and I have figured out that I might have been born to someone Mother went to school with."

"What did that DNA test tell you?" Jacob asked.

"Yeah. It leaned toward Southwestern. Maybe plains," Adam said.

"Close enough." Jacob smiled.

"Tell me about what happened at your place. When Gracie was taken," Jacob said.

Duane and Adam pieced together the events at Adam and Gracie's. Then Jacob began to inform them about the attacks on the council.

"Do you know any more about what has happened to your other council members?" Duane said.

"Nothing we can prove. I don't think we will ever know." Jacob looked out the window as the cigarette between his fingers quivered over the ashtray. He tapped off the ash, took a pull, and let the smoke trail out thoughtfully. "I know Wally Anemki's family quite well and I talked with Carl Odjig's wife. It was sad." He stirred his head back and forth. "There was nothing I could tell them. I didn't know what to say."

"What about Dr. Kakegamic? Where is she?" Duane said.

Jacob snuffed out the cigarette. "Well, I'm afraid that's another matter. Something maybe your agents will have to help us with. It is not good. Sad." He paused, then smiled at Duane. "By the way. *That* was a good smoke."

Ginny returned to the room just in time to roll her eyes.

"You're welcome. But what should we be concerned about?" Duane asked.

Jacob carefully gathered his long hair into a ponytail, snatched a band off the table, flipped his hair through the loop, and deftly set the tie.

"As you probably know, she disappeared while on sabbatical down in South America. But I don't think she disappeared at all. I think she went underground," Jacob said.

"What do you mean?" Duane asked.

"I've known her a long time and I knew she was doing research on medicinal plants in the jungle. She was a natural fit," Jacob said.

Ginny interrupted. "Her mother was a medicine woman and that's why Dr. Kakegamic was inspired to get her PhD in plant biology."

Jacob grinned. "Yes. Ginny was one of her students. That's how we met."

"Yup. I was one of Dr. Sophie's grad assistants and this old Indian shows up one day to do a guest lecture. Then he and I collaborated on a project or two and, as they say, the rest is history." She chuckled.

"I would not say it was that easy. We had to do a lot of *field work*." Two of his long fingers making quick air quotes.

"Oh, but the extra credit was—" she said.

He flapped his hand. "Now stop. You will embarrass our young guests."

He turned toward Duane and Adam. "We became concerned about the direction of Dr. Kakegamic's research. She got into all that peyote, mushrooms, hallucinogens, and crap. She wasn't just learning how to heal anymore, and I was getting real concerned about some of her associates."

"You mean at the university?" Duane said.

"Well, yeah, them too. But they were just kooks at a university trying to set up retreats and other events to use and promote those drugs. You know." Jacob waved his hand.

"Ayahuasca." Adam said.

"Are you talking about that hallucinogen?" Duane said.

"Yeah," Adam said. "Every conference I go to talks about it. In everything I read, there is always a lot of buzz about using hallucinogens for treating depression, bipolar disorder, or whatever."

"You are a shrink. So, does it work?" Jacob asked.

"I'm a psychologist, so I'm not prescribing or working along those lines. But I think some of the research is promising—using low doses under careful supervision," Adam said. "But do you think that is why she is in South America?"

"We're sure of it," Ginny said.

Jacob blinked. "And worse. I have a hunch that she ran into some associates down there who are worse than those clowns at the university."

"What happened?" Duane pressed.

"Some of the communications that her family received didn't make sense. The council believes that now she may only exist as a Social Security Number, an e-mail address, and a drug pipeline that probably leads through her university and to who knows where."

"To the Dark Council, that's where." Duane was intensely tapping into his phone. "Yes! That's it."

"What?" Adam said.

"Some test results were funneled back to me on that syringe that was found in the exam room at the clinic. But it didn't make sense," Duane said and looked from Jacob to Ginny. "I texted you about that assault on Gracie at the clinic, right?"

They nodded.

"They tested that syringe, and we knew there was probably Ketamine in it—which would make sense, it can knock you out and put you in a sort of suspended animation. But the other elements weren't clear. There was something like an antihistamine. But then there was other stuff. I will bet it was ayahuasca, or something very similar."

"These guys are serious. This must be something massive," Adam said.

"We already know it," Duane said, staring at Jacob.

"You should tell him." Jacob tilted his head toward Adam. "About the drugs."

Duane inhaled and moving both hands over his knees. "We learned much later that my mother died of an injection of Ketamine and something else. But in addition to whatever killed her, there had to be something weird, something um...spiritual, like the ayahuasca I figured later, because..." Duane paused.

Jacob dipped his head, encouraging.

"When I was a kid. When my friend Scotty was killed, we saw her. She rescued me."

"What do you mean? From what?" Adam asked.

"Maybe Gracie has told you more of the story. But that was when I believe that she...I mean that's when she *did* rescue me from the underworld. Even though we know she would have passed away by then."

"I heard the story, but never in detail," Adam said. "After the last few years, I am a believer in just about anything."

Duane was staring at the floor.

"So?" Ginny asked.

"What?" Duane said.

"It doesn't make sense. Your mom, the drugs...How is it all related?" she asked.

"Sorry." Duane ran a hand across his forehead. "Well, I have come to suspect that she believed that those men were able to put her into some sort of induced state, or coma so that she could pass over and rescue me."

"They were using those drugs?" Adam asked.

"Yeah. Or something like those drugs."

"What happened?" Ginny said.

"They gave her an overdose. They killed her."

"But the drugs worked," Jacob added.

"Exactly," Duane said. "Because she found us in the underworld and rescued me. Even though she was never able to come back."

"So, they have been using these drugs for a while," Jacob said.

"They perfected them. And now they are using them to traffic women or something?" Adam said.

"Yes. That's what we believe."

"So, Sophie may have gotten in over her head in South America. But I only know a little about the missing women," Jacob said.

Duane told them about the investigations into the women and his curious experiences in that strange lodge in the underworld. And about meeting Ron.

"Yes. This is beyond the FBI and anything more the Lake Council can do," Jacob said. "Now I see. It was a whim, but now I know why I put together that medicine scroll rolled in birchbark that I gave you for Ron Jarvin." He looked at Adam. "Eventually it will all make sense."

After refills of coffee and another cigarette, there was much more to discuss. But too soon, they heard the drone of the plane in the bay.

The men stood to leave and to offer thanks and farewell. Ginny handed them a paper bag that showed a smudge of grease on the bottom. "The good stuff. And it's all legal." She smiled.

Duane peered into the sack. "Thank you. But I'm afraid we will have to share some with Stan, or he may drop us off in the middle of the lake—without a parachute."

Jacob walked them to the door, and they shook hands. Duane stepped through the door and onto the deck holding the door for Adam, but Jacob grasped Adam's elbow and spoke slowly. "I lost my first wife, too. So, I can imagine how you must feel. Our Gracie is precious, but I strongly believe this will turn out well. I was not sure how to tell you something else, knowing your faith may not be strong, yet." He hesitated and Adam bobbed his head. Jacob looked out the patio door and over the water. "A while ago, I dreamed of a white doe, and that white doe had a fawn. But this little doe was different than her mother, different from her grandmother or any other woman."

"How so?" Adam said.

Jacob looked at Adam. "When this little one looked at me," Jacob pointed two fingers at his eyes, then rotated his fingers toward Adam, "she had a face surrounded in white hair and eyes that went right through me. She is a force that this world needs. Now."

"What do you mean?" Adam creased his eyebrows.

Jacob squeezed Adam's elbow. "Just give that birchbark to Ron. And tell him this." His grip tightened. "There are some things only a father can provide for a daughter."

Chapter 32

Peep Show

AT THE MOUTH OF the cave, Ron's heart was racing, but he knew it was meaningless to run. Wasn't this what his subconscious had prepared him to expect? With fingers outspread, he braced the sides of the cavern to feel the cold damp and assure himself he was awake and not dreaming.

He also needed to steady himself.

"You are not dreaming, Father Jarvin."

Ron turned reluctantly. The swirling pressure faded as the billowy white shirt appeared to float upward from the darkness until the form of the man stood before him. The being spread fingers through his hair and flipped his head, tossing the dusky gray mane streaked with red and brown. His bare feet padded deliberately up the narrow passage. He jutted his chin, his nostrils flaring briefly as if seeking scent. "You are not dreaming, and you have nothing to fear."

Ron's response to this unreality was instinctual. It was based once again on decades of training in therapeutic crisis management and through countless harrowing situations. He knew to impassively examine his emotions, to decompress his response, and to consciously determine that he would not act afraid. And he would force himself to remain rational enough to be cautious.

Because everything may be on the line. Especially for his daughter. Maybe that is why he had allowed his nagging subconscious to lead him back to a place where he might have to face this entity again.

Lately everything had been coming at him in a whirlwind of the supernatural. It was too much to process. And Duane and Adam's flight to connect with Jacob Payment would only stir things up more.

Ron had to stand his ground. The stakes could not have been higher; not only for Duane seeking help for his sister, not only for Adam seeking the rescue of his wife, but now for Ron seeking deliverance for his daughter.

Ma'ii paused at a distance and folded his arms. With the full light from the mouth of the cavern on his face, he regarded Ron carefully. "So, our conversation resumes." His smile was surprisingly disarming. He did not seem as sinister as Ron had remembered. Or was it just another side of the Trickster?

Ron relaxed. "What do you want to talk about?" A psychologist's opening.

Ma'ii tilted his head. The string of lights suddenly flickered on, leading back down the cavern. "I have something to show you."

He pivoted back down into the cavern talking over his shoulder or pausing momentarily in his leisurely descent. "I think I told you. I am fascinated by you. Because you have much to offer. Not only does your lineage fascinate me—I am always intrigued to study lineage and how it relates to human events. But I've been fascinated by your insights. For example: How you have reconciled what you have learned about the supernatural factors of the big lake with your faith. In the last few years, you have seen ghosts and mythological beasts." He turned and pointed at Ron. "Now the old man has even dreamed dreams and seen visions."

Then bringing up his elbows and sweeping his hands down the length of his torso, he presented himself to Ron with an extravagant gesture. "And now there is me." He grinned. "I am intrigued by what you think, what you can offer."

"Is that how you regard your friends? Only by what they can offer?"

"Oh, so you are my friend, now. How quaint." Ma'ii pressed a finger to his chin and thought for a moment. "But I suppose you are my friend. Though you could not imagine some of those whom I have called my friends. And few are of this earthly realm, I can assure you."

"No, I am sure I could not imagine." Ron was captivated despite himself.

"You say that with a tinge of skepticism, Father Jarvin."

"I suppose I say it with...fascination. Maybe I am intrigued, like you," he said, plying the god's ego. "But cautious might be a better term. And I am no longer a priest."

"But you are a *father* once more." Coyote smiled to himself.

He's playing with you. Resist the devil and he will flee from you. But Ron was probably beyond resistance or even beyond making an effort to evade this entity.

"I am not the devil. There are more things under Heaven and Earth, Horatio. I am here to enlighten you."

He reads my thoughts. He had no template for any of this, and only a scrap of the knowledge he had inherited from his father and grandfather. Nor could any of his research apply to anything like this. But he decided to follow, and he would expose himself to whatever the creature wanted to reveal to him for the good of everyone involved.

In his heart he had crossed a threshold, and he was stirred with a sense of mission, for something much larger than himself.

At the bottom, they entered the small chamber with Duane's bare furniture. The narrow fissure that cut deeper into the rock had been too tight to enter just moments ago now yawned wider. Ma'ii waved him forward.

They sidestepped into the slim vault and slipped into darkness. Ron reflexively slowed to avoid being too near to the being. As he sensed the cavern widening, a gray light ahead began to outline Ma'ii. The space continued to widen. The diminishing crevice where Ron had shown his light and thought about looking for artifacts had grown much larger, becoming vast as they went further along. The ceiling broadened until it seemed so large they could have been outdoors. He was certain they had found their way out of the cave under a gray sky. But that was impossible because only moments ago, the sun was rising outside. And they were not outside, but deep under the rocky mounds. A scent of muck and stagnant water arose, and the gray "sky" revealed a dirty pink ribbon at the horizon attended by the sound of swamp creatures. But these were not the musical notes of crickets and peepers. These songs were guttural dirges, harsh and discordant. In the grim light, trunks of long-dead trees teetered like grave markers leaning toward a swamp edged by ragged reeds and brittle thistles. Slime laced across the face of black water like a corpse's veil.

Another step and Ron felt his shoes sink in mud and he stepped back. "Ugh. What is this? What are you doing?"

"You think that I am the devil, the evil one. You think that you humans are merely the victims of wicked temptations from evil devils and demons. And if not for these tempters you would be clean as the driven snow."

Ma'ii plodded a few steps and paused. "In this Dark Council, as you call it, you must know what you are dealing with. You must know the real source of evil that is threatening your daughter and that has threatened all of humankind." His gaze was serious. "Often, you do indeed battle flesh and blood. We shall see who the evil ones are. Everyone talks about draining the swamp. I am about to show you what that means. Let us drain the swamp."

He swept his hand across the scene and the dark waters began to worm away from the dead shore until all around them were heard sucking and gurgling sounds. Uneven black muck glistened and was dotted with sporadic pimples of bursting gas bubbles. A fetid draft held a gagging corpse scent. Ron covered his face with a sleeve.

"Ah, there we are. Our first catch." Ma'ii pointed with his lips.

A withered shoulder emerged, jutting a shard of bone. As the water subsided tangled gray hair woven with feathers settled like tentacles around a bloated face. The man lay partially overturned and was dressed in shreds of a ribbon shirt stretched over his massively bloated stomach. Buckskin leggings strained at the seams.

"Some of your daughter's handiwork, I presume. And you cannot help but feel partially responsible. You should recognize him." He grinned. "Though he has not aged well."

Covering his mouth, he spoke into the elbow of his sleeve, his voice muffled. "James Graves."

"The sham shaman," Coyote said.

"Why are you…?"

Ma'ii held up a finger and directed Ron's attention to the next mass laying in the ooze. "And what do we have here? A lost and forgotten loved one," he said sadly.

The straps of a moldering gray bikini sliced into the sodden flesh: A bleached thigh above a crooked knee, a wrinkled gray arm buried to the wrist, and black hair matted with moss and strewn over a shoulder.

"I'd bet Adam would recognize her. Though I would surmise not quite as lovely as the day she went missing," Ma'ii said.

Ron brought his arm down from his face.

"No," he whispered. "Julie. Adam's first wife."

"In the…um…flesh."

"You're a monster. Stop this. I don't have to see this. It was no one's fault."

"I'm not blaming anyone. You're the ones who love to lay blame. We are just draining the swamp and seeing what lies at the bottom. For some reason, everyone thinks draining the swamp is such a good idea."

The waters receded until only a squalid slick remained. And another corpse. She lay on her back, black hair blending into slime. Ron jolted as the head slumped toward them, eyes skinned over, charcoal tongue lolling. Her arm lay over her chest, and shriveled flesh in ribbons snaked over a white buckskin dress now mottled gray.

"Dee," Ron whispered to himself. "Dee. Oh, why?" Ron's jaw clenched. "You foist your horror on humanity, tempt us and entice us, and use us as playthings. You enjoy the carnage, and then have the gall to throw it in our faces?"

"It's *your* carnage. And I knew you'd go there. That's exactly why I showed you this. You want to blame others. As if you humans are the victims and not the perpetrators. You have no idea how any of this works, do you, priest? You are missing the entire point." Ma'ii faced him and took a step closer. "Can't you see what I am trying to show you? Look." He tilted his head toward the corpses. "Who has taken your daughter? What sort of people—yes people, are you dealing with? It has little to do with me or anything going on in spiritual realms. This is what I am trying to get through your thick head." He jabbed a finger into his temple, then his voice rose as he pointed the finger in Ron's face. "I don't enjoy *your* carnage. It is, after all, *your carnage*, you know. It is so like humans to deflect the blame. Your species will coerce each other to agree with your sin and shame, dilute your debauchery, stifle everything decent. Any true prophets are bound and gagged like swine to the slaughter."

"The devil is the king of lies and deception and—"

"Shut up! The *devil.* You fool. Your Church never taught you anything about who I am. Your church is unable to tell you what humanity is, much less who I am."

Ron began to speak, but the being stifled him, holding up his palm. He took another step toward Ron. "Do you not know that the demons quarry the human psyche to mine their gems of evil? Don't you see it? Dee was killed and her daughter held captive by dumb human evil."

He spun on his heel. "Follow me."

A short trail led to a mossy hummock. Torches burst into flame and Coyote tilted his head and proffered his open hand to an anomaly yet more bizarre.

At the crest of the little mound stood a circus caravan. Ma'ii spread his arms like an orchestra conductor and with index finger and wrist he counted down *three, two, one* and swept his arms with a flourish. Ominous, sad, and discordant calliope pipes burbled from the caravan. In the flickering light were twining carvings with chipped and fading paintings that decorated the sides of the wagon. Garishly portrayed were bloodied bare-chested pugilists, valiant fencers with swords red to the hilt and mustaches meticulously curled above jutting chins despite mortal wounds to their chests and limbs. Next to these portrayals were duelists dying in blood-misted clouds exploding from their flint lock pistols. At the corners of the caravan were voluptuous mastheads, their figures worm-eaten and missing a nose, an arm, or a breast.

Ron started to protest but Ma'ii waved him off then motioned him toward the back of the caravan where rickety wooden steps led to an open door. Springs squeaked mournfully as they entered, and the calliope music grew yet more ominous. The interior glowed with anemic light and the room was sparse except for the walls hung with dusty red velvet. A loose and ragged swag with tassels swayed beside a window.

At the center stood an ancient penny arcade peep show. The machine stood atop a similarly ornate blue metal base. Forged in the shape of a clamshell, the device had a shield around the binocular viewer and a metal crank at the front. An elaborately framed placard proclaimed *The Mysterious Mistress* above an illustration of a woman, sad and fleshy with a thin robe pulled apart to expose her deflated bosom.

"Take a little look in here and see what you may conjure," the coyote said, pressing a hand to the back of Ron's head and pushing him into the viewer.

"I do not want to..." But he already saw.

The crank on the machine began to turn of its own volition and images ticked by in jerky succession. Drawn in the old Speedball font of silent movies, the title flickered: *The Mysterious Mistress*. As the old black and white frames clicked by a woman gyrated, her painted expression unchanging. She turned around once and dropped her robe to display slack flesh. Ron tried to pull away, but his face was melded to the viewer like a tongue on a frozen flagpole. And in the worst of nightmares, he could not close his eyes.

With sinister themes, the calliope music blared while the woman continued to twist, her pendulous breasts writhing to her belly. Another caption card was displayed: *A Curious Suitor?* And through a curtain a man stepped onto the tawdry set, burly and shirtless. He twirled his mustache and slicked back greasy hair parted down the middle. The woman covered her mouth with the back of her hand and rolled her eyes in feigned despair. In moments they were engaged in clumsy foreplay and deeds despicable. Ron mumbled trying to rip himself away again. But as the slides clicked away, the curtains of the movie set tore away and fluttered to the floor and the walls of the set fell backward, hitting the stage and raising a cloud of dust. *Now, Who Shall Visit the Amorous Twosome?!* The couple lay exposed and naked surrounded by jeering masses. Several people from the audience, deformed and leering, limped or crawled on stage to join the pageant.

"Stop! Stop! I don't want to see anymore," Ron pleaded above the music as the display became yet more bizarre and vulgar.

"I am not doing anything." Ma'ii said. "Everything you see has been summoned from your own imagination. I merely wrote a script. You conjure the horror. You are making up every image in your head."

Defending His Damsel in Distress. The naked man brandished a sword and hacked at and carved up the misshapen interlopers until a man with a tricorn hat sporting a sweeping feather stepped up with a cartoon blunderbuss and blasted the man and the dancer to bloody smithereens. Then gunfire was met with cannons as the violence rippled from the ancient movie studio to the streets of a black and gray cardboard city. Thousands of shambling hoards rippled outward, trying to escape the violence. Craven urchins and beggars naked and angular held forth their cups toward the carnage.

The End of Days!! Then overhead flat biplanes made of more cardboard and strung onto stage gear and pulleys clattered overhead. Into the midst of the crowds fell bulbous hand bombs that screamed as they fell. They were shaped like tear drops and fletched with tiny rudders.

Oh Dear! The End of Days. None were spared as the earth split open and earthquakes shook and sifted the squalid, broken corpses and they fell into a canyon infinitely deep and black.

Swept toward the precipice of the bottomless chasm, Ron wept and begged to see no more, to be rescued.

Until he wailed, plunging into darkness.

He was jostled from his sobbing fit, someone shaking his shoulder. There were voices. He opened his eyes to see the string of lights leading upward along the tunnel and found himself sprawled in Duane's reclining lawn chair in the small chamber at the bottom of the cavern.

He expected to see only Ma'ii, but someone else was engaged in a fervent conversation with the entity. He plied his memory, trying to place the friendly face, but only movies came to mind. He dreaded the horrible arcade and for a moment feared another show.

"He alone conjured it. I did nothing," Ma'ii spoke from a distance. "Everything conjured was conceived in the human mind. Nothing was whispered in the ear by a demon or made up by some craven entity more debased than humans. It is inherent in their brain. Standard equipment. It has all been provided to them free, compliments of the human condition."

"You may leave now—*Your Eminence,*" the man said to the retreating god and then glanced toward Ron again, smiling. In a flash Ron recalled. It was once again the kindly man from the restaurant in Cadillac who had so generously assured Ron that he would make a good father.

Ma'ii pivoted. "He had to see what they are dealing with. Human evil arising from human minds. This Dark Council has only raw human evil. Ultimately, only humans can battle human evil. Their evil is the most temporary, impermanent force in the universe. Yet they wield it with such pride and smugness."

"If that is the most impermanent force, then what is the most permanent?" the man asked.

"Oh, you know," the god said.

"You will not say it?"

Ma'ii did not reply.

"Malachy?" Ron whispered to the man.

"He's awakening. There will not be much time. Leave before I must command it," Malachy said. He patted Ron on the shoulder. "He is leaving. I am here to minister for a bit."

But Ma'ii continued. "Humans take care of human events. Ants build ant nests, and birds build bird nests. Elohim takes care of the cosmos. Humans must take care of their world."

"Don't get ahead of yourself. Some of us are here to help," Malachy said. "Stay in your realm."

Ma'ii sniffed. "Our task is not to interfere. Because if we did, our help may be wildly beneficial or wildly catastrophic. Beavers build their—"

"Leave now," Malachy said. "Your machinations are not helping. Who put *you* here, elohim? Who set the stars in space, the oceans in their place? Who laid the continents in their space and appointed you to be a prince?"

Ma'ii did not respond and spoke only once more, his voice an echo in the depths of the cave. "Tell him. There was never anything running in that arcade. Every image conjured comes from their own mind. Their own mind. Tell him."

"Now," Malachy said.

"I only write. You make up the pictures in your own twisted mind."

Chapter 33

It Comes Down to This

"What's going on with you, Ron?" Adam said. "I have known you for a long time. You were the steady hand and if I were your therapist, I might tell you to commit yourself for observation."

They sat at the dining table and a bright ceiling lamp cast the room like a stage. Having checked on the twins, Maura entered and sat at the table.

"You're telling us about a coyote god, weird visions of the afterlife. It's not like you," Adam added.

"But by now, we've seen enough to believe you," Duane offered.

"I'm not disputing the existence of what he's experiencing. But why now? We need to examine every thread if we are going to find Gracie." There was exasperation in Adam's voice.

Ron finally spoke again. Since he had left the cave and wandered back to the house at sunset, he had told them everything. He had woven the random threads of all he'd seen and who he believed he had met since he had first ventured into the inn and awoke on the red couch to the sounds of gunfire.

Ron scrubbed his face with both hands and ruffled his hair. "Gracie's in the Soo. Somewhere in the infirmary with the rest of them."

"What? The rest of who?" Adam nearly launched from his chair.

"Ron, you must mean those women. The ones we saw." Duane swiveled toward Adam. "It's like I told you when I saw Ron...on the other side." He took the tie out of his hair and shook his head.

"You'd mentioned that room with the stained-glass window with the...with that snake, the one I thought was in the infirmary," Adam said. "You think they are actually in the infirmary?"

"I have to believe so. It's all we have," Duane said. "And they actually call the place *The Infirmary*, now. They had the balls to rename Maggie's beautiful Sainte Marie Inn *The Infirmary*."

"Yes. I know the place too well," Adam said. "The old infirmary from Fort Brady is a huge two-story brick building with big doors and arched windows that is attached right to the back of Maggie's inn. But how do you know Gracie's there?"

"Just before I woke up. After I first saw that being, that coyote in the inn by your house. It must have been around the time they took her from your home. I think I saw her lying in that room. The one with the stained-glass serpent. She was on one of the slabs."

"Yes," Duane said. "That makes sense. They must have drugged her. That's the only way they could have taken her without harming her. The only way they could have taken her alive."

"But that was just a dream. Right? What you saw. That was just a dream," Adam said. He looked from Ron to Duane. "Right?"

"I don't think it matters anymore. It doesn't matter if we call it a dream or a premonition—or something else. It seems for us that the barriers may not matter anymore," Duane said.

Ron nodded.

"What else did you see before you woke up in the inn?" Duane asked.

"Nothing else. I woke up," Ron said. He leaned toward Adam. "I am so sorry. I wish I had told you all of this sooner. About the coyote god and all. But it was just so strange and beyond comprehension. I could not get my head around it and it has been so confusing for me."

Adam made a fist. "We gotta do this. We have to get her. But there is no way we can just barge in. They'll kill her. Look at what they were able to do at our house when they snatched her. They will be armed to the teeth," Adam said.

"We have options. We are getting people in place, and we have a few resources they can't expect." Duane motioned for Adam to produce the tiny birch scroll.

Adam handed it to Ron.

"What's this?" Ron asked.

"Jacob told us to give this to you. Maybe you would know what to do with it," Adam said. He paused thoughtfully. "Jacob also told me to tell you that there are some things only a father can provide for a daughter."

A smile tugged at the corner of Ron's mustache as he thoughtfully regarded the scroll.

"It's called a wiigwaasabak." Duane said. "A scroll used for centuries by Native people to relay messages. Especially by men like Jacob."

Turning it over in his fingers, he said, "I've heard of them, but I don't think I have ever seen one and I have no idea what to do with it. Should I unroll it?"

"No. I don't think so. Jacob would probably tell you to wait for the right moment," Duane said.

"Whenever that is..." He took out his glasses case and slipped it beside his reading glasses. "But I have a feeling that I will find out."

Ron took a deep drink from his coffee, folded his arms, and pressed his back into his chair. "The Dark Council works on pure evil. Using purely human resources. If they are employing anything supernatural, they don't even know it. They have an inkling about the other side, they are trying to break through. But I have a feeling that it is still something that only we know about. It is our only advantage."

"Tell us more," Duane said.

"The coyote had a reason for draining the swamp and then showing me that disgusting peep show—*my* disgusting peep show. The things I was making up in my head. I believe he always has a reason."

"He's helping us?" Duane asked.

"I doubt it. Um...but I don't know. He's the Trickster. Capricious. I don't know if we *can* know—exactly," Ron said. "I believe the Dark

Council has nothing but their own twisted resources at their disposal. Their human evil. But we may be able to tweak our advantage. At least that must be what Jacob believes." He patted the pocket where he had slipped his glasses case.

"If they only have human capabilities, then how did they store the women in this—this dungeon in another world?" Adam asked.

"I thought of the same thing," Duane said. "But I don't think they know that the women are manifesting in the underworld. I have to believe that I was led there. Maybe by Ron's coyote friend."

"You mean they didn't *put* them there?" Ron asked.

"The Dark Council doesn't know that they put the women there or what their drugs are doing. Except maybe one guy. And we cannot be sure about him," Duane said.

"Who?" Adam said.

Duane swiped at his phone a few times and held it up. "Here. When Eddie was interrogated he told us a lot about this guy. And we're pretty sure he's the guy that attacked Gracie at the clinic." He swung the phone around the table. "This is Ggorchik," he said.

"Yes! The face that we saw in the underworld, just before those horrid creatures emerged and I was snatched back to life," Ron said.

Duane agreed. "And like I said. We have resources. Their biggest mistake was to go digital. They thought that their power was built on some ancient paradigm, but all the while, the fools allowed themselves to be ensnared by technology. Our ICT tech guys, Korey and Kyle, are booting up the boxcar on that abandoned train even as we speak. Hopefully they will be able to take down The Infirmary's security. They are also focused on knowing who is at the inn and even who their guests may be. Their clientele. I'm getting more info here and there. The big guns from the Dark Council's connections arrive in a few days. Ggorchik and his side kick, Schmidt, are getting everything nailed down."

Ron added, "They believe they have powers, but it is nothing but human vice alone. I told you about the horror I saw in that arcade. And that was from my own mind. This coyote creature wanted me to know that the Dark Council is motivated by nothing but their wickedness. Their stock in trade is human frailty and vice."

Ron told them more of what he had seen. And then repeated to them the moment he'd seen Gracie just before he awoke to gunfire at the inn. "But I will not forget seeing Gracie at the last moment lying on the slab with the other women." He trailed off and felt Adam squeeze his arm.

"They are practically out in the open at The Infirmary. They must be confident in whatever they are up to. Probably over-confident." Duane paused. "But so were we. We already made enough mistakes. We thought—and the Lake Council thought—that laying low and taking a defensive stance would protect us. It failed. We all failed. Now we must sure as hell be carefully prepared to take it to them."

"How?" Adam said.

"The feds never give us what we need up here unless it affects something in Detroit. It will be up to us to get our foot in the door, but we might already have someone on the inside, and we'll have plenty of force by tomorrow."

"You have someone on the inside?" Ron asked.

"We might. We have a whiff of something playing out with either ATF or the gambling commission. Very secret. But they still have not given us anything about the women who might be held there."

Adam was staring at the floor.

Duane watched him for a moment. "Don't worry. By this time tomorrow, Gracie—and damn sure every last victim, will be safe. We must stop them. Or The Infirmary will be only the beginning of what they will be able to do. If an organization like this gets a foothold, it will be devastating. The Dark Council wants inroads into tribal affairs for one reason: Money, casino dollars, federal grants, you name it. They will soon have their mob in every state and on every reservation."

Chapter 34

Dawning

IN THE CAMPER, RON slept poorly that night. This was a night when spirits were thin on the wind. Their fingers screeched on the panes and worried the branches, playing notes and singing lyrics in ticks, creaks, and a harrowing whine.

Duane had sketched a plan, but they had to be realistic. They knew that it could go poorly. If their cover was blown, not only would they be killed, but more importantly they would lose the opportunity to rescue Gracie and any other captives in The Infirmary.

Duane would weave together the details as best as he could, and they had to hope that support would be there when they arrived at The Infirmary. If Ron and Adam got involved, they would not have Duane's training. They would be going in blind.

Restless, Ron eased out the narrow door of the camper and down the aluminum steps. Cool and troubling, the morning was paling as he looked to the west where silent lightning flashed on the horizon, as though Hell's welders were at work fashioning chains and shackles.

His thoughts were sharp and roving. In moments like this, the earth seemed to pause and then grind backward into an age of darkness. From dark ages to enlightenment then back to a dark age, humanity swaggers through history. Despite oceans of information humanity, at any moment, was primed to slide back into ignorance and darkness.

He pondered how only a generation ago, when he was a boy, the world seemed to lay in ignorant bliss, as archaic and oblivious as the ancient poets. His parents still told him that heat lightning was flashes of light created by the nighttime release of the heat from the day and that sheet lightning was a flat pane of ectoplasm that splashed across the firmament, heralding a hurtling storm.

Northern lights were caused by reflections off the ice in the land of a midnight sun was another myth he'd grown up with. If you looked real closely, you could see the reflections of an Inuit hunter stalking a polar bear—Or vice versa.

Ron rubbed his face with both hands and scanned the yard amid the flashes of flat light. In a world awash in weather apps, *yet drowning in knowledge and fear, more ubiquitous is ignorance and rare is beauty and cheer.* Even in the present age, wisdom was rare as moon rocks.

Then his thoughts were interrupted when something that defied wisdom or knowledge approached. He knew that what he saw was not intended for this world.

Detached and floating like a child's lost balloon, a figure hovered along the path that led from the rock mounds and the cave. It appeared faint as the lightning on the horizon and moved hesitantly toward the houses as if lost or bewildered.

Ron stepped back behind the camper as the apparition neared. Her face regarded him and seemed to look right through him with a countenance puzzled and sad.

"Julie," he whispered. Adam's first wife drifted on toward the house and vanished without a trace.

Indeed, a night of wonders, Ron thought. "The veil is thin here," he whispered.

THEY WERE ALL AWAKE before dawn. No one needed alarms. And soon they were steering onto Highway 41. The eastern sky was a breath of blue, and in the west vigilant stars surrendered their night watch behind them.

For the first half hour, except for Duane's brief phone chat with the two tech guys in the train car, the three men rode in silence, the tentative sky illumining Duane and Adam's solemn and thoughtful faces in the front seat.

"It should not take long in Marquette. They have everything ready to go. We stop there and then we should make it to the Soo by midafternoon. They're saying that there could be some heavy thunderstorms later," Duane said. "I hope it doesn't affect our communications."

Adam sighed, wiped under his nose quickly with the back of his hand. "I had a dream about Julie just before I woke up."

Thoughtlessly, Ron began to speak, "I, um..." and immediately clamped down.

"What were you going to say?" Adam asked.

"Nothing. What was the dream?" Ron said.

"I don't actually remember much of the dream. It's just that I haven't thought of her much. Trying not to. Maybe that's wrong."

"Did she say anything?" Ron resorted to the only psychologist thing he could think of.

"Nope. I don't remember. I just feel like she was trying to say that everything would be all right. I've felt that before when—Wait. No, that's wrong. It's coming back to me. Now I remember why I woke up feeling frightened." He pressed his palms together between his knees. "How could I have forgotten? Terrible."

"Are you sure you want to..." Ron said.

"I thought she was telling me everything would be all right, but the last thing she said disturbed me and I asked her to clarify. But she was gone."

"What was it?"

"She said, 'Where I saw you last.' That's why it bothered me."

"On the beach. Before she, um, before she...was lost? Isn't that where you saw her last? Where else would it be?" Ron asked

"No. It was distinctly '*Where I saw you.*' I knew what she meant. But it's confusing." He glanced back toward Ron. "Either of the places where I thought that I saw her seems unthinkable. It seems impossible that Gracie would be on that beach. It would either be at the beach where Julie drowned or..."

"Or where?"

"I saw Julie as an apparition in that old infirmary. That was the last place I saw her."

Chapter 35
The Infirmary Club

THE CLOUDS BELOW WERE mounded upon the Irish Sea like heaps of snow. Maggie Steward looked out the window as the plane eased toward Edinburgh and she recalled the inn after a particular November storm.

Horizontally, the snow lay white, and vertically, the gray trees and older homes on the block enfolded her Sainte Marie Inn. The only angles that contrasted with this grid were on the inn, which was still rimmed with snow from the previous day's blizzard. Two towers rose from the sprawling house, one at the corner and one in the center. Dormers receded into darkness on four or more roof lines that swept in several directions. The broad, dark porch wrapped the east side and came around the front to brow the windows like sleepy eyes. Behind the inn, mostly hidden from the street, was a long, hulking, brick infirmary that stood two stories high with tall arched windows. It was older, more decrepit, and seemed awkwardly attached to the back of the main building.

She drew a finger across a tear under her eye while in her mind she walked through the front door. Like those ghosts in that old brick infirmary, she pined for a life that was no more.

In her memories, she saw the low light that crept along the hallway from an open doorway, far at the end. Two or three yellowish wall sconces were lit, but barely illuminated the high, coved ceiling, criss-crossed with plaster moldings. Shards of patterned plaster were missing in places. The walls were painted mossy green, but small gray patches were visible where it had flaked near the top. Despite the wear, the dark emerald was vibrant against cherry woodwork that surrounded every door and trimmed the long hallway. "It was so old, and so hard to keep it all up since Mr. Steward—I mean, my husband, Leslie—died," Maggie said to the Irish Sea. She imagined the first room on the right off of the foyer. *This is the sitting room. They used to call it a drawing room or reception room, but I suppose that room across the hall would be considered the reception room now. But I never use that room.* She recalled saying this a thousand times as she led guests through the rooms and saw the gleam of wonder in their eyes. She had loved the sitting room with coffered ceilings, and walls of recessed walnut panels that reflected the orange glimmer from the fireplace. Tiffany-style lamps sat on low tables on each side of the mantel. A large couch was set between two stuffed chairs facing the fire. Velvet pillows patterned in midnight blue flanked the ends of the couch, enhancing the muted hues of antique rugs. A painting of a ship was propped on the mantel with a blue glass net-float on one side and a lantern on the other. Lighthouse paintings hung on each side of the fireplace.

"Please check again that your trays are up, and your seats are in the upright position."

She wiped her nose with a tissue. "All will be fine when I see Sis and the kids," she whispered. *But just to see my inn one more time...*

Yet before the wheels of her plane had touched down in Edinburgh, rooms full of antique trim had gone to salvagers, the hallways gutted, walls busted out and thrown in dumpsters along with all the lights and remaining furnishings. Stained glass, much of it damaged by clumsy contractors, had been replaced with glass that let in little of the light of day but was entirely more sustainable and energy efficient.

A shady deal had been made with the Dark Council's handpicked city councilwoman which allowed the contractors from Detroit to pull permits authorizing them to completely renovate and modernize the historic inn.

But they were only allowed to go so far. The limits of their contacts and their corruption forced them to maintain pristine and unharmed the attached nineteenth century Fort Brady infirmary. They would leave intact all its historic features, along with the troubled entities that traversed unknown realms and haunted its mortal depths.

The contractors who had surveyed the infirmary were pleased that they could finish their scant repairs and preservations and be out of there. The Dark Council had gotten all that they needed by renovating the inn. They could leave the infirmary for another day and for *other* endeavors when the time came.

The lovely old walls of the inn had been transformed into uniform panels of white, gray, and black accented with baffling broad bands of silver paint. The vertical surfaces were interrupted by lurid paintings, garish plumes of aluminum feathers, and other atrocities procured by an art dealer in Chicago who had commissioned a prominent artist whose sole qualification was having a grandmother who was purportedly one quarter Cherokee.

Functional doors and windows sank into the outer walls without drapes or trim. And all the floors were carpeted with a vomitus of swirling greens, purples, reds, and yellows.

Messrs. Schmidt and Ggorchik strolled along the main hall, inhaling the scent of fresh paint, their hands in their fine jackets, chatting with the inaugural guests who had checked into the Dark Council's new enterprise. Between them Ggorchik held a leash that restrained a huge pit bull. Its body-builder chest flexed as it waddled and its white face a specter with shark eyes and no brows. Its wide gash of a mouth dripped foamy slobber. Ggorchik was dressed impeccably, but Schmidt thought it raffishly Northwoods to retain his khakis and hiking boots. Despite protests, Ggorchik insisted that Schmidt lose the stupid, floppy hat. Most of the clients who had made reservations for accommodation had already toured their second-floor suites. There was a crowd of many more clients who were only there for the presentations and to sample the goods. And all awaited the welcoming where they would hear what sizzling temptations were about to be drawn from the old infirmary and served up for them on the third floor.

The area casinos were a draw, but not all clients in this cadre were high rollers. Though the appetites of big spenders would produce some of the Dark Council's hungriest lodgers. Much of the clientele were drawn from circles much darker and more secretive than casinos. These were the bleak individuals that the Dark Council had catered to from the start of their enterprise decades ago.

Local tribes had quickly disassociated themselves from the Dark Council and had condemned the establishment. But since *there is no such thing as bad publicity,* the tribal condemnations had only spurred the arrival of customers even more nefarious. The stock-in-trade were primarily non-Natives existing on the outer reaches of tribal culture, who had subverted Native customs for their own prurient interests. They came from all walks of academia, government, the arts, and finance. Government-sanctioned trade in *legitimate* vice from tobacco to gambling and even recreational marijuana had unbarred the door for illicit investors like these miscreants from the non-Native world. They were hyenas circling the carrion, waiting to pick up the scraps.

The men were interrupted by a voluptuous blond woman whose strange retro attire could have placed her inside any similar establishment from a 1970's Playboy mansion to a restaurant chain that would feature women's breasts with the hopes of attracting its clients like infants to a nursery. To the ogling delight of a few clients, she stood on tiptoe and whispered something into Ggorchik's ear while she pointed to a door at the back of the main room. He dipped his chin thoughtfully, touched Schmidt's arm, and tilted his head toward the door.

The men strolled to the back of the room, entered a small office, and closed the door. Ggorchik stepped behind a trim ebony and aluminum desk while Schmidt dragged a chair from a corner. A woman was sitting near the desk and began speaking before the men were seated. "I'm worried about her. You said it would only be a day or two. This has gone on too long. When will you wake her up?"

"Nessa, stop. What about her infant? How is the infant?" Ggorchik asked and leaned back, sucking on his big teeth.

"The nurse said everything is fine," she replied coldly.

"Well, fine it is, then," he said, showing her his palms then folding his hands on the desk. "Your niece is only a vessel at this point." He dabbed at his swollen nose and looked at the speck of blood on the tissue. For the grand opening, he had determined to leave his nose un-splinted while the staff was instructed to spread a rumor that he was an MMA fighter. That would certainly sound better than getting his nose smashed by a five-two, one-hundred-twelve-pound gal who happened to be eight months pregnant.

He thrust the tissue into his jacket.

The woman bolted out of her chair, leaned over the desk, and shook a finger at the ghoul. "No! This is not what you said. You said Gracie would be fine. That you would take care of her."

Schmidt launched out of his chair, swerved around the desk, and took the woman's arm. "Sit."

"I want answers," Nessa said. She struggled free. "You said—"

Schmidt tried to ease an arm around her shoulder and guide her back to her chair. "It's all taken care of. Gracie will be fine." He shushed. He glanced at Ggorchik wide-eyed—*Say something.*

"Fine. She will be fine. Arrangements have been made for her release." He shrugged. "When we have the baby, and we know it is well. That child is the key to the future. We have it on excellent advice that she is the key to a new age of..."

Nessa seethed in her guilt and anxiety. "And what about my husband? What about Donnie? Leo? When you picked me up on the highway, you said no one got hurt except for that Eddie kid. I heard a hell of a lot of shooting from out by the highway where I was hiding out. How can I trust anything you say?"

"What did we tell you?" Schmidt said.

"You said you would pick up that wasi'chu Jarvin that got my sister pregnant. That's why I got involved. But you couldn't even find him." She pounded her fist on the desk. "I swear. You are all alike. Wasi'chu!"

"We are looking for him," Schmidt said.

"Bullshit. No, you're not. I told you I would help you if you got him, because of what he did to my sister. You promised you would get him. Where is he?"

Ggorchik was looking at his phone, ignoring her. Ggorchik knew it was not Ron Jarvin who had destroyed her sister. Maybe Ron had gotten her pregnant, but Ggorchik had just come on board with the Dark Council when Dee was killed. He knew who, how, and why Dee died.

"Now I'm trapped here and I'm going to get blamed for all this," she said. She slapped the desk. "Dammit! Are you listening?"

Ggorchik glanced up. "Your alibi will always be that you were taken to protect your niece. So what?"

"And dammit, I *will* protect her."

Like a snake, Ggorchik's hand struck across the desk and grabbed her wrist. She winced and groaned as her wrist was twisted back.

"You will stay in that damn room with your niece, locked in, chained if needed. We need you to keep her calm if she wakes up or goes into labor. That is your job. And you will speak to no one, not even the nurses unless we ask you to." He twisted further until she squealed. "Is our *agreement* quite clear, Auntie Nessa?" His lip curled away from his teeth.

"Call the guard and get her out of here," he said to Schmidt.

Chapter 36

Abomination

THE SIGN ON THE front lawn might have been more appropriately set over the entrance to a Botox clinic located within one of Detroit's ostentatious suburbs or in one of the near-suburbs like Ann Arbor or Gross Pointe. But it was out of place amid the historic buildings and plain-spoken inhabitants of a city like Sault Sainte Marie. The white oval sign was scrolled with black lettering that announced *The Infirmary Club. Members Only.*

Easing up to the curb, a black SUV displayed a rideshare sticker slapped onto the darkly tinted windshield. That pretentious sign on the front lawn looked less out of place than the man who emerged from the back seat of the vehicle. He adjusted himself in the tight-fitting orange pants, rolled his shoulders in the matching suit jacket, then reached back in the SUV to retrieve his leather satchel. Beefy ankles were exposed above sockless feet and brown loafers. He nodded to the driver and gave a quick salute to another rider in the front seat and headed up the walk as the vehicle pulled away.

He twisted his head quickly to adjust a flap of hair that ran over the top of his head and down the left side of his forehead, partially covering one side of his face and half of his round sunglasses. The right side of his head was shaved, and a razor thin moustache arched above his lip.

The color of his red hair nearly matched a jacket that was not only jack-o-lantern orange but patterned with the delicate outlines of skulls and other ghoulish countenances, as if he had consumed souls of the lost.

He represented *The Infirmary Club's* ideal demographic.

The sweeping old porch had been mostly dismantled and replaced by a clean landing with a black awning and steel posts. A black glass door hissed open where once there hung a heavy oak door graced with a frosted-glass landscape.

Through the door stood a metal scanner. A brawny man with a suit jacket seemingly painted onto his chiseled physique waived him through the scanner. The man held up a thick hand and approached him with a wand and proceeded to pat him down. Behind the guard waited another man, bored and withered, slumping in a tuxedo at a podium while running his finger across a tablet screen.

With a small polite smile, the tuxedoed one said, "Mr. Cronkite, I presume."

"Correct. Call me Walter."

"Thank you. And this is Tristan." He swept his hand toward a nervous bellhop. "He will be happy to carry your bag for you. Are there more bags in your vehicle?"

"That won't be necessary," the man in orange snapped. He hugged his pack, pausing for a moment to take in the open architecture, darkened windows, and modern appointments.

"Splendid. Then Tristan will introduce you to—"

"Are Brinkley and Sam Donaldson here yet?"

"Yes, and—"

"Good. I will know to avoid them." He laid a hand on the podium. "I want to get through preliminaries and get to my suite."

"Of course, sir. Tristan will escort you to the lounge. In a few minutes, we will have our brief overview from Mr. Ggorchik and Mr. Schmidt. I am afraid because of the err...unique nature of our establishment," he cleared his throat, "our briefing is quite mandatory. There is a reception to follow, but we will show you to your accommodations immediately after the welcome if you prefer. It should only take about ten minutes. We know travel in this area can be exhausting and we—"

"Will *we* please shut up," Walter said to the maître d', then lifted his chin to Tristan. "Let's get it over with."

His laptop keys crackling, Kory's fingertips punched through his keyboard as he cursed. "No! No! Kyle, look at this. Pull up my screen."

There was more furious typing as screens full of graphs and schematics swiped up and down and data flew across their computers.

The boxcar was darkened and the rat-a-tat of rain on the metal roof only fueled their desperation.

"I see it. I see it. Damn. Damn. No!" Kyle said. "Call Duane—if we can get through."

"As this will be our inaugural run, we beg your patience." Ggorchik grinned to the room of lowlifes who were knocking back their drinks in quick succession, crunching ice, and looking about in anticipation. Wait staff flitted back and forth and the voluptuous blond in her brief retro attire refreshed their drinks and their appetites.

"If we may get started. Kitty here is only a sampling of the rich delicacies we will be serving up. Fresh delicacies. One of the advantages of participating in the inaugural run is that every treat is *certified fresh*." Ggorchik paused for the laugh, Schmidt giggled foolishly, but the rest of the mob sat silently unfazed or scoured the waitress with their eyes. Ggorchik cleared his throat and continued. "Welcome, gentlemen, and also Miss Roosevelt and Miss Walters in the back. I do not have to remind you that while you are here, it is essential that you only address one another by your aliases. We have labeled our inaugural run *The News Makers.* Each and every one of you were the handpicked influencers from among your peers because we want to get the news out. Everyone that you communicate with and share files with online needs to hear the news. Certainly, each of you has a VPN, but one of the benefits of membership at The Infirmary Club is an even more powerful and secretive VPN with lifetime access to our highly encrypted networking systems." He grinned. "I am sure you will find this a valuable perk to your, um...businesses and to your...proclivities, shall we say."

Schmidt laughed like an idiot again. Ggorchik spun and gave him a stern look, leaving Schmidt to fuss with his jacket and stare at the floor.

Restless as a bowl of maggots, the mob paid less and less attention as the meeting proceeded punctuated by more of Ggorchik's inane humor. He presented an overview of the strict *no weapons* policy that would be enforced throughout their stay. After boring details about sanitation, health certificates, disposal, and limitations on the use of violent sexual practices—*maintaining the integrity of our product*, the meeting adjourned. Walter hailed Tristan, circled his finger, and pointed upward. Tristan bobbed his head and motioned for Walter to follow him, then proffered his hand toward the elevator that had been cobbled into the wall where a grand staircase had soared toward the upper floors. The staircase had been dismantled and the remaining space was occupied by a flight of narrow, functional steps.

The light above the elevator registered a red *B* for basement but soon hummed and rumbled then brightly *dinged* when the *L* for lobby appeared. Tristan handed Walter a room card as they waited for the doors to open. But the doors remained closed.

"So sorry, Mr. Cronkite. That's weird. The elevator guy just did the inspection." Tristan hammered the buttons and stammered.

Finally, the doors stuttered open. The interior was lined in red velvet and a man stood at the center in bare feet. His long silver brown hair fell over the shoulders of a blousy white shirt and a grin spread above a sharp goatee. His gaze scanned from Walter's brown loafers to his jaunty red hair.

"Well. A surprise, indeed, Mr. Jarvin. Don't you look rakish. I would not expect to find you here as a guest. Not in an establishment like this," Ma'ii said.

IN THE PARK ACROSS the street from The Infirmary Club, they pulled the black SUV into a slot facing the river. Duane could watch the front of the inn from rearview mirrors. "Kory and Kyle are banking that the rest of the Dark Council's tech is outdated by at least a couple of years. At least that's what they found out about the facial recognition," Duane said. "Ron's shave, his hair-over-the-eye, sunglasses, and the faces on his jacket will only work for so long to disrupt the algorithms. We don't know everything else they might have."

His phone rang, he looked at the SUV's display and furrowed his brow. "What the..."

Frantic, garbled speech came over the car speaker.

"What's wrong?" Duane said. "I can hardly hear you, Kory. Why didn't you text?" Duane glanced up in the mirror toward the club.

Adam tried to follow the crackling voice.

Kory continued, "It's cloaked. A shell. We never hacked it. We couldn't reach you. We had to jump onto this backup line and—"

"Explain," Duane barked.

"We thought we'd hacked the security system, but it was only a shell. We can't do anything with their alarms or hardware. We have no eyes inside. That's how we picked it up. The cameras were just on a loop. We realized that we were just seeing the same thing over and over. No live data."

"What can you do?"

"We can only pull up barebones stuff like room assignments, schedules, and..." Kory crackled into oblivion.

"Shit," Duane said.

"Do we go in?" Adam said.

"Hell no. Not yet. Let me think." Duane gripped the steering wheel. "Ron had everything in his pack. Kory and Kyle might be able to get a few pieces of data as he's checked through. And they might be able to anticipate some of Ron's movements as they monitor his tracker. But what good is a tracker if we don't know what's inside or what's waiting for him in any room that he enters? And what if he doesn't move for a long time? That would be the worst case. We wouldn't know if he's dead or alive. We have nothing."

Adam slumped; his hands lay with palms up on the seat beside him. Defeated. He sighed. "What now?" He scanned the river as it grew dark and roiling. "You mentioned ATF or someone else. Do you know who or what you might have inside?"

They flinched at a brilliant flash. In seconds, there was a rumble like great rolling boulders that grew to raging thunder stretching across the sky. As if shaken from the clouds, a sheet of rain was thrown over everything.

Duane's phone pinged. He looked at the text.

"Impossible," he said.

"What now?" Adam asked.

"The guys from Lansing are grounded in Pellston because of the storm. And they are saying high winds may close the bridge. It will be at least two hours, maybe three. There may be some backup over in Marquette, but it would be at least four hours before they can be pulled from their assignments and drive over here." Duane bit his lip.

"THIS IS GOING TO be so much fun." Ma'ii smiled to himself.

Ron tried to maintain his disguise. "What did you say?" he said. But it was futile.

Ma'ii yanked Ron into the elevator.

Tristan signaled and two beefy guards came out of nowhere and lunged as the elevator doors began to slide shut. A big hand clawed at the edge of a door, trying to force it open, but the coyote god poked at the air as if pressing a button and the doors slammed shut on a wrist.

"Going down," the coyote said, pressing the *B* button.

Clutching and clawing, the hand stayed in place as the elevator descended. The frantic eyes of the big man peered through the crack in the door, yanking on his trapped wrist with his other hand while he went from standing, to crouching, to kneeling. His angry grunts scaled upward an octave or two as he sprawled on the floor outside the elevator and his arm made contact with the edge of the elevator shaft.

Ma'ii held his thumb and index finger in front of his face and quickly pinched. "Snap," he said.

There was a muffled crunch and wet slap like a dropping plate of pork chops as blood drizzled between the doors down to where the hand twitched on the floor. The wailing crescendo of the man's cries moved farther away overhead as the elevator descended.

"Ugh." Ron put his hand to his mouth and dropped his sunglasses.

"Anyway, Lefty is a better bad-guy moniker." Ma'ii grinned.

Ron edged against the side of the elevator in revulsion. But he also needed to distance himself from the irresistible gravitational field of the entity that left him feeling as though he were teetering at the edge of a great chasm.

"Where's Gracie?" Ron blurted. He needed to focus. Ma'ii's appearance on the scene was shifting everything and finding Gracie was Ron's only purpose for being there.

"I thought you might like a tour, first," Ma'ii ignored his question.

PISTONS OF LIGHTNING AND thunder pounded the city. "Let's get closer. I can't see through this rain." Duane reversed the SUV, sped out of the park, and slowed to a stop in front of the club again.

A big guy in a too-tight black suit stumbled into the rain, howling and clutching the spurting stump of his wrist as he tumbled down the steps. The blood and rain immediately formed a black apron around him, where he lay writhing on the walkway.

"What the hell?" Duane said.

THE ELEVATOR DOOR SIGHED open. Stepping over the hand, the coyote led out the door into the basement. Amid the cellar odor of moss and mustiness, a line of bare bulbs led down a narrow alley with walls built from thick blocks of red sandstone. Damp blots crept from where walls met the floor.

"Follow," Ma'ii said in way that could have meant *heel*.

Inconspicuous and unpretentious at the end of the alley stood a simple panel door that had probably been added in a recent century. It had once been painted green, but near the floor there was a gap where the bottom edge had rotted from the damp. Ma'ii turned the rusted knob, opened the door, and reached inside patting along the wall inside, searching for a switch. When he couldn't find it he fluttered a hand, and another set of dusty lights lit a small waiting room set about with a few moldering wooden chairs.

Ron pointed when he saw the door on the opposite side of the room. A stained-glass panel was set into the upper half of the door, but it was twisted, missing pieces, and was nearly falling out of its frame. But preserved on the panel, a serpent coiled around a wooden rod, its eye leering at him.

"That's it. That's the one I saw. With Duane."

"Of course it is," Ma'ii said. "And there is another just like it on the floor above here. Layer upon layer." The coyote pushed open the door and dim bulbs lit the ceiling of a much larger room.

Ron covered his face from the stench and looked about in disbelief.

"I was here. How can this be...? I don't understand."

"The place you stood with Duane was like a mirror image of this room. You were not really here," Ma'ii said.

Twenty or more cots were haphazardly crammed into the space and displayed sheets that were rumpled and soiled in abstract renderings of bodily fluids. Tubes coiled and bags hung lifeless like spent parasites.

The coyote tilted his head toward a spiral staircase built of stone and carved into the wall. Next to the stairway, the wall had been hacked out and an elevator had been crudely installed. "They've been moved above into the old infirmary and after they were hosed down and scrubbed, they were moved into make-up and wardrobe." Ma'ii's finger slid over his moustache pensively. Almost sad, the entity seemed affected in a strange way that Ron could not decipher.

"Gracie," Ron insisted.

"Not here."

Before Ron could ask again, the coyote god strode across the room intently toward a bricked-over archway where, at one time, there would have been a doorway. "I hate this shit. This is the worst of your kind." He seemed agitated and thrust once with his bare foot, plowing through the brick wall. Angrily, he smashed again and again until a black maw gapped. Dust fogged the room, and fractured debris littered the floor.

Looking into the darkness, Ma'ii braced his hands on his hips, waiting. While staring into the menacing breach, Ron edged backward toward the door.

There was a phlegmy grumble from somewhere in the depths far beyond where Ma'ii watched. Then a thin whining like the first notes of a mother grieving. It built to a wail like a hyena punctuated by porcine squeals.

"For God's sake..." Ron mumbled.

"Hardly for God's sake. God's vengeance, maybe. But run. Now!"

Ron tore past the door with the stained-glass serpent, across the small waiting room and down the narrow hallway. He was first to the elevator and hammered at the *Up* button, but the god stepped beside him and laid his hand on the door. It parted with a hiss. Ron stepped high over the hand and pasted himself against the wall, away from Ma'ii again to avoid that sense of being pulled or of falling into something bottomless and unfathomable. As the doors closed, it became silent as a tomb inside the lift. They were not moving. Ma'ii patiently folded his hands in front of him, looked at the floor, and waited as if for a cue.

The elevator was not moving and felt stifling as a sauna. Ron felt the gravitational pressure mounting and carefully removed his jacket. In a jacket pocket he felt Jacob's birchbark scroll. It was like an unexpected assurance or currency; like finding that hidden twenty-dollar bill just in time. He held it out to Ma'ii.

"Find the key," Ron whispered to himself, suddenly remembering the words spoken to him by Salvi Lopez in his vision of the women in the room. "Truth is the key. The Truth will make them free," Ron said.

"What are you mumbling about?" Ma'ii asked.

"Maybe it will make sense to you. Maybe it's something. A key." He held the birch scroll to the god. "Gracie's husband, Adam, gave this to me. It is from Jacob Payment. He's the old—"

"I know who Jacob Payment is." The god made a sideways smile and snatched the tiny tube of bark. It made a cellophane crinkle as he unrolled it. A piece of paper had been rolled into the scroll and he held the paper to the side as he read the few symbols that had been scratched into the silky, fawn-colored cambium of the bark. The symbols merely pointed him to the piece of paper.

He unfolded the small piece of paper and tried to read the cryptic scribbling. He looked up, his brow furrowed, then read it again. He swept a hand across his forehead and through his hair.

"It's Latin. Latin." Exasperated. "How would that old Indian...? Latin." He looked at Ron. "But I can't read the writing. It's like an indecipherable scrawl. What does it mean?" Ma'ii asked.

Ron shrugged, widened his eyes, *As if I would know.* He remembered some Latin, but he was certain it would be less than the god would know.

"Latin." The coyote was already agitated, but now his ire grew. The elevator began trundling upward while he seethed.

"For centuries, the people of this continent have had a covenant with me," he said. "In return for their small acts of devotion, if they perform certain favors, I will accept a plea for help." He held up the birchbark. "On the birchbark he tells me what he wants. To read the paper." In his other hand he fluttered the slip of paper. "This piece of paper states what holds me to our bargain and what I get in the end if I carry out the deal." He ground the two together furiously. "But I do not know what the hell the paper says—yet."

The pressure in the elevator seemed to be mounting and Ron pressed himself further into the corner.

"I am certain that charlatan shaman Jacob Payment is asking for the release of all the women and particularly the White Doe, Gracie Bird. But there must be more to this message. Something he is hiding from me. So, since I came here to do it anyway, and since Jacob is such a fascinating soul, I am forced to help. But if I have to hold up my end of the deal, then not only will I do it," he stuffed the crumpled bark and paper into his shirt pocket, "but I will do it—Big."

His voice rising, he jabbed his finger at Ron. "But by God, none of you—not your bastard daughter, her half-assed husband, her tin star sheriff of a brother, or a failed priest like you will be allowed to leave this planet until I find out what is on this piece of paper and what this bullshit means." He patted his shirt pocket.

The elevator doors opened to reveal that something *other* had been unleashed.

"We have to wait out here," Duane said. "We don't know what's going on in there. In Marquette they put together Ron's costume and did all that stuff when we stopped there on the way over. It was supposed to foil facial recognition. But if Ron's disguise, his jacket, and all the other things didn't work, then they probably got him. They will hold him as bait to lure anyone like us."

Suddenly a number of the tawdry clients began spilling out the front door of the inn clutching at each other's throats, punching, and clawing in frenzied and vicious warfare.

Thrashing and slipping across the slick lawn, one baldheaded, portly man dressed only in a tank top and chaps had another in a head lock and was stabbing at his face with a jagged shard.

"What the hell is this? I can't wait. I'm going in," Duane said.

"Stop. Should I…?" But it was too late. Duane dashed for the inn, his feet slapping through sizzling rain. Adam followed.

The space was filled with torrents of screaming and violence. People tore at each other. Ma'ii swept from the elevator, and Ron stayed back and watched as the terror seemed to move away from the god in a ship's wake of writhing violence.

Near to the elevator, Ggorchik was pulling his snarling dog up the stairway with one hand and shoved Schmidt up the steps with the other. The dog was straining to return to the fray, its mouth bathed in red and its tiny eyes wide in bloodlust. It yelped and slobbered.

Suddenly, the dog froze. For an instant it was allowed to see something that his human companions could not. In a brief vision, the cruel and stupid brain of the pit bull could see back through the millennia of lupine deformations. Back through darkness. Back to when canines were not human mutations but noble, fierce, and formidable wild animals. Standing before the dog was a creature beyond its wildest fears. The pit bull whined like a scalded pup until Ma'ii casually turned his thumb and forefinger in the air like a key. There was a choking, meaty, crackling sound that started with the dog's gash-of-a-mouth widening until it was impossibly wide open, its shark eyes wild in fear. Its snout drew back over the top of its head and the bottom jaw onto its throat. The rift continued along the length of the animal all the way to where its tail had been guillotined when it was just a pup. Blood washed the flapping organs as the dog was turned inside out.

Ron looked away, covering his face, though it was only more carnage in a room ravaged with butchery.

"Ah. It is a shapeshifter," Ma'ii snarked.

Ggorchik looked at his dog, squealed, let go of the leash, and hurled an explosion of puke across Schmidt's chest.

When Ron spun around again, he saw an enormous coyote crouched where a man had been. Shaking its head and snarling, it plunged into chaos.

STILL OUTSIDE, ADAM FALTERED on the porch, not knowing what to do. With gun drawn, Duane slipped through the door, twisting and turning through chum that scattered the floors. Other miscreants were pouring down the stairs past Ggorchik and Schmidt. Out of doors along the main hall, countless staff and other lowlifes were streaming onto the killing floors. When Duane saw the two leaders on the stairway, he angled toward them but was intercepted by the blond woman. She'd drawn a gun from somewhere in her skimpy suit.

Duane swiveled.

"Stop. I'm Agent Crandell," she shouted.

He paused for a fraction of a second, and the heavy *pop* of a gun came from Ggorchik's gun and cut through the screaming racket. Duane caved like he had been punched, his hand scrambled for the wall as he slid to the floor, his eyes glazed, and foamy blood blooming at the corner of his mouth. The woman swiveled toward the stairs in the direction of the shot, but Ggorchik and Schmidt were gone.

The blast from Ggorchik's gun had snapped most of the combatants out of their spell, though a few still struggled and grunted. Adam had stepped through the front door just as the shot was fired.

After his first wife died, Adam had stayed in this inn with Maggie when he had returned to Sault Sainte Marie. Now his disorientation was compounded because the place looked entirely different—and the carnage only made it more overwhelming. He saw Duane go down and he sprinted toward him, but the woman already had her fingers pressed to his brother-in-law's neck, feeling for a pulse.

Thunder rolled and the lights flickered. People were milling around bloodied or sprawled moaning or dead. The coyote had disappeared somewhere, its appetite sated. A flash pulsed through the tinted windows, followed by deafening clouts of thunder. The building went dark except for murky light through the gray windows.

The woman seemed unfazed. "Adam, I am Agent Crandell. I know who you are. I'll take care of him." She lifted her chin toward Duane. "There is nothing you can do. I think Ron went back in the elevator. You probably know areas in here better than me. I've never been back in that old infirmary, and I just learned that the women are being moved to the floor in there."

"Where is Gracie? I haven't been here in—"

"I was told that the layout of the infirmary has not been changed. There were no major renovations," she said. "And I don't know what personnel is back there or if the women are guarded or not. I found out that your wife was on the second floor of the infirmary. She was in those rooms on this end." She motioned. "Unless they moved her again. I think she's with her aunt."

"Her aunt—?"

"Stay clear of Ggorchik and Schmidt. They are the only ones with guns."

Adam snapped his head around at the white and silver walls splattered red, the shambling injured and the grisly dead. He tried to find his bearings in the wrecked and renovated inn. The open and modern meeting rooms and lounges were drastically different from the confined and elegant spaces he remembered. Along the right side of the hallway there had been the sitting room and library. On the other side would have been the parlor and dining room. He scanned to the end of what would have been the wide hallway. A wall stretched across the space that would have been Maggie's bright and delightful kitchen. On the other side of that wall, he hoped he would still find the old entry to the infirmary and also the servant's stairs that led to where his room had been on the second floor.

Nearing the wall, he shouted back to Agent Crandell, "Are the servant's stairs and big infirmary door still there, and—?"

The floor quaked. Behind the wall, it sounded like someone was being tortured and ripped limb from limb. Crashing and tearing were followed by more inhuman squeals and squalls.

Suddenly the wall exploded into plaster and splinters that showered the shambling and the dead.

Adam cowered.

Chapter 37

Second Wave

Adam pitched away from the crashing wall and dove into the dark elevator. He scrabbled toward the back wall. He rolled into the knees of a man who was crouching with his back wedged into a corner of the elevator. The man recoiled and pushed Adam away. "No. Damn it. No," the man pleaded.

"Ron. It's me," Adam said.

"Oh, Lord. Thank you," Ron said.

Outside the elevator and throughout the inn the cacophony rose into a gale as the painful screeches from the vile clients and staff mingled with the inhuman squeals from the creatures and their floor-rattling roars. It reached a crescendo as a second tsunami of butchery coursed across the meeting rooms and along the broad hallway. As if mastodons had been unleashed, a mangled body flew past the elevator, a bloody leg slapping the edge of the door. Ron and Adam pressed to the back of the elevator. Gluts of gore coughed ahead in the tide as if a human chipper had been deployed. A great paw like a bloodied gorilla claw waggled in front of the door and a head more human than an ape lowered from above and glowered in, eyes wide like polished obsidian lenses, lips moist and thick. Lashing its tongue, it curled its lips back and grimaced sharp teeth, shook its head, and huffed.

The men recoiled, trying to paste themselves tighter to the back of the elevator. The creature stared at them pensively a moment longer with dead liquid eyes, blinked, and moved on. Further away from the elevator door, another massive ape creature shuffled past, gripping a torso in one hand and employing a human leg as a scythe to clear the hallway.

"Where's Duane?" Adam shouted. "He was just ahead of me. He went down." He covered his face with his elbow and peered out of the elevator and along the hallway. The meaty, brine odor of blood and the gagging scent of excrement were overpowering. As quickly as they had arrived, the creatures had vanished. Duane and the woman, Agent Crandell, were also gone. Ron pulled Adam back into the elevator.

"They're gone. Everyone. Gone," Ron said.

"We have no time," Adam said. Slipping on offal, Adam pushed Ron ahead of him as they tumbled from the elevator. "We need to get to the second floor of the infirmary."

They twisted through the wreckage of the broken wall where the creatures had busted through. Ahead, a narrow door faced them.

"That's where the servant's steps used to be when I stayed here. My room was at the top of those steps. The main entry to the infirmary is over here." Adam angled right to where he expected the big oak and iron door to the infirmary. But Ron yanked his shoulder and he skidded to a halt at the rim of gaping darkness in the floor. A chasm was busted in the floor where the creatures had emerged from the basement.

"If the servant's stairs are still accessible, we can get to the second floor. I know another entry into the infirmary from up there."

The narrow door was open, and the servant's stairs were intact and led upward toward the second floor and came out near Adam's old room.

Other than paint and carpet, Adam was surprised that the second floor had changed little. It seemed a quiet, distant refuge from the hell that had played out below. He pushed through the door of his room. It had been converted to an office. He stepped quickly to the window and looked out toward the arched windows of the brick infirmary.

A memory.

"I just remembered that in my dream last night. I told you that I had dreamt of Julie," Adam said. "She said I would find Gracie where she—Julie had last seen me. That would have been over there." He pointed at the arched infirmary windows. "Years ago, I stood there looking out that window and I imagined that her ghost could hear me. I forgave her. But I believed she was long gone, that she had not heard, and she would not actually know that I forgave her."

He paused a beat then withdrew from the window. "In the room next to here." He pointed at the wall. "There was a door to the second floor of the infirmary. But it was locked and nailed shut when I lived here. Let's check."

The next room had also been converted to an office, but the old door to the infirmary had been replaced with a metal fire door that was slanted open. Adam jogged through.

The second floor of the infirmary had also been cleaned and painted but was otherwise the same. On the left side of the narrow corridor the tall windows soared to the ceiling. For a heartbeat, he paused at the middle window where years ago he had spoken his last words of mercy to his first wife.

He hustled away.

Across the hallway several doors faced the big windows. And just as it had when Adam lived there, a stairway led downward between the last two doors.

Before they had gone further, a woman flung a door open and stepped into the hallway. When she saw them, she darted toward the steps.

"Nessa? My God. Are you...Wait." Adam ran after her and down the steps.

Pausing, Ron felt his heart racing. He inhaled and peeked into the room that Nessa had departed. On a narrow bed in a room lit by a single candle, Gracie lay peacefully. He approached cautiously, fearing the worst until he saw the slow rise and fall of her breathing. Standing at her bedside, his heart swelled. The tiny cubicle of a room did not feel large enough to contain all that he was feeling.

Into his soul, where there had existed unfamiliarity and separation, there poured a lifetime of connection and knowing. Onto a relationship bereft of memories or photographs was applied the mortar to inseparably bond father and child. Daughter and father.

As if all those moments that he could never have fathomed were knit into a past that could not have been. He imagined a little girl turning her face toward him in glee as she took her first steps. A child in a little jean jacket with a backpack, her black hair in pigtails on her first day of school. Graduations and parties, scraped knees, and kisses teemed in Ron's grateful mind and were enfolded into his tender care.

He extended a hand and brushed a strand of hair from her damp forehead. Her eyes fluttered, and a hand promptly swept to her abdomen and rested, her fingers arching and falling.

"What are you?" she whispered with a slightly drunken smile.

Your father, he wanted to say over and over. He ran a finger over his patch of mustache and mussed his hair. "Ron," he said hoarsely.

"Ron." Her intoxicated smile broadened. "Right. Where are we…Ron." Her eyes narrowed, looking up and down at Ron's strange hair and orange pants. "You look ridiculous. Are you really my dad?"

With his eyes brimming, not caring from where or why her question came, he slipped his hand into hers. "Gracie, I'm your…dad. Proud of it. Really proud."

She let go of his hand and grasped her stomach with both hands. "Ho." She grinned. "She's doing backflips in there. This child wants to be here." Suddenly, more alert, she began to sit up.

"Wait. Are you okay?" Ron said.

"Where is Adam?" Her head swiveled. She rubbed her face with both hands. "Leo? Donnie? I need to get home."

"We are in Sault Sainte Marie. You were taken. We must call an ambulance. It's not safe to move until someone can help you."

Holding up the palm of her hand, she swung her feet over the side of the bed and waited, then stood beside the bed, steadying herself. Ron grasped her elbow, but she gently shrugged free, stretching her arms and shaking out her legs.

"Wait," he said.

She shook her head, determined. "I will be fine. I feel like I've just had the best nap of my life," she said.

ADAM WAS TRAILING AFTER Nessa and followed her down the stairs.

On the first floor was a narrow hallway with a row of windows similar to the one above. Adam remembered all of it from years ago. She pushed through a door and darted into the old lobby of the infirmary.

"Nessa. Stop. It's Adam. What are you doing?"

She ran through the lobby. Like the other rooms that Adam remembered, the lobby had been cleaned up and was no longer strewn and dusty, but had been painted and set with ill-suited modern furniture. Across the small lobby was the big oak and iron door that he and Ron had tried to access from the other side. Years before the lobby had been littered with shards of plaster and broken-down wooden chairs left over from a century past. He paused when he saw one feature in the lobby that had been restored instead of removed or destroyed.

In the basement Ron and Ma'ii had entered through a door with a sagging stained-glass panel. The panel on the main floor was in good repair and set in a heavy oak door separating the lobby from the main ward of the infirmary. In the glass, the garish green serpent entwined around a wooden rod: the medical symbol of the Rod of Asclepius.

Nessa avoided the serpent door but was rattling at the great wooden door that led back into the inn. She kicked at it and raised the latch. The door began to creak open.

"No. You can't go out there. The hallway is gone. We almost fell in," Adam shouted.

He lunged at her, swiped for her arm, but missed. At the last moment, in the scant light from the darkened inn, she saw the gaping wound in the floor, teetered for a moment, and fell over the edge, twisting and clawing at the broken tile floor. Adam slammed onto his stomach, braced his legs in the doorway, and caught her wrist.

"Let go. Dammit. It was all my fault. I'm sorry. It was my fault." She tried to shake loose from his grasp, swinging her legs in the chasm.

"No. I don't care. You can explain later," Adam said.

She screamed.

"Best nap of my lifetime." Gracie rubbed her face again quickly. Dressed in scrubs, she went through her typical warm up routine, rolling her shoulders, stretching each arm, and flexing each knee.

She froze.

"Gracie. What is it?" Ron asked. "Are you okay?"

"I'm here, but Leo and Donnie are not." Her expression was flat.

"They...they—"

She stopped him with a waggle of her chin, gazed down, and pressed her fist to her lips.

"I didn't know if..." he began.

"No." She sighed. "Later. Not now." Her eyes met his for an instant. "Tell me later."

She headed for the door.

"No. Stop. You can't," Ron said.

"I know my body. Besides..." Her expression changed as though she had drawn a curtain over her fear. She looked at him up and down again. "I'm not taking advice from a clown." She smiled. "Are you sure you're my dad? Swear it."

He smiled thinly for a moment, caught off guard, marveling at her discipline. "We...we have to get out of here," he said. "This is that old infirmary, next to Maggie's old B&B. That pack of dogs has turned it into some kind of brothel. They brought you here. Nessa ran out your door, trying to get away, and Adam ran after her."

"Adam's here? Nessa? She's here? Where's the bad guys, those Dark Council guys?"

"Butchered. It was mayhem beyond belief down there. I think they're gone."

"Good. Where's Adam?"

"This way."

They hustled down the steps that Nessa and Adam had taken. They found the infirmary lobby and Ron bolted across the floor toward Adam and grabbed Nessa's other wrist. They pulled her out of the hole flailing and screaming. Adam turned to see Gracie and was quick to abandon Nessa to Ron. He grabbed Gracie and flung his arms around her.

"Careful." She laid a gentle hand on his chest and one on her stomach, smiling. "We're fine. She's riled up, though."

He grabbed her again. "Are you sure she's okay?"

"Hell, I think she's ready to join the fight." Gracie grinned.

Nessa sobbed and Gracie went to her. While they talked over one another, Nessa tried to apologize, tried to explain, but all the while throwing an eye of disdain toward Ron.

"I don't care about any of that. Not now. I don't want to hear it. Explain later," Gracie said.

Adam was working on the door with the stained-glass serpent.

Ron came beside him. "It's what I saw in that underworld lodge with Duane. They are behind here. The women and girls. I am sure of it."

Adam fumbled with the latch.

"Yeah. That's probably where they moved them, now," Nessa mumbled.

"Let me try." Gracie cocked a leg and thrust her foot into the door. It buckled.

"Enough, already!" Adam took her shoulders and gently moved her aside, giving her a look. He put his hip into the door and pushed it open.

Gracie gathered Nessa. "We talk later." She pointed into her aunt's face. "Later."

More than a century had passed since the big open ward had been used for men whose minds and bodies had endured a horror similar to the women, only under a different guise: War instead of trafficking and abuse.

Gracie led them into a space as large as an auditorium. After the electricity had gone out, a lone emergency spotlight glared like a bright gash along a far brick wall but left the middle of the big room in shadows.

In a circle of beds were corralled twenty or thirty young women.

The low light was enough to expose their garish make-up and revealing costumes. Two large women in scrubs kept them hemmed in, assisted by two of Ggorchik's thugs.

Adam pulled at Gracie's shoulder, but she shook him free and approached.

"What the hell is this?" she asked.

The first guy reached inside his jacket, but Gracie's first kick broke his wrist while her elbow shattered his jaw and sent him sprawling. The next thug had her by the shoulder, but she twisted and thrust both hands into his face, breaking his nose and blinding one eye. Before his hands reached his face, she had delivered a knee to his groin.

Adam grabbed him by the shoulders and threw him aside.

Gracie charged the women in scrubs, who were twice her size, but they only shrieked and rushed away from the beds to huddle in a corner.

The beds screeched on the old floors as Ron and Adam dragged them aside. The women clustered nearer to each other.

All but one.

A girl stepped forward with black hair flowing like a cape nearly to her waist. Her bangs were cut in a crisp line above her brow, and she had strong yet graceful features that not even the gaudy makeup could mar.

"Find the key," she said.

"Find the key. Truth is the key. The Truth will make them free," Ron said. "Salvi Lopez."

She grinned and took Ron's hand. "Gracias. We saw you when you came to us in that dungeon."

"But how? I thought—"

"I knew we would be found," she said. "Thank you. Thank you for not giving up." She opened her hand to reveal a blue stone. "My grandmother told me that if I held this stone, I would be found, so I never let them remove it from my hand. I gripped it so tight."

Speechless for a moment, Ron looked back at Gracie and Adam. "We saw her in that dream, or vision. Duane and me. In the underworld. She was one of the women in that room."

Nessa began babbling to herself again. "I didn't know. I didn't know any of this was happening. They never told me anything about these women."

Something occurred to Gracie, and she scanned around the room. "Duane should be here. He would have been involved. Where is Duane?" Gracie said. She immediately tuned into their silence. "Adam. Ron. Where is Duane?"

Ron looked at Adam.

"Where is he?" she asked.

"He went down. I don't know what to say. Someone was with him, and when Ron and I came out of the elevator, they were gone. I don't know where he is," Adam said.

They tried to explain to her all that had happened in the inn when the insanity had taken over and later when the creatures arrived.

And earlier when Ggorchik had fired the shot.

Gracie pondered. She inhaled. "He can take care of himself. He always has. But I need to find him."

Nessa continued to stare at the girls and mumbled. "I know where those bastards are. I know how to find their office. We cannot let them escape."

Gracie was silent only an instant more. "Let's go."

Chapter 38

The Inn Undone

IN THE LARGE WARD of the infirmary was the narrow elevator that hauled human cargo from the basement to the infirmary. It continued up to the second and third floors. The elevator door stood open, dark, and out of order. Nessa pushed through a side door that opened from the ward to the outside. Along the mossy brick of the infirmary, a narrow walk of broken concrete led to a small door that was tight in the corner where the inn had been built onto the infirmary.

Nessa pointed at the door. "Those are the back steps they showed me to use as an escape. They go up to the second floor near Ggorchik's office. If they were going to escape, it would be down these steps."

Behind them came a bustling commotion and Ron's comforting murmur. From the side of the infirmary, he ushered the bevy of girls into daylight. The storm had passed, the day was fresh, and the late afternoon was washed with slanting sunshine that sparkled like faerie dust. Shielding their eyes, one by one the women took tiny shuffling steps out of the infirmary and onto the grass. Some embraced, some stared at the sky, while others slumped onto the wet grass and wept silently.

Nessa watched sadly for a moment, then turned the handle of the narrow door leading to the second floor. It was unlocked. "They are probably gone," she said.

Gracie opened the door and started up the narrow steps with Adam and Nessa following, and Ron stayed with the women.

"Slow down." Adam touched her elbow.

"Duane," she said. "I have to find him." She continued up the short flight of stairs that led to a narrow landing. She took a breath, then turned to follow the second flight that led up to the second floor. When they reached the top, they were standing in an alcove built off the side of a hallway.

They waited. Listening. Down the corridor, they heard voices in a heated exchange: one or two men and a woman. Nessa motioned them forward. The voices were coming from behind a closed door. Further along the hall, a man sat crumpled against the wall.

"Duane," Gracie whispered. Hurrying past the closed door, she could hear shouts, a crash, and the muffled rumble of struggle.

Duane was propped against the wall with his legs outstretched. The main stairs down to the inn and to all the carnage were on the other side of the hallway. Gracie knelt beside him, and his hand slid toward his chest. He searched her face, grimaced, then smiled weakly. "They'll need to issue better vests," he said. "This hurts like a bitch. But I'll be—"

"Shh…It's okay, I've got you," she said.

"Nessa, wait." Adam wrenched Nessa's shoulder as she hustled toward the closed door of the office.

The commotion inside had subsided by the time Nessa reached the door.

Gracie stood. "Wait," she said. In a few strides she was back at the door, but Nessa had already opened it.

Inside the door, a blond woman in the scanty hostess uniform lay motionless. Her vacant eyes stared up at them from a head wrenched awkwardly backward.

Three tall windows set with stained glass transoms bathed the large office in bronze sunlight. Ggorchik stood behind a sprawling desk. In a corner, Schmidt slumped in a leather chair with his eyes focused somewhere in the distance, his jaw slack.

Ggorchik did not seem alarmed by their intrusion. "Mr. Schmidt has already left us, and I shall soon catch up with him. We have found the elixir." With a coiled smile, he reached for a syringe, swept it off his desk, and plunged it into his arm. Gracie stepped around the body of the woman as Ggorchik dropped into his chair. He knit his brow and seemed lost and confused for a moment. Fearing that he may be concealing a gun, she rushed around the corner of the desk and yanked his arms behind him. He gave no resistance. She released him and his head hit the desk with a crisp thump.

"Should we call the police? What should we do?" Adam asked.

"I am in no hurry to help these monsters," Gracie said. "I need to be sure Duane is okay."

Nessa was standing in the doorway, wide-eyed. Gracie crouched beside Agent Crandell, felt for a pulse, but could see that the woman's condition was hopeless. She pushed past Nessa and led Adam down the hallway.

They returned to Duane and helped him to his feet. Gracie continued to hold onto his hand as he leaned heavily onto Adam. Avoiding the butcher shop stink that seeped up the stairs from the inn below, they walked past Ggorchik's office again. Duane paused at the open door where Ggorchik slumped on his desk, Schmidt sprawled dead in the chair, and Agent Crandell lay on the floor.

"She saved me," Duane said. "When I woke up, she told me that the impact on the vest must have stopped my heart. She told me she had done CPR to revive me. We should..."

Gracie shook her head. "Her neck is broken. She's gone."

Carefully, Gracie stepped to where Ggorchik slumped over his desk. She felt his neck. "But I suppose we should call help or try to—"

"Hell no," Nessa said. "The verdict is already in."

Clutching her stomach, Gracie braced her hand on the desk. "Whoa." She bit her lip and her knees bent to the contraction. She looked up helplessly at Adam.

Nessa slipped beside her. "Is it..?"

"I think so," her eyes widened. "Oh..."

"Can you sit?" Nessa asked.

Gracie teetered a while, taking a few deep breaths. Duane leaned on the side of the doorway and Adam went to Gracie.

"The contraction is passing." She stared helplessly at Adam. "But it's too early."

"It is a little early." He slipped his arm around her. "You've been through a lot. And laying off the foot work might have been a good idea." He smiled. "But I would have expected no less. Let's get out of here. I heard sirens. Someone will be here to help."

Gracie smiled weakly up at Adam. She felt Nessa's arm around her shoulder and Adam retuned to help Duane.

"I am so sorry," Nessa said as she led Gracie into the corridor.

Gracie waved a hand. "I know. I think I understand. But I told you: Explain later."

Nessa inhaled. "Let's get out of here." She looked once more into the room and shut the door.

"We have to tell them about Crandell when we get downstairs," Duane said.

They edged down the narrow back stairs. As they emerged from the inn, more sirens were tearing down the street. Surrounding the inn, the manicured grounds were crawling with police, plainclothes, and rescue personnel. Ron was helping ease the women toward help while Salvi Lopez led two of the youngest girls, barely pre-teen, one in each hand.

A bank of thunderheads with their yellow manes in the firmament deserted to the east. Their backs were scoured pink by the sun, and they grumbled like Titans reassembling the broken earth.

Gracie and Nessa stood nearby while Duane leaned on Adam and scanned the bustle of activity. "By the time we go through everything here, examine their guest list, and sift through their files and computers the Dark Council will be finished." Duane nodded at Gracie. "And I don't think that you or the Lake Council will ever have to worry about them again,"

A policeman and plainclothes woman approached as Duane dredged his wallet from his pocket. He held up his hand to pause their questions for a moment and called Ron.

Ron hunkered beside one of the girls on the grass and he looked up with surprise that melted to a smile. "Thank God," he called to Duane. "You made it."

Duane gave a weak thumbs-up. "The SUV is open. Can you take Gracie over there? We'll be along soon."

Ron hurried beside Gracie. "What's the matter," he said. "Are you okay? Come on, it looks like you need to sit. I told you—"

"I'm fine. It's okay...*Dad.*" She grinned, only slightly sarcastically.

Nessa seemed uneasy as she held to Gracie's other side. "Any more contractions?" she asked.

"Not yet. But I feel certain there will be," Gracie said.

"Contractions?" Ron asked. Gracie slipped her hand into Ron's elbow.

Gracie nodded. "I said, don't worry—yet." She smiled.

They threaded through the garden and across the sprawling lawns that were teeming with cops and officials. Most of the women sat dazed in the damp grass or gazed at the commotion with quizzical smiles.

Ron opened the door to the SUV and another contraction seized Gracie. She gripped Ron's elbow and leaned against the car. "I don't want to sit. Just wait."

"You're early. We need to get to the hospital," he said.

Gracie shook her head slowly. "They seem far enough apart. But yeah. I know, I suppose we should go, soon."

After the cramping subsided she sat on the seat.

Nessa leaned in. "I'll tell Adam." She was silent for a moment. Then she tipped her head toward Ron and said to Gracie, "He did all this for you. And more. I believe you are in good hands."

Gracie lifted her chin. "I know."

Ron and Nessa stared at each other for a few beats. Nessa began to speak, paused, then spoke again.

"I'm sorry, Ron. I was wrong to feel that way. So wrong. I can't..." Nessa glanced at Gracie and walked away.

"What do you think she means?" Gracie squinted at Ron.

"It can wait. There's always more to the story. She's had a hard time trying to accept me," Ron said. He was not good at being evasive and added, "I guess she doesn't approve of my new look."

Ignoring his hedging, she chuckled. But she couldn't help being distracted as she studied her father: his silly hair lit red; his face bathed in golden light. Late afternoon sun always seemed to confer a sense of reckoning.

"The thin mustache looks silly, but you're rockin' that hair."

He mussed with his head, scratched the shaved side, and ran a finger over his mustache.

"You know." Gracie sniffled. "When I woke up a while ago, the first thing I saw was your face. And even with the bad disguise, I think that I knew who you were. And who you were to me."

Ron shrugged and grinned.

"It was stupid to try to draw their attention with the DNA, but I realize now that I was taking that risk for a reason. Maybe without even knowing what I was doing." She wiped beneath her eye. "All my life I had looked at the faces of a thousand men, maybe more. Always pondering which one might be my father. Then I saw your face again...to know that you were the one, that you are that man. My father."

Ron ran his arm across his eyes. "Thank you." He made a crooked smile. "I am honored to have you as my daughter." He leaned in. As he hugged her, he felt Adam's hand on his shoulder.

"Let's get to the hospital," Adam said.

Ron took Adam aside. "You guys go ahead. Let me catch up with Nessa. Someone needs to tell her about Donnie."

Adam laid a hand on Ron's shoulder. "I will tell Gracie everything."

ONE MAN GASPED AND opened his eyes wide, head swiveling, then the other man did the same. In a dim room heavy with the scent of mold and carrion, they sat naked on damp stone with their backs against the rock.

"Where are we?" Ggorchik whispered hoarsely. "What is this?"

Schmidt ratcheted his head side to side.

Far away, down a dark cavern, a squabble and wailing echoed and subsided. A glowing light grew near then receded; a woman wept pitifully—pity for the two men.

Ggorchik grappled to rise, but his legs seared with pain and flopped and twisted aimlessly. Schmidt also tried to move, but his legs thrashed and slapped together with Ggorchik's, making them look like a fleshy cephalopod with two bodies.

"Someone will pay," Ggorchik whimpered.

"Yes. There will be a reckoning," someone said. "The part I so enjoy." The men snapped their heads toward an approaching man, his bare feet padding softly on the damp floor. He rolled the sleeves of his white shirt deliberately and folded his brown arms across his chest.

"Who are you? What have you done to us?" Ggorchik demanded.

"I did not want you to escape before I had the pleasure of meeting you. And you no longer needed the bones: The femur, the fibula, or tibia. The countless bones of your feet. You won't need any bones in your legs or feet while you are here."

"What the hell?" Schmidt said.

"Yes. What. The. Hell?" Ma'ii said. "You are close, very close. But no cigar. In fact, no cigar, no food, no water, no sex, no pleasure, no nothing. Nothing. Ever."

The men tried to flap their naked legs again, but the result was only thrashing pain like burned meat, recoiling and sizzling with pain.

They groaned and sniveled.

"Time to sleep," the coyote said.

"Now, just one minute. We have connections. Connections," Ggorchik said.

"Don't let the bedbugs...bite."

Tunnel vision closed around and cinched their existence to a puckered sphincter. Until there was only a pinpoint of light that wavered for an instant like a firefly and blinked out. Forever. Their actuality would consist of nothing larger than the height, width, and depth of a blank screen.

An eternity of dead silence.

Chapter 39

Ma'ii's Revenge

WITH A HAND BRACED on the rim of the kitchen sink, Jacob gazed out the window contemplating the sun-spangled waters of the big lake.

The steam rose from his coffee and entwined like the delicate wrists of a dancer. *No better time for a smoke.* He lumbered to his chair in the living room, retrieved the blue bag of Cherokee tobacco from next to his chair, and returned to stand near the sink, intently rolling his cigarette. For an instant, the glimmer off the water flashed like lightning, but when he looked up, the face of the rising sun remained unwavering and pleased.

Behind him, there was a bold knock at the front door.

"Who the hell...?" Ginny said as she padded out in her robe, a towel around her shoulders and her hair damp and tousled.

"I'm right here. I can get it," Jacob said.

"Never mind," she replied with an edge of exasperation.

Jacob rounded the corner as Ginny stood at the open door, speechless for a moment. "Can...can I help you?"

A man with a mass of long hair that flowed in colors of gray, red, and black made a quick and courteous nod, then twitched the hair from his face. "Good morning, Ginny Payment, may I have permission to enter?"

"Let the Old Man in," Jacob piped up. "He is here for a little reckoning. Some bookkeeping, I imagine. But only with me. Isn't that right, you old coyote?"

"Correct. Quite...painless." Ma'ii smiled.

"And again: only with me," Jacob said sternly. "You are only here for me."

"Precisely."

Ginny was nonplussed. "It's a bit chilly out there, isn't it?" She swept her gaze from his blousy shirt to his bare feet.

"Never gets very chilly in that corner of hell his kind come from." Jacob grinned.

"Never been there. To be sure," Ma'ii said.

"You never said a word about anyone coming over." Ginny threw a nervous glance at Jacob. "Will everything be okay?"

"Never better," Jacob said. "I'm sorry. I should have told you that he might show up. But you can never be certain about this one."

"Are you sure you're okay?" Ginny asked.

"I would like to say that our very distinguished guest knows how to behave, but that would be a lie. He can be a trickster."

Ginny understood at last who their guest may be. In their years together they had welcomed many unusual guests into their home and Ginny believed that some may not have been entirely from this world. But none would have rivaled the storied coyote.

Jacob shuffled over to his chair and hefted the bag of Cherokee tobacco. "Will you share a smoke?"

Jacob swept his hand toward the couch and Ma'ii sat.

"Am I not compelled to accept?" he said.

Jacob methodically rolled the cigarettes and listened.

"I have much to say to you, Jacob Payment."

Jacob looked up and presented the god with a roll-up.

"In a fleeting time," the coyote said. "Maybe fifty thousand years or less—quicker than a toad's tongue, as you would say."

Jacob fumbled with his lighter, but the entity's cigarette had already lit itself somehow and he was taking a satisfied pull. He blew smoke in a circle within a circle.

"As I was saying, in an instant every remnant, each particle of this place, this year, and of this day will be deleted and utterly forgotten.

Dust. Think of the Maya. Or I should say imagine those who came before them. Not even a millennium went by, and every trace of their existence was erased." He circled his cigarette in the air. "Every squeal uttered in joy, or in childbirth, or in pain is now silent and not even an ancestor is left to recall. It was never recorded." Leaning forward, he rested his arms on his knees and motioned again with the cigarette. Smoke trailed like a banner. "When you die, every grave is an extinction, a holocaust, and every holocaust like a single grave. When you are gone, when a human dies, it does not matter if it is one old Indian dying alone or an entire civilization swallowed by an earthquake or buried by a great volcano. You're gone. They're all gone."

Jacob sipped his coffee and raised the cup, but Ma'ii shook his head, took another drag, and grinned. "Tobacco. This is one pleasure that never gets old."

"You were saying? Are you trying to tell me that someone is about to leave this plane of existence?" Jacob held the cigarette in the corner of his mouth as he packed up his bag of tobacco and papers. His eyes flicked toward the coyote.

Ma'ii took another drag and let the smoke trail from his nostrils. He waggled the cigarette between his thumb and finger as he spoke. "So, in time, all of humanity will be seen as your contemporaries. From the first cave painter in France, the Phoenicians, all the way to that future handful of survivors of the great plague that arrives in a millennium or two. Humanity is a blip, an anomaly."

Ginny was still standing and listening cautiously but took the cue from Jacob and settled into a chair. She rustled her damp hair with the towel.

"You could not fathom how much the world has changed," Ma'ii continued. "But more fascinating to me, you could not fathom how things stay the same. Exactly the same."

They sat in silence for a while.

"I didn't recall that you were such a gabber." Jacob grinned.

Ma'ii ignored him, set down his cigarette, and withdrew the birch wiigwaasabak scroll. Jacob blew smoke slowly and watched him. The bark crinkled and Ma'ii unraveled the crumpled note. He held it up and said nothing.

There was a reflexive rumbling that seemed to start in Jacob's chest and swelled until it burst into laughter. "So. You did not like my...prescription?" he said.

"It's nothing but Latin scribbles," the coyote said severely. "You're a shaman, a medicine man. You're not a damned doctor."

"You thought that *I* wrote it? C'mon, old man. You're the trickster. Can't take a little fun?" Jacob said. He laughed again.

The coyote continued to hold the paper.

"I told my doctor that I sure as hell didn't need that prescription, but he scribbled it anyway," Jacob said. "I didn't need them boner pills. But I tried to remember if I knew any other old codgers. And I could not think of anyone I knew who was as old as you are. I thought you might need a little help." Jacob set his cigarette in the ashtray and laughed until he coughed.

Ma'ii stood and tore madly at the prescription and crushed the birchbark in his hand.

"I took a gamble," Jacob said. "I gambled that you would not let Gracie, Ron, or any of them die until you understood what that note said. I thought it might buy enough time, and I knew you had to honor my request—if you could figure out what it was." Jacob grinned. "And I heard from my old friend Duane that it must've worked."

"Your mortality is now." The god threw the pieces at Jacob and went to the door.

Jacob continued to laugh, and he coughed some more. And coughed. He wheezed and brayed as his chest shook. Ginny rushed to his chair.

"Jacob. My God, are you all right? Jacob."

The old man clutched at his throat and continued to cough, his face becoming ashy and his lips blue.

"Jacob!" she said. Desperately she spun toward the door, but the coyote god was gone. Jacob slumped to the side. She felt her husband's neck and laid a hand on his chest. Ginny patted her waist then hurried to the kitchen, looking for her phone.

Jacob remained silent and still.

Ginny's hand shook as she rustled through her jackets and rattled through drawers, trying to find her phone.

The cuff of Jacob's calico shirt stirred. Like an inchworm, his finger moved toward his cigarette. Ginny was standing in the doorway tapping madly into her phone when he looked at her out of the corner of his eye.

"You bastard," she said. "You scared the shit out of me."

"That was the plan. I had to convince him I was dead."

"He will find out. You know what he is."

"Of course, he will. But so what? There is nothing he loves more than a good prank."

"But he does not like it when the prank is on him."

Jacob paused and shrugged. "Yeah. Then there's that."

A MASSIVE COYOTE BOUNDED across the grass, heading for the lake. A searing light poured in through the big window that faced the bay. Ginny hustled to the window in time to see a great arch of meteoric light blaze across the sky.

Watching a fluttering glow disappear into the clouds, she asked, "Will he return?"

"He never leaves."

Chapter 40

And Then…

"She looks like one of those troll dolls with the big hair," Adam said.

"Your daddy is not going to be allowed anywhere near you. Ever." With the back of one finger stroking the infant's cheek, Gracie smiled adoringly.

Framed by a blast of white hair, the baby's face was scrunched thoughtfully, and her dark eyes brooded as she measured her father. .

"No. You're beautiful, Aaiden," Adam said.

Gracie looked up. In a corner chair, a man dressed in scrubs was leaning forward with his hands pressed flat between his knees. He was trying to remain invisible, and his eyes studied the floor like a kid in class who did not want to be called on.

"She won't bite." Gracie grinned.

He looked up, shyly.

Adam motioned. "C'mon…Grandpa. You won't scare her, you lost your orange clown suit."

"It seemed like a family moment, and I didn't want to…" Ron said.

"Exactly. A family moment," Gracie said. "And you are family."

Ron edged to the side of the bed. It might have been his imagination, but it seemed to him that a glow enfolded his daughter and her child.

The child turned her intense dark eyes toward Ron, and he felt immediately enchanted and disarmed.

"You want to hold her?" Gracie asked.

The End

Dear Reader...

I deeply appreciate that you bought or borrowed Dead Silence. I hope it was a good journey for you and please check out the "Also by" page that follows.

Reviews are precious to writers. Every book hangs on the generosity of readers like you. Please take a moment to drop a rating or even a review on Amazon, Goodreads, or wherever you can.

Sincere Thanks
Craig

PS: Feel free to contact me:
craig@craigabrockman.com
Or visit my website:
http://craigabrockman.com

Also by

Marty and the Far Woodchuck: A middle-grade novel

Lake Superior Trilogy:
Dead of November: A Novel of Lake Superior
Delirium Wilderness: A Coming of Age Dark Fantasy in Michigan's U.P.
Dead Silence: They Steal Your Thoughts, Your Body, and Leave You in the Afterlife

Curve of the Earth: A Novel of Lazarus

Surviving to Thriving: Living Your Best Life with a Hospitalized Child
Co-authored with Jessie Huisken

Acknowledgements

My wife, Sally, is a ready ear and reads draft after draft. There is no better reader and no one's BS meter is more in tune to blather and inconsistency. She is in every sense a co-author because everything I write is filtered through her eyes and her generous heart.

I am blessed with a family of readers who were more than willing to really dig in and find the flaws and offer (very honest) advice. Son Jonah, daughter Sarah Bertolini, and granddaughter Naomi Chae who offered a wide-ranging critique. Granddaughter Makaiya Griffin who was willing to throw in a woman's perspective on a chapter or two.

Neighbor Barbara Hanselman was the first to devour an early draft and offer great insight. Author Matthew Hellman was generous to read an early draft with his law enforcement attention to detail. Any problems with tactics or ballistics are my fault because I may have glossed over some of his great advice for the sake of the story.

Thank you Michaela Bush and her Tangled Up in Writing for another excellent edit, proofreading, and great collaboration.

A little appreciation should go to the late Michael S. Heiser and his Divine Council perspective. I was just starting to chew on his concepts of gods and principalities when I started this manuscript. Now he sees face to face. Our God is an *awesome God*.

Everyone who has read my books, given reviews, and offered encouragement—or criticism—is part of this book and your role is genuinely appreciated.

About the author

Craig A. Brockman has spent his life near the Great Lakes, especially Lake Superior. In 2017 he completed the final 140 miles of his meandering hike across the entire Upper Peninsula of Michigan from Detour Village to the Montreal River. His diverse portfolio spans everything from a middle-grade novel to historical fiction, anthologies, and even a solo music album. He lives with wife Sally in Tecumseh, Michigan.

Visit his website at http://craigabrockman.com
Contact: craig@craigabrockman.com

www.ingramcontent.com/pod-product-compliance
Lightning Source LLC
LaVergne TN
LVHW041754060526
838201LV00046B/1002